Now Rahn stood over her, looking down at his naked captive who knelt with huddled shoulders heaving raggedly, her bowed head just inches from his crotch.

"So you want me to treat you like a princess, do you? And why should I? Even if you were called 'Princess' once, you certainly are not one now," he said in hard, precise tones. "You are nothing! A mere slave. A sex slave who, if she is allowed to live at all, lives at the pleasure of the King. And if I let you live…it will be only as long as you please me. You make no demands here; you live only to obey."

Also by DON WINSLOW:

The Secrets of Cheatem Manor
The Insatiable Mistress of Rosedale
Claire's Girls
Gloria's Indiscretion
Katerina in Charge
The Many Pleasures of Ironwood
Private Pleasures

The Fall of the Ice Queen

DON WINSLOW

MASQUERADE BOOKS, INC.
801 SECOND AVENUE
NEW YORK, N.Y. 10017

The Fall of the Ice Queen
Copyright © 1997 by Don Winslow
All Rights Reserved

No part of this book may be reproduced, stored in a retrieval system, or transmitted in any form, by any means, including mechanical, electronic, photocopying, recording or otherwise, without prior written permission of the publishers.

First Masquerade Edition 1997

First Printing April 1997

ISBN 1-56333-520-4

Manufactured in the United States of America
Published by Masquerade Books, Inc.
801 Second Avenue
New York, N.Y. 10017

> Sex is power. It lays waste to our defenses. It overrides good sense, short-circuits the higher functions. Our universe constricts until it approximates the contours of our bodies; our breasts thud concussively as we grind into each other, our vocabulary reduced to paleolithic grunts.
>
> —Cliff Burns,
> *The Illustrated Guide to the Masters of the Macabre*

CHAPTER ONE

It is strange to think, dear unknown reader, that, having discovered this manuscript, you will be seeing words written by someone who, like you, was once alive—but who now is dead, and, most likely, will have been dead for quite a while. For if the gods are kind, I trust I will indeed be long gone by the time these pages are opened. For it is always dangerous to be alive and know too many secrets—especially if they are royal secrets. It is even more foolhardy to allow oneself to witness the folly of kings and sheer madness to record those follies.

So I have taken the manuscript with me to the grave, and only when this tomb is opened, if ever it is, will these words once more see the light of day. These precautions are necessary, as you will soon discover, for it was my fate to be in attendance at one of the most depraved and decadent courts known to man. And it was there that I was witness to, and recorded, these remarkable happenings—the events that led to the undoing and ultimate downfall of one of the most beautiful and wicked women ever to have worn a crown.

I don't know whether the fame of King Rahn will survive the ages, so perhaps it is best if I tell you the story of his most glorious and most infamous reign from the very beginning.

The people of the Two Lands, who stand in awe of him, sing the praises of Rahn as the greatest of the warrior kings. But he was not born to the purple. No, he had to fight his way to the top, hacking away ruthlessly at enemies, and even, in the end, his own brother, till he stood alone—crowning himself King of the Two Lands.

A tall, powerfully built man of iron will, cruelly handsome, with an aquiline nose, angry eyes and a stern, commanding visage, Rahn was a man of fiery temper, a man born to lead, even though he was not of royal blood. At one time, some of the bolder members of the old aristocracy whispered that the upstart king was no more than a brigand, the bastard son of a family of thieves, but nowadays such words are seldom uttered.

I had known of Rahn before he took the crown. For he was a warrior of great renown, a chieftain who led his clan into battle with ferocious effect, cutting through enemies whom he utterly destroyed without the slightest drop of mercy. He was a big, rapacious man who roared through life, demanding food and wine, women and wealth with an appetite that was insatiable.

And King Rahn's sexual appetite was also legendary. No one was safe: Man or woman, boy or girl—it made no difference to Rahn if his blood was up. In the heat of lusty passion, he was not very discriminating. It was rumored that his close companion and favored general, Gan, had yielded to him when both were young soldiers.

But though Rahn might dally with a soldier who caught his eye, or perhaps the occasional male slave, his preferences were clearly for women. Here, too, he wasn't very discriminating, for he would take whoever caught his fancy, and if she belonged to another man, well, that was of no matter to the King. Lovers and husbands were expected to offer their women freely, and they all did—to a man, for no one defied the royal will…and lived.

It wasn't always so, but I remember when the King's profligate ways first began. In some ways, I suppose I was responsible. Rahn was loud and crude, and totally without imagination. But he was clever, quick to learn about this business of being a King. I had once mentioned to him the custom at some of the remote courts I had visited of having young boys and girls serve at court as pages. He was surprised to learn that it was the custom to invite the children of aristocratic houses to serve their liege lord in this capacity.

It was a bit unbelievable to Rahn that the hostages might be used to force concessions from the fathers since he himself would, without hesitation, sacrifice a child or two, his consort, or even his mother, if he thought he could better gain his own nefarious ends.

Still, I assured him that the mere presence of children at court was enough to ensure the loyalty of their fathers and the clans that fell under their sway.

For some reason, the King took a fancy to the idea, and word was sent to his barons that they each must give up two children, placing them at service in the court of Thralkild. As it happened, by that time Rahn's court had already acquired a rather unsavory reputation, and so there was some understandable reluctance on the barons' part to yield their offspring to the King. When Rahn heard of this foot-dragging he was, predictably, furious, and he swore to make an example of any baron who defied the royal will.

Now, these barons were an unruly lot who would have been restless under the hand of any man. In that manner, they were no different from their liege lord. Proud, arrogant, ruthless and greedy, they would cede no possession without a fight. One of the most rebellious was a certain Baron Andur, who had become a thorn in the King's side. Andur was always an untrustworthy ally in war, treacherous and of questionable loyalty in peace. It was widely rumored that he had his own eye set on the crown of the Two Lands.

He was a brute of a man, thick set with a chest like a barrel, coarse in manners and appearance. Alea, his consort, was so unlike him that the contrast was quite remarkable! She was a tall, well-endowed blonde, a woman of the hills, born of the proud northern people. As the gods would have it, her offspring (mercifully) resembled her mother in all of the most important aspects. She was the apple of her father's eye—a fetching girl on the edge of womanhood, a young woman by the name of Gwin.

Andur guarded his women jealously, and seldom let them out of his sight. But Rahn had caught a glimpse of them once, at a country fair. His roving eye passed quickly over the solid, ugly form of the Baron, before going on to linger with considerable interest on the tall, long-legged blonde: her full figure corseted tightly, regal lines cinched to a narrowly constricted waist. He admired her thick golden hair, the pleasing curve of her shapely bosom, the top curves of those rich, full breasts left so casually bare by the fashionable gown that cupped and lifted them up for obvious display. And in her wake, like the filly trailing the mare, came Gwin, her slender nubile figure laced up in a shortened version of the long gown her mother wore, budding breasts peeking saucily out at the top, small and tentative and infinitely appealing. Her pale blond hair was braided, pulled back from the innocence of her neat youthful face. Andur's women had pleased the eye of the King, and this was a King who never forgot a pretty face.

It came as no surprise that the stiff-necked Andur happened to be the first to throw the gauntlet at the feet of his sovereign. Rahn took up the challenge with relish, an evil gleam in his eye. It all began when the King's messengers, sent to deliver the proclamation, had been received rudely at the Baron's grim hilltop castle. After being shown the road unceremoniously, they rode off empty-handed, only to be set upon by a band of well-armed "highwaymen." The messengers and their escort managed to fight their way out, but they barely escaped with their lives. The line had been drawn.

Rahn let it be known that Andur was to be destroyed, his women taken, his lands confiscated by the crown. The House of Andur would cease to exist! He plotted and waited and watched, but he made no move. Months passed, and some began to question his courage—even his manhood—as the challenge went unanswered, for it was well known that Andur was a formidable foe. But I knew better. One should never underestimate a King.

Now it was well known that Andur was a deeply superstitious man. The mighty Baron Andur feared no man, yet lived in constant terror at the thought that he might, in some way, offend some supercilious god. This religious streak could be traced back to the time when, as a young man, he had been on the battlefield, fighting at his father's side. The old Baron, an impious old sot, was struck down by a bolt of lightning just as he raised his sword in the very moment of triumph. That act of divine retribution had made a deep and lasting impression on his young son. Of course Rahn knew of this weakness, and he plotted to use it in laying his scheme for revenge.

The chief priest at that time was a man named Druz, a fawning sycophant, corrupt even by the standards of that most degenerate court. He was summoned to appear before the King, who informed his chief priest that he had some concerns about the upcoming Feast of the Crimson Moon. This was the rite of propitiation, a time of atonement when tribute was paid to appease the gods.

Womenfolk were not allowed to participate in this all-male ceremony, except of course for the female slaves. But all able-bodied men were called upon to attend, so these religious occasions regularly brought together the squabbling barons. Fights broke out frequently. And since the wine flowed freely at these gatherings, more often than not they degenerated into drunken brawls. Skulls had been broken, blood spilt. This was an ancient practice.

And so it was with utter astonishment that the chief priest heard his monarch now express dismay that such a thing should be allowed to happen! Before the dumfounded priest could reply, the King graciously suggested a remedy. Why not a "peace of the gods"—a brief truce in which old quarrels were set aside, along with the all weapons, to be left at the gates of the city. The chief priest would personally proclaim that all worshippers would be accorded divine protection. Moreover, he was instructed to see to it that all the priests throughout the lands would inform the faithful of this novel idea. The noose around Andur's neck had tightened just a bit.

One can only guess at the thoughts that went through the helmeted head of the obstreperous baron as he rode to the city confident, yet perhaps uneasy, even in the company of a strong guard of his most trusted warriors. He must have been deeply suspicious; yet, driven by his religious obsession, he was unable to stay away from the call to offer sacrifice. Rahn, watching down from a secret chamber in one of the guard towers, must have smiled to himself to see his enemy and his escort dutifully hand over their weapons. Andur's face was set, his lips turned down in a stoic, glum expression. He must have felt quite naked without this sword as his horse carried him through the massive wooden gates and under the dread battlements of Thralkild.

The Baron and his men were graciously invited by the smiling, bowing priests into the holy sanctum, and there they were surprised to find they were the only worshippers to be admitted. The doors were barred swiftly, and a group of the King's guards slipped into the room through a hidden side entrance, their swords drawn and ready. It was a slaughter. The unarmed men were hacked down quickly and ruthlessly, before the eyes of their devout but very foolish master.

Andur's life was spared, for he was to await the King's pleasure. But when, after a few minutes, Rahn entered the room with sword in hand, the smell of fresh blood was in the air. And when the struggling, outraged Baron screamed his insults and spat into Rahn's face, he so provoked our sovereign that the King struck at once, thus depriving himself of the pleasures of seeing his enemy die a slow, lingering death.

Even as he was dispatching his enemy with one hand, the King reached out with the other for his prize. Under the ruse of having a message from the Lord of the Manor, a delegation of the King's men had gained entrance into the largely unguarded castle. After a brief but furious skirmish with the few remaining guards, they captured the Lady Alea, her daughter, and their servants, bound them, and hauled the lot of them off to Thralkild.

Now the captives were brought before the King, frightened, disheveled, barefoot, and still in their night clothes, for they had been roused from their beds by the untimely arrival of the horde of armed men. Rahn still wore the short warrior's kilt, although he had changed into a fresh tunic and washed his hands of the blood of he who had dared to challenge the King. He sat enthroned, his powerful thighs half-exposed, knees well spread, sandaled feet flat on the floor, hands resting comfortably, gripping the arms of the massive throne lightly.

We of the court had been ordered to turn out, for Rahn loved spectacle, and he was especially pleased when he could have his triumphs witnessed by his admiring subjects; we courtiers certainly qualified. He would have a most appreciative audience when he humbled the memory of his vanquished foe…by taking his women before our very eyes.

CHAPTER TWO

Helmeted guards stood at the side of each of the captives. They took them by the arms, hauling them forward, presenting them to their King. The prisoners stood dejectedly, barefoot and naked under their thin white shifts, paralyzed with fear, their eyes rigidly downcast, hands tied in front in front of them. Without a word, the King raised a jeweled hand and stabbed a long pointed finger directly at Andur's widow. Before she could react, the shift was torn from Alea's lush, twisting body and she was dragged forward to be placed, naked, on her knees before her sovereign. Her blue eyes were wide with terror, and she might have cried out, but she was too afraid to make a sound. Everyone knew it was forbidden to speak at a royal audience unless one was first given permission by the King.

Now Rahn let his lecherous eyes play over the ravishing beauty who knelt at his feet, her blond head hung in abject submission. It was well known that our King had an eye for those pale northern beauties, with their fair skin and incredible silky blond hair. Some of his most favored slave girls had been acquired by his raiding parties that were regularly sent across the northern frontiers in the hunt for women for their insatiable monarch. They were hardy women, lean and long of limb; handsome women with hard bodies, strong thighs and splendidly muscled legs.

Apparently, when she retired for the night, it had been Lady Alea's habit to twist her long hair into a single braid, which she wore pinned up while she slept. It was a bit bedraggled, but more or less intact, still coiled and pinned in place. Rahn beckoned to a slave and whispered in the girl's ear. Obediently, she approached the kneeling woman and, standing behind her, undid her hair deftly so that the soft blond mass was released to tumble down over bare shoulders and fan out halfway down her back. As his captive bent her neck, the freed hair fell forward, partially shielding her face.

I watched Rahn's lips curl in a grin of pleased satisfaction as he studied his prize: the smooth top of her shiny blond head with hair shimmering in the candlelight, the huddled shoulders, the flattened cones of her gently mounded breasts with pink nipples that were wide and slightly uptilted, and below the silken thicket of pale blond curls that shaded the pubis tucked between her robust thighs.

The Fall of the Ice Queen

With a commanding gesture, Rahn bade her rise. The big blonde, her hands still bound, struggled to her feet, rising to her full height to stand before her liege lord.

"Raise your head up, woman," the King ordered curtly.

Obediently, Andur's proud widow lifted her chin, and stood with her shoulders thrown back, chin held high, her clear eyes on some distant horizon. Her smooth, high brow seemed curiously untroubled, her blue eyes calm and steady under their fine blond arches. She gave no sign of her true feelings. It must be said that while she was fearful for her life and that of her children, as any sensible woman would be who was the wife of a declared enemy of the King, Alea could hardly be called distraught over the death of her brutish boor of a husband.

If the facts be known, the beautiful young widow was undoubtedly relieved to be free of him. And although not exactly pleased to find herself being eyed as an object of desire in the King's lecherous gaze, she may have seen more hope for herself here than in the dreary isolation of that grim pile of stones at Andur. It was hard to tell what thoughts went through her pretty head, for there was not a trace of emotion in those soft blue eyes and that vacant stare, impossible to know what she thought as she was made to turn around so as to present the man with her back so he might appraise her handsome, well-made bottom; the splendid ass that had once been Andur's and now was his for the taking!

And what were the feelings of this elegant woman? Did Lady Alea feel the heat of the King's longing gaze on her naked bottom? Could she even dream of the perverse humiliation she would be made to endure at the hands of that vengeful monarch? Could she even imagine what it meant to be called upon to submit and to serve in the most debauched and decadent court known to man?

Only after his greedy eyes had leisurely devoured that magnificent behind did he allow the young woman to turn and face him once more.

"Release her," the King commanded; the captive's hands were freed. "You may approach," he said imperiously, scanning her pale, expressionless face.

Moving as though in a trance, the stately nude stepped forward, placing a bare foot on the thick fur rug that lined the steps to the throne. We watched in silence as she mounted the steps, moving with measured dignity—one, two, three steps, till she brought herself to the place where our monarch pointed—a patch of fur rug just between his opened legs.

By now there was an unmistakable bulge in the King's kilt. His blood was fired with lust, and he could no longer keep from enjoying with his hungry hands what so far he had savored only with his eyes. He reached out for his latest acquisition. Large masculine hands curved around naked feminine haunches as he brought her hips toward him. Strong fingers curled around her hips and dug into the cheeks of her meaty ass as he held her, tightening his grip, squeezing, testing the firm but yielding resiliency of her twin mounds. The woman leaned back and closed her eyes, swaying slightly as the King ran his cupped hands over her splendid loins.

"Look at me!" he hissed, suddenly infuriated by the blonde's quiet composure, that maddening detachment that seemed to him to border on disdain. The big blonde stood straight and tall, her hands loosely at her sides. And as she looked down on her enthroned sovereign, she saw him brush back the short hem of his kilt and expose his obviously ready penis which lifted its head eagerly and stood proudly erect.

I saw Lady Alea's blue eyes widen as she stared fixedly at the phallic apparition, studying the King's erect manhood, transfixed, suddenly taken aback to realize what was being demanded of her. The angrily impatient King made his wishes perfectly clear.

"On your knees, woman!" he spat, pointing to the spot on the rug between his spread thighs. With quiet dignity, Lady Alea lowered herself till her eyes were even with her sovereign's erect manhood that stood pulsating with lust only inches away from her lips.

He watched her closely as she reached for him, wrapping her fingers around his swollen shaft, holding him lightly in her curled fingers. Then she tilted his stiffened sword forward to bring the taut ring of her lips down over the throbbing crown, docilely accepting the turgid prick of her Lord and Master into her receptive mouth.

I saw Rahn's eyes flutter closed and the edges of his drawn lips curled up in pleasure as Lady Alea went down on him. The golden silk of her hair spilled over his thighs as she buried her head in his lap. Her soft breasts shifted seductively, swaying heavily beneath her as she leaned forward. He reached down, placing his hands on her head, running his fingers through the mass of hair, holding her lightly, while she worked him over with mouth and lips and tongue.

I glanced over to where the daughter stood watching from the shadows, curious to see her reaction as her mother was forced to her knees to show her subservience —paying tribute to the King's mighty rod in front of the entire court! The girl stood perfectly still, looking on, obviously intrigued. There was fear, it is true, but there was also a note of sexual curiosity in those wide blue eyes—eyes that were so much like her mother's, I thought.

I turned back just as the King threw back his head at the sudden stab of pure delight that shot up from his loins. His head lolled back and fell to one shoulder and his eyes opened—to fix on me! He gave me a truly wicked grin as I stood transfixed, watching my King being pleasured by the humbled consort of his beaten foe.

I heard a groan escape his lips. Now he, too, let his gaze fall on the observing daughter, watching the lass through dark, half-lidded eyes. Perhaps, like me, he was curious to see her reaction to the sight of her mother paying obsequious devotion to the royal staff. In any event, his study was cut short as the blond head bobbed with mounting vigor, bringing a shock of pleasure that forced his eyes closed so that he might savor the exquisite thrills rippling up from his loins more fully. Rahn threw back his head, tightened his grip on the throne, and strained backward, raising his hips, arching his back and thrusting himself even deeper into the ministering woman's mouth.

He struggled to hold his control till the last possible moment and then, when the crashing wave of ecstasy overtook him, he reached down, grabbed the captive woman by the hair, and pulled her head back, thus freeing his erupting manhood from her mouth. Aiming the head of his pulsating prick right at her face, he splattered her fine aristocratic features with his sperm, decorating her forehead, trailing down her closed eyelids, along her nose, down one cheek, painting her lovely face with thick ropy gobs of semen. The creamy residue soaked the edge of her hair and dribbled down over her lips and chin.

Now the King dismissed his aristocratic cocksucker with a contemptuous wave of his hand. I wondered about her fate. Would he keep her as a concubine in the House of Women? Would she be raised up to become his consort? Or would she be humbled even further, kept naked to serve the court as a sex slave? One never knew about the capricious King.

For now, she was dismissed. The guards came forth to pick her up by the arms and drag her back into the shadows. Now they tied her hands again, but this time her wrists were bound behind her. Shoulders back, her breasts jutted nicely, taut and firm. They placed her on her knees and she knelt upright, head hung low, the

King's spendings slowly drying on her face. Next, she was gagged; forced to wear the leather strap around her mouth, although I failed to see the reason for that refinement. Perhaps the King saw it as a precaution lest she forget herself and cry out in anguish at what she was about to witness. For now her sovereign turned the royal eye from Lady Alea to the children of his vanquished foe.

At his gesture, the young woman was brought before him and at his command, one of the male servants of Andur's house, a young tousled-haired stable boy. I wondered what the King had in mind. When he nodded to his guards, the captives were swiftly stripped of their thin clothing. Naked, they were shoved forward toward the King. I judged them to be in their late teens, perhaps eighteen or twenty-one; it was hard to tell. The young man was wide-eyed with terror. He stood tense and expectant, holding himself rigidly erect as though frozen in fear to be within reach of his terrible Monarch in such an unprotected state.

Rahn eyed the lad's wiry young body and somnolent sex, a skinny drooping soldier that hung shriveled with fear. Rahn nodded at the boy's pitiful state and dismissed him with a leering grin. The pleasing shape of the young woman's body however, held our monarch's lecherous interest for quite a bit longer. Even in his depleted state, having been satiated so recently by the mother, the old satyr felt a twinge of desire as he examined the comely lass.

The girl stood before him with her head bowed

submissively, eyes lowered demurely. Her hair had been twisted into two ropes that were coiled in place. As she stood before him she couldn't help noticing the royal member, which even now seemed to stir itself into a semihard state, swelling as the King took in the clean lines of her youthful beauty.

Again there was just the slightest gesture from the throne, and a well-trained slave girl leapt forward to quickly undo the girl's hair. Unlike her mother's hair, which had a deeper golden hue, hers was of spun silvery gold, pale, like fine cornsilk. Now her hanging hair was split over her fragile shoulders so that a long silky strand fell down the front at either side, while behind a curtain of finely textured hair covered her bare back.

The King studied that hair, the fresh appeal of those neat blond features, the pleasing nubile shape of the girl's slender, almost hipless body, and the breasts, two delicate pendants with soft pink nipples that were small and precise. She stood with her bound hands before her, holding them down as far as she could to shield her blond sex. That annoyed the King.

"Untie them!" he ordered gruffly. Then, to the girl: "Raise your hands up—on top of your head—both of you."

The fearful captives assumed the pose he ordered, standing there, side by side, their arms raised up, fingers intertwined, hands on their heads. He had them pirouette slowly, turning their backs to him, just as he had made the girl's mother do. This gave him the opportunity to compare their bottoms: the hard boyish butt, small and tight; and the more softly rounded shape of the girlish ass—two nicely contoured, perfectly symmetrical domes.

When the young captives completed their circles and faced him once again, Rahn eyed them up and down, not saying a word, letting the tension build. They shifted uneasily under his unblinking stare, tense and expectant.

"Your young mistress is quite pretty, isn't she?" Rahn murmured at last, addressing the stable boy while leering at the young girl who had fallen into his clutches. Now he reached for the thin pointed scepter that rested against the throne, using it to point out the girl's charms. Starting at the chin, it was drawn down the front of her throat in a straight line that ran right down the sternum between her choice young breasts.

"Tell me, what do you think of these, eh?" And then without waiting for an answer. "As pretty a set of tits as you'll ever see. A bit on the skimpy side, some might say, but a frisky pair, to be sure. See how they bounce!" And with that the point slipped into the tuck of the undercurve of the girl's left breast so that the Sovereign of the Two Lands could flip that small, neat globe with his scepter.

He kept up this ribald banter while he played with the poor girl's tits, tracing the sloping contours, agitating those fleshy globes, rubbing the nipples with the tip, zeroing in on the sensate tips, pressing a hard nubbin into the soft, crinkled disk of its surrounding aureole. Throughout it all, the girl bit her lips but held herself still. Once I saw her close her eyes. Her lips parted as she drew a sharp breath through clenched teeth at the light scratching that tickled her sensitive nipples. The mischievous King, using nothing but the very tip of the scepter soon had the young girl's nipples stiffening with excitement till they stuck out hard and pointy. Restless and insatiable, our wicked Monarch soon tired of this diversion, eager as he was to move on and explore other territory.

"You must have lusted to get your hands on that pair, eh? a randy young fellow like you growing up with those titties bouncing around before your very eyes. But maybe you've sampled those treats before? Felt up your sister now and again when the two of you played games behind the barn?" Suddenly he turned on the terrified lad.

"*Well?*" he exploded.

"N-No…my my Lord," the youth managed to stammer out in a choked voice.

"Hmmmm," the King speculated, the point of the scepter playing now under the maidenly breasts and down the center of the flat belly that flinched with its tickling passage. Rahn continued his line down, lightly indenting the soft skin, heading slowly but inexorably over the smoothened contour of the lower belly and on to the small, gently mounded pubis.

"And what about this? Your young mistress's little treasure box? Surely you've dreamed of slipping your cock in there, a young stud like you?"

The rigidly tense young man seemed to have lost his

voice, paralyzed with fear that he might give his sovereign an answer that displeased him. Meanwhile the pointed rod was tracing its way through the light whisper of soft blond fuzz that furred the slight mount of Venus. The point was heading for the neat cleft tucked demurely between the girl's tightly pressed young thighs.

"They say your lord was quite a cocksman," the King went on, scratching absently at the delicate netherlips. "You've got his blood. A healthy young stud like you must be fucking half the girls in the shire. Maybe there's a little slave girl who's your favorite…but you must have lusted after this pretty piece, eh?" The King grinned, hugely pleased with himself.

"No…no, my Lord," the youth stammered out, clearly scared witless by now.

"Oh? And why not? You don't fancy the boys, do you?" the King leered. The youth shook his head, but the King was ignoring him, intent as he was on the spot where the scepter pointed inquisitively right at the center of the girl's pussy just at the top of the dainty petals. The King paused to consider. "Then maybe it's her ass you lust after? Some men do, you know. Turn around, girl. Show us that pretty little ass of yours!"

Young Gwin, her hands still on her head, turned obediently, with small steps, till she stood sideways to her King, her back to her erstwhile servant.

"See that?" The King tapped the solid object of his affection with the scepter. "Well…*look at it!*" he demanded.

The poor boy, standing with his eyes locked straight ahead, now turned to regard his naked bottom.

"A fine ass she's got there." The King nodded approvingly. *"Isn't it?"* he screamed suddenly.

"Yes, my Lord," came the instant reply in a high, strangled voice.

"Yes, *what?!*"

"Yes, it's a n-nice ass," the terrified youth managed to get out. He was undoubtedly convinced that his next words might well be his last. But the Monarch of the Two Lands, his lust satiated temporarily, was in a playful mood. He grunted, acknowledging the youth's tribute to the proferred posterior.

"You there, girl, bend over! Hands on your knees. Stick out that saucy little tail of yours so we can get a better look!"

The girl seemed flustered and a bit hesitant, but she, too, knew the price of disobedience. And so she did as she was told, bending from her hips, holding herself rigid, bracing herself with hands just above her knees, arching her back and jutting her ass back in the lewd pose the King demanded. She closed her eyes and waited tensely.

"Go on, touch her! I know you want to—probably wanted to for years." The King laughed. "I'll bet you used to dream about that ass when you stroked yourself, eh?"

I was not surprised by this turn of events. No one who knew Rahn could be. Such perversity was typical of the games that degenerate King ordered for his private amusement. Confused and fearful, the stable boy seemed unsure, but he did as he was told, dropping his arms, reaching out to touch the proffered bottom lightly.

"Not like that!" The King spat in disgust. "Feel her up good! I want you to make her feel like a woman! What sort of a man are you, anyway?" he shouted, his terrible eyes blazing in anger. "Didn't that worthless father of yours teach you how to handle women?"

The lad licked his lips nervously, fumbled a bit, then, renewed his grip on that sweet little butt. Clasping her more firmly now, he began to massage the taut domes.

"That's better," the King crowed. "She loves it—you see? Don't you love it, having your servant play with your ass?" he asked the girl, who maintained the position with her eyes still closed tightly.

"Yes, my Lord," she whispered, tense and afraid.

"And you?... Don't stop! Doesn't it feel good... having that pretty little ass in your hands?"

"Yes, my Lord."

"Then why don't you show it?" the King asked in sudden dismay. "A healthy young lad like you should be sporting a good stiff one by now. But what's this?" the King demanded, moving his scepter to where the young man's penis hung drooping sadly. He was enjoying himself immensely, amusing himself by tormenting the lad. As well I knew, at times like this, Rahn could be most dangerous.

Now his eyes roamed over the youth's tightly knit body. It was a body sheened with a patina of sweat—the sweat of fear. The King let his gaze fall down a narrow chest with only a modest trace of golden down, small

The Fall of the Ice Queen

swirls that trailed down the center of that taut belly to thicken into a light bush of pubic hair from which sprouted the boy's fear-shrunken, dormant sex.

The King brought the wicked scepter into play, placing the very tip delicately under the drooping head of the youngster's cock, flipping it up playfully, as the fearful lad stood stock-still, still holding his mistress by the hips.

"When a real man's blood is stirred by the feel of a woman's behind, his prick rises up in proud salute," he lectured calmly as he brought the scepter up between the boy's legs to lift the somnolent prick, as though to demonstrate.

"Come, now," he coaxed, "I want to see this proud soldier snap to attention!"

Needless to say, the King's command had not the slightest effect on the shrunken cock that hung limply on the thoroughly frightened youth. The King feigned a puzzled expression as he prodded the lifeless prick with the royal rod. Then the light dawned!

"I have it!" he announced to those of us who stood by, watching his bizarre game unfold. "A sure nostrum for the pitiful condition from which you suffer. It is your sister here who holds that cure in her very hands! Go to him, girl! Take your friendly servant's cock firmly in your hands, and use your feminine wiles to restore his sagging spirits."

The young woman straightened up and stood there, anxious and confused.

The King was impatient now. "Go on, lass! Surely you know what to do? Hold him. Stroke him! Hasn't your mother taught you what to do? I presume such skills are passed on from mother to daughter. You can't be as innocent as all of that...or are you?"

Suddenly a thought struck him! "Surely you're not a virgin?" The king demanded in a loud, clear voice.

The poor distraught girl clenched her eyes tightly and shook her head from side to side.

"Just as I thought!" the King crowed triumphantly. "You're a randy little minx, I'll wager, and you've probably played your share of games with the lads, eh? A tumble in the hay with a stable boy or two? Come, now, nothing to be ashamed about. Go on...why don't you show us what you do? Take this sad servant boy in hand and make him happy!"

Now the two young people saw fully what was expected of them, realized that they were to perform for the perverted King of the Two Lands. There was no choice; Rahn must be obeyed! From the shadows the girl's mother watched, her wide blue eyes staring incredulously over the top of the leather strap that gagged her so effectively.

The young woman came to the terrified lad, and, reaching down, she placed a hand on his limp penis, curving her fingers to cradle his manhood, while the boy straightened and tensed visibly at her touch. The small hand slid down to cup his scrotum in a curving palm as all the while the lad stood rigid, clenching his fists in nervous spasms and trying not to look at what his mistress was doing to him.

King Rahn snapped his fingers and a sprightly slave

girl came running. Naked but for the leather collar that banded her throat, she fell to her knees before her Master. Without waiting for him to express the royal desire, she reached up between his legs and molded her small hand to his swelling prick. She moved her hand, flexing her fingers, fondling his soft prick adeptly with both hands. Her efforts, more skilled than the inexperienced young girl's, brought immediate results. Before our very eyes, Rahn's prick surged with renewed vigor, becoming semihard, thickening, elongating once more. Rahn always kept a slave girl nearby for just this purpose as he much enjoyed feeling the touch of soft feminine hands cuddling his masculine equipment while he sat enthroned, his gaze riveted on one of the sex shows he had ordered to be performed in the palace.

Meanwhile, Gwin lifted the lad's flaccid cock, holding it between her fingers and rubbing the head experimentally between thumb and forefinger. I saw his tongue peek out to rim his lips as she sampled the velvety smoothness of the head, running a thumb along the underside while cupping the shaft lightly, working with fingers that were curious, yet showed definite interest in the job at hand. Now, under these tender ministrations, the rise of excitement began to overcome the fear, so that the lad's cock uncoiled a bit, stirring, twitching in the girl's hand with the first sign of awakening.

At the same time, the slave girl had Rahn's member fully erected. The turgid head of his prick swelled proudly and darkened with lust. Small fingers were curled loosely around the royal shaft; she was yanking on him with slow, even strokes. His hand came down to clamp the girl's wrist, stopping the tantalizing movement abruptly. He removed the hand and placed it down lower, between his legs, encouraging her to fondle the hairy sac with its royal jewels while he watched the young man's cock swell into prominence under the manipulation of the slim blond girl.

By now the exciting touch of that curious feminine hand had the boy's cock firm and fully expanded. Long and slim, the healthy young lad's invigorated prick stood upright, bowed slightly so that the head curved back almost to his belly, the young prong rigid with excitement. Looking over her shoulder at her liege lord, the girl got a nod of approval from the leering King, who urged her silently to continue what she had started. Now she flattened her hand and used the fleshy heel of her palm, sliding it down the taut underside of the boy's straining manhood, pressing deeply as she did so, sending a delicious shudder of lust surging through the weak-kneed lad who swayed at the powerful rush of unbearable pleasure.

The lad's hands shot out to hold the girl by the hips, perhaps to steady himself, perhaps because the raging lust she inflamed in him made him ache to run his itching hands down the naked lines of her desirable body, only inches away.

"Now play with her pussy!" Rahn ordered harshly.

Rhyn stepped closer till the two siblings faced each other. The young lad was taller than his erstwhile mistress, and she looked up at him and held his eyes as he slipped a hand down between her legs. The girl held him in a loose fist while his inquisitive fingers pressed into the soft folds of her cleft. The two youngsters played with each other's sex under the stern eye of their Monarch.

While Rahn kept them at it, toying with each other, his gaze shifted to Uta, the slave girl who crouched at his feet. She was one of his favorites.

Uta was a small-breasted, slightly built lass, her dark brown hair close cropped like that of all slaves. Her thin body was tight and wiry, with straight limbs and a small, hard butt. Rahn favored her with a thin curl at the edge of his cruel lips as he reached down and hauled her up off her knees, drawing her onto his lap, pulling her down till she lay draped over his spread thighs, her naked hips pressed up against his monstrous hard-on. He shifted the girl's passive weight till he had her in the classic spanking position, head hanging down one side, spindly legs angling down the other, taut bottom upended and served up nicely. Now he cupped a choice buttock and worried that little mound while he let his gaze once more fall on the two young people who were working each other up for his edification and amusement.

"Use your finger. Stick it up her cunt!" he shouted at the stable boy.

By now both young people were showing signs of healthy arousal. The boy was panting, his shoulders heaving; his taut prick seemed to be straining to explode, and I noticed that he drew his hips back to keep the swollen head from actually touching the naked body of his mistress, lest the inevitable eruption take place; he was apprehensive that such understandable consequences might anger the wildly unpredictable King.

Gwin's pretty face was flushed with sexual excitement, her cheekbones tinged with a blush of pink. Her eyes were narrowed, her moist lips parted; she, too, was breathing heavily, her small breasts rising and falling raggedly. I saw her fine lashes flutter, her eyes close as her body shuddered with pleasure at the delicious moment when her brother slid his middle finger between her slick netherlips and began to explore her well-lubricated vagina. Her fingers clenched in instinctive reaction, squeezing the lad's throbbing cock as she swayed against him. The sudden tightening of her fist threatened to set the boy off, and he staggered back.

"Kiss her!" Rahn hissed, his own increasing excitement evident in the vehemence of his forceful tone. He was absently stroking Uta's young bottom as she lay still across his lap, running a cupped palm up and over the taut, satiny skin of those twin domes, pausing now and then to deliver a light slap. Rahn was an avid devotee of spanking, although it was Queen Lohr who would later raise spanking to an art form at the height of the court's debauchery.

His cupped hand rose and fell in short, choppy blows, each solid *splat* echoing in crisp staccato in the silence of that huge pillared hall, while before him the two children embraced and kissed, their arms twining around each other, naked loins pressed together, hips writhing with the fires of passion that pulsed through their eager young bodies.

"That's enough!" the King called out. "Now, girl, get down on your back…and spread your legs for your servant. Be quick about it!"

The girl slid to the floor, and lay back propped up on her elbows. I watched her quivering breasts rise and fall in deep undulations; nipples protruding, taut with excitement. Her eyes were hooded, glazed with passion, and her legs moved sensually, opening and closing in a languid scissoring motion on the thick fur rug, while the young man stood there with limbs rigid with tension, his prick jutting out obscenely, swollen and painfully stiff, the throbbing ache of lust quite evident.

"Go on, mount her!" the king commanded the obviously ready lad. "Look at her—you can tell she wants it! Fuck her…*now!* Fuck your young mistress!" he roared.

Wild with feverish excitement, the youth flung himself down on the writhing lass, who welcomed him with opened arms. Her legs rose instinctively, and she bent her knees as his hips plunged between her moist young thighs and he drove his prick into her hot wet womanhood, penetrating her, thrusting so deeply that she tossed and moaned with inescapable pleasure.

We watched the boy thrust his hips forward, tightening his butt, plunging in and out, fucking furiously. The highly responsive female was soon meeting him with her own bucking movements, thrusting her pelvis up at him, thrusting and bouncing in wild abandon. The coupling so excited Rahn that he leapt to his feet, spilling the slave girl on the floor. His cock stood out red and angry, a monstrous lust-swollen erection.

Little Uta scrambled up to her knees and reached for her Master's throbbing manhood. Small fingers wrapped around his shaft as she guided it to her mouth, taking him in, sliding her lips down the shaft, enfolding the head of that prick in her sweet little mouth. Rahn never looked down at the sucking girl, but kept his eyes on the fucking couple, urging them on.

"That's it! Fuck her. Fuck her! *Fuck her!*" he yelled. The boy was grunting like a rutting animal, while the girl whimpered and tossed her head from side to side, flailing the soft fur with her long blond strands. She arched her back, straining up high to meet the lad's pounding cock, to force him even deeper into her burning, grinding cunt.

Rahn's hands shot out and he clamped the sucking girl's bobbing head, holding her in a viselike grip while he bucked his hips, fucking her mouth.

A sharp cry from the skewered blond girl followed by a low quivering moan from her partner told us that they had reached their moment of climax. With hips still raised high off the rug, the girl shook and trembled while convulsions racked her tight young body. Meanwhile, the lad's lean body had tightened into a single rigid line, his buttocks clenched as he held himself deep in her core, his sword ensconced to the hilt in the slick, churning, wet pussy.

Rahn guided the slave girl's head up and down, bucking furiously to speed up his climax till he, too, threw back his head, squeezed his eyes shut, and erupted into the pleasuring mouth, coming for the second time that night. Twice was not very much for him. Rahn admired sexual prowess and sometimes held contests which he won inevitably, one time being sucked off five times in one long marathon night.

For a moment, he stood there swaying, holding onto the slave girl who obediently kept his still-pulsating cock in her mouth, swallowing every drop of the royal seed he deigned to give to her. At last he extracted himself. His softening cock plopped free, wet and gleaming, still swollen, but no longer rigidly hard. His dark eyes were alert and excited, wanting more, as he looked on the depleted forms of the two lovers, who lay, still in position, recovering gradually.

Rahn nodded to his guards who sprang forward and began binding up the couple, looping leather straps around their exhausted, limp, sweat-soaked bodies, tying them so they fitted snugly together in the lovers' position with the girl's legs wrapped around the young man's loins; his depleted cock, limp and wet, pressed against the damp, mossy lips of her saturated pussy.

And in that way the two young people would spend their first night in captivity. "Getting to know one another," the king sneered. He grinned at the joined couple squirming at his feet, threw back his head, shook his dark mane, and laughed uproariously. It was a gleeful, triumphant laugh, and a thoroughly evil laugh. Naturally, we all joined in.

CHAPTER THREE

By Rahn's time, the court at Thralkild had reached the height of its imperial splendor. It was on the wide dry plain atop a great hill that overlooked the town of Thralkild that Ank, the first and greatest of our warrior kings, had chosen to build his fortress, a squat, formidable structure designed to be impregnable. It was Orr, Ank's dissolute, pleasure-loving grandson who ordered the mammoth expansion of that powerful fortress into the largest and most comfortable castle in the world, a pleasure palace to rival anything to be found in the Indus or Cathay.

The court of the Two Lands had come a long way from the spartan simplicity of King Ank. Our armies were everywhere victorious: pillaging, raping, and looting so that a steady stream of wealth poured daily into the King's coffers. And with this newfound wealth, the palace rose into magnificence.

Behind the enormous walls was a small city, and within that, an inner circle that held the actual court itself. The grounds of the massive palace dominated the inner circle. Stone walls stood gleaming in the sun: a sprawling series of buildings with open courtyards, terraced walkways, fountains, gardens, and verandas, all of it interconnected by porticoes with tall marble columns that covered more than one square mile.

This was the most wondrous court in the world, a court where luxury, riches, and sheer opulence surpassed that of any Eastern potentate. Brightly colored banners marked the way to the throne, and there mighty King Rahn held audience, receiving the spoils of war: Defeated princes, vanquished foes, and newly acquired slaves were all paraded in, naked and in chains, forced to their knees, to pay their humble tribute. The wealth of conquered lands, gold and jewels, tapestries, precious silks and cloth of gold were laid at his feet. And here, in all his imperial splendor, he received the ambassadors from faraway courts who came to behold the magnificence of the enthroned King of the Two Lands, and left in awe.

The basic plan of the palace was laid out east to west. There were hundreds of rooms—no one knew how many. Long corridors twisted and turned from meeting halls and dining rooms, through the chambers of government clerks and court officials, connecting them with the quarters of the growing retinue that always surrounded the King at court. There were suites of private apartments with bedchambers for the King and his women, the concubines he kept always close at hand, all connected by secret tunnels and hidden galleries.

At the eastern terminus, the magnificent throne room was designed to impress mere mortals, and here the scale was larger than life. Massive pillars circled the room and lined the way from the huge double door to the throne. These stone sentinels served to draw the eye to the enthroned monarch, who sat alone on a raised platform under a golden arch at the far end of the room.

The central passageway led from the raised throne through the double doors and along the spacious main hall to a second set of doors at the far end of the axis. When these were flung back, one was confronted with the blaze of a thousands candles that brilliantly illuminated the splendid opulence of the grand hall. Here the King held his "feasts," decadent revelries with an endless supply of food and wine and sex; banquets that would begin with all proper decorum just after sundown and degenerate inevitably into the most outrageous sexual indulgence, riotous orgies of unbridled lust that would go on throughout the night.

Invitations would go out to the aristocracy to gather at festivals and fetes that would be held at the royal command at Thralkild. The feasts were more frequent than these large gatherings; a few lords, their wives and mistresses, favorites of the King might be invited, and, of course, we courtiers were expected to be in attendance.

Finally there were those more "intimate" parties the King had arranged for his pleasure. For these it was Rahn's habit to invite those women who had caught his eye, or whom he'd heard of by reputation. The guest list might include the most beautiful women of the Two Lands. Often as not, their husbands, fathers, and brothers were pointedly not included.

Naturally, an invitation from the palace could not be declined. On the contrary, husbands and fathers would gladly send off their womenfolk in response to the royal summons, hoping they would please the King and return with the Monarch kindly disposed toward their house.

Of course, there was always the risk that matters might go differently. Should the King be inordinately pleased with the female's companionship, he might easily command an extended stay—in his service as one of his concubines. She would then enter the House of Women to dwell at court until such time as he might tire of her.

On the other hand, should the King be displeased for any reason, the unfortunate female might well find herself relegated to enforced servitude to the court as a common sex slave. Neither wealth, age, or beauty, high status or family prestige could save a woman who had fallen from grace from this fate—a fate which might have her used indiscriminately, called upon to provide personal service at the slightest whim of any bored courtier, lord, or lady who took a fancy to her.

The King's revelries took place in the grand hall, a

The Fall of the Ice Queen

large circular chamber with high vaulted ceilings and seven arched entrances. Invited guests in their finest garments passed through these archways to enter a room whose walls were adorned with mirrors and resplendent with rich tapestries. Elaborate candelabra bathed the walls of the spacious ballroom in the glow of hundreds of candles.

A series of low couches or divans were set end to end to form a square, whose center was left clear as a space for the entertainers to perform. Thick, soft pillows and fine upholstery allowed luxurious dalliance, as the King and his guests reclined, sipping their wine, waiting to be served the choice meats and delicacies that were brought forth in an endless parade of exquisite treats.

On such a night, one would find gaily clad courtiers mingling with the excited guests, all in a convivial party mood. The lords would be dressed in their tightly fitted tunics, booted, and wearing the snug riding trousers that were so popular in those days. The ladies would be dressed in their long satin gowns, flowing dresses made of sleek, shimmering fabrics that they wore with brightly colored hosiery and the high-heeled shoes that were all the rage with the women of the court. Tight corseted belts were worn on top of the gowns, constricting the waist and uplifting the bosom; the open bodice cut so low in front as to provide a generous view of the breasts.

There were other women present, of course—the King's beautiful concubines who wore gowns that were even more revealing than the ladies', since in their case the bodice was cut away so that the front of the gown was made to curve down under the breasts, thus leaving the women's bosom beautifully exposed. These long, flowing gowns were sleeveless affairs, with low-cut backs and silken ribbons that bound the shoulders with narrow straps. The upper part of each concubine's bare arm was banded with a wide bracelet of burnished gold, marking her as the property of the King. Unlike the lady, who might wear a breast halter, short underskirt, and often a full-length chemise beneath her gown, the concubine was always required to be naked under hers.

These tall, elegantly made up, bare-breasted beauties were much admired as they moved through the raucous crowd with such majestic ease and exquisite presence. As I have mentioned, Rahn had quite an eye for women, and only the most attractive females in the Two Lands were chosen to be his concubines. It was considered quite an honor.

Kept in their own separate chambers—called the House of Women—they were a class apart. Educated, and carefully trained in the art of love in all its many manifestations, they also received lessons in dress, deportment, manners, art, and music. And they were taught the gentle skills of femininity—most of which were hopelessly lost on their crude, bawdy Master, although there were those of us at court who truly appreciated these most refined and delicate feminine virtues.

Fortunately, we could do no more than admire these desirable creatures from afar, for they were designated as the King's exclusive harlots. Rahn could be most generous, particularly if he had been drinking. Then he would share the girls freely. It was considered a particular sign of royal favor if a lucky courtier was singled out for the privilege of enjoying the services of a royal concubine for an evening's pleasure.

Finally, in attendance at these affairs would be a handful of pages along with a generous number of sex slaves. Pages were instantly recognized by their gay attire and their short hair, cut in what came to be called the pageboy cut: far shorter than a lady's or even a lord's, but still longer than the close-cropped shag of a slave. Boys and girls were shorn identically and dressed in the similar uniforms of bright, solid colors, reds and greens and blues and yellows: fitted tunics that ended snugly at the waist, worn with matching tights that molded the pleasing contours of their supple young thighs and slim, coltish legs.

Lowest in order were the sex slaves. Chosen from the vast army of slaves that served at Thralkild, only the prettiest girls and handsomest young men were privileged to serve as sex slaves. Unlike the concubines, they were given no formal instruction in the arts of love but had to learn on their own as it were, often from each other or at the greedy hands of an impatient courtier. Some of these slaves were instinctively talented and became quite adept at giving pleasure so that they rivaled the best of the concubines. Their services were much sought after.

Except for the broad leather collar that banded their necks, slaves were kept naked when required to attend

Rahn's feasts. On other occasions, they might be allowed a skimpy outfit, a short kilt perhaps, or a brief tunic of fine-spun silk, a thin flimsy garment that would partially cover, but not conceal, the lines of their taut young bodies. The duties of both groups at these affairs were much the same: Pages, like sex slaves, were expected to wait upon the courtiers and royal guests, to be instantly available to provide whatever services—including sexual services—that might be required of them, whether by lord or lady.

I well remember the feast that the King ordered to celebrate his triumph over Andur. On that occasion, I was reclining only a few feet from where His Majesty was lounging, stretched out beside one of his favorite military commanders, a lean, hard-muscled, weathered veteran of the eastern wars, one General Turhan. The party was well under way and the men had gotten comfortable, allowing the slaves to undress them completely and wrap their naked bodies in brief, wide-sleeved silk jackets. Loosely belted and open down the front, these hip-length lounging robes were lightweight and cool, and had the advantage of being slipped off easily in the heat of passion.

Turhan had been the King's right-hand man throughout the eastern campaign, and now those two old campaigners were swapping war stories, shouting, roaring with laughter, and demanding more food and drink and women.

And there were women aplenty. Lively dancing girls who stripped off their skirts as they performed before the

King, and then went on to dance with fully clothed guests while they themselves had been reduced to nothing more than a string of beads around their necks. There were tumblers and acrobats who performed in tights, both sexes naked from the hips up: muscular, bare-chested men with strong arms that easily lifted slim, agile girls with wiry limbs and compact tightly knit bodies, their small, taut breasts pleasingly bare as they performed their gymnastics for us, delighting the court with the twisting, straining contortions of their limber athletic bodies.

Sex slaves were everywhere, slithering between lounging couples, or lying languidly well within reach so that their young bodies might be toyed with leisurely by a lord, his wife, or his mistress as they sipped their wine and engaged in idle gossip. Slaves learned quickly that they must be always at the beck and call of the lascivious guests who, having the followed the King's lead, wasted no time in shedding their clothes. The men slipped on the brief lounging jackets, in the fashion much favored by the King; while the women sprawled about in various stages of undress.

Since Rahn always chose the girls whom he invited as his special guests most carefully, there were quite a few ravishing creatures on hand, and they lost no opportunity to show the King whatever seductive charms they possessed in that highly competitive atmosphere where the women heavily outnumbered the men. They would do whatever was necessary to catch the King's roving eye, for it was rumored that Rahn had been overheard expressing the desire to take a queen.

Of course, the court abounded in rumors, yet to this one I gave some credence. I myself had heard Rahn express the need for a son—no, for many sons, healthy strong lads who would grow to fight at his side, and someday to rule his kingdom when he was gone. In short, he was now coming to an age when he was beginning to feel the first stirrings of immortality, the time of life when a man might dream of a dynasty.

So the ladies, having removed their dresses to prance about in their underwear, would throw a glance his way, favoring their randy monarch with a sly smile, a seductive flutter of the lashes, or a brazenly sexy grin. A dwindling number still retained their breast halters, but by now most had dispensed with even that garment so that they might parade about bare-breasted, loins wrapped in thin underskirts of fine spun silk that barely grazed their knees. A few of the bolder ones had gone even further. They lounged about pleasingly naked but for stockings, garters, and high-heeled shoes.

It was rumored that the King might select his consort from among his concubines; that caused considerable consternation on the part of the highborn ladies. Near the far wall directly across from the King, a low bench had been placed, and behind that bench knelt the royal concubines, lined up in a single row, bent legs tucked under them, their bottoms resting on their heels as they knelt facing their Master.

From where I sat, I could study and compare their magnificent bare-breasted forms at my leisure. Only seven were in attendance that night, which was not

THE FALL OF THE ICE QUEEN

unusual, for at any given time of the month one or two women might be excused from attendance. But among those present in that lineup of splendid beauties was the fair Alea, formerly the Lady of Andur. She wore a blue silk gown, and she knelt perfectly still, eyes lowered, hardly touching her food, sipping her wine occasionally. The wide bracelet of burnished gold banding the soft skin of her upper arm marked her as one of the King's stable.

The King was bragging to his old crony about his defeat of Andur, and that seemed to remind him of Alea. He sent a slave scurrying over to summon the statuesque blonde to him. She rose deliberately and crossed the room slowly; her chiseled aristocratic features calm; golden hair magnificent in its shimmering array. The flowing gown draped her tall frame, suspended by the thin ribbons that looped her bare shoulders. The satiny material was gathered at the midriff and then allowed to fall in pleated folds that ended just above her ankles, an inch or two above her delicate high-heeled sandals.

The young woman moved with her usual dignity, those full-mounded breasts with their big nipples displayed so proudly. Her chin was held high, her blue eyes untroubled and serene. I had seen her retain that marvelous composure even when her sovereign's sticky spendings were trickling down her noble visage.

Now the King presented her to Turhan, inviting his general to admire his prize, who stood before him with bowed head. For a few moments, he kept her standing there while the wise general, knowing he should appreciate—but not too much—the King's latest acquisition, was suitably impressed and then praised the King's good taste. Rahn smiled, pleased that it was so.

"Come here." He beckoned the big blonde to him. "Lift your dress. Show the general your cunt."

I watched Alea's face closely, but the crude words of the King made no impression. Still expressionless, she bent forward, moving to obey, reaching down to gather up two handfuls of the slippery blue silk. She hauled the dress up, raising the hem and uncovering her long, shapely legs, their splendid lengths sheathed in the finest hosiery of a soft sheer blue. The men watched captivated as the curtain rose to reveal her lush thighs, the smooth contours banded halfway up their graceful lengths by lacy garters. Gradually, the rising hemline uncovered the naked skin beyond the snug stocking tops, smooth columns of the upper thighs that came into view as did her mount of Venus with its silken thicket of tiny pale curls.

"Higher," the King commanded gruffly, leaning forward in his chair.

And the hem was lifted a few more inches obediently, till Alea held the bunched-up dress across her belly, letting the men's greedy eyes drink in their fill of her naked womanhood. For a moment they studied the lightly furred vulva displayed before their eyes, not saying a word. I wondered if the King would take her right then and there, or perhaps offer her to his victorious general, for the rumor had it that although the King had used her on several occasions he had yet to dip his sword into that choice honeypot. But he did neither.

The Fall of the Ice Queen

Instead, he ordered the woman to turn around and lift up her dress in the back.

As I had sat entranced, watching this seductive display, a slave named Gar, a skinny girl with cropped blond stubble, came up to replenish my wine. She stood beside me as she bent down to pour the wine into my cup and, inspired by the blood-stirring sight of fair Alea showing herself, I reached up to run my hand up the girl's bare leg and over the curving fullness of her naked haunch. Being a well-trained slave, she froze in place, letting my hungry hand savor her firm naked flesh.

Now, as the statuesque woman turned her back on her admirers, I relieved the wiry girl of her jug and pulled her to me, inviting her to sit on my lap. I cupped her trim waist as she perched with her legs dangling over my thighs and let a hand explore her hard young body, meanwhile never taking my eyes off the beautiful concubine who was lifting her skirts in back to expose her naked ass to the King and his most appreciative general.

Alea's clenched hands held fistfuls of the thin dress up across the small of her back so that she was totally exposed behind, from the sweeping mounds of her shapely buttocks with their firm undercurves, all the way down the long stockinged legs to her slim high heels. The King looked expectantly at his general, who was attentively examining those delectable pale hemispheres, so smooth and rounded, with a neat shadow line separating them precisely. Turhan turned to his sovereign and smiled, nodding his enthusiastic approval.

The King grinned from ear to ear and clapped his hands. A low table was brought out and set before the men, a padded footstool placed on top of it.

At the King's impatient gesture, the fair Alea placed a high-heeled slipper on the table and stepped up, still holding her dress up in back so they might watch her bare bottom as she mounted the platform. With her back still toward them, Rahn had her kneel on the table and lean down over the low padded stool, all the while keeping her dress hoisted shamelessly.

Alea did as she was ordered, lying over the padded stool, her bottom raised boldly. The dress, falling across her lower back, formed a parted drape through which her naked ass peeked out provocatively.

"Well, what do you think of her? Nice ass, eh?" Rahn inquired of his appreciative officer. "I've not yet tried it myself, but I'm sure she's had a prick up her ass before, since she had to submit to that old goat Andur. He probably murmured his holy prayers while he was fucking her up the ass!" The King roared at his own joke, and those of us within earshot joined in the raucous laughter.

Now he turned to face his general. "You must be the first at the court to have her ass, old friend," he offered generously.

The general made the ritual protests, but his gracious and most generous sovereign insisted on presenting this trifling gift; so General Turhan sat up and unbelted his jacket, letting us get a good look at his engorged passion-swollen prick.

"Prepare her!" the King commanded, and a slave girl hurried up with a small jar of ointment used to ease such a passage as was now being contemplated by the clearly excited soldier whose eyes were fixed on the female bottom that was jutting out before him in lewd invitation.

The clever slave knew her job well. She applied the slippery ointment, running a finger up and down between the clenching pillows of Alea's ass, tickling the seam, probing the anus. We watched as she used one hand to open up the twin mounds, splaying her fingers to part the straining rearcheeks while she applied the ointment to the cringing anus, a pale rosette that spasmed at the touch of the impish fingertip.

Once she was assured that the girl had been prepared properly, the slave removed her hand and allowed the twin pillows to snap back. Then she turned her attention to the old warrior's massive hard-on, its purplish knob darkened with lust. Coating her hands with the slick oil, the little slave used both hands to lubricate the soldier's equipment carefully, lavishing oil on cock and balls most meticulously. Now, with a bow to her master the slave receded into the background. She left the general on his knees before the proffered ass, his prick sticking up, aching with intolerable readiness—a proud phallus gleaming with a bright sheen of oil.

Fascinated, I kept my eyes on the riveting action while sliding a hand up the smooth rises of Gar's breasts, feeling my way over their slight ridges, two flattened crescents. I let my fingers play with the taut flesh that yielded softly to the press of my fingertips. I scissored a pert little nipple between two fingers and gave the girl a playful squeeze, which caused the impish vixen to squirm in my lap and grope for my stiffened cock. She wrapped her small hand eagerly around the rigid shaft.

Kneeling behind the bending Alea, Turhan grabbed her rearcheeks, mauled them roughly, and spread them apart viciously. Holding her open, he shuffled up on his knees, bringing his vibrating prick up to the vulnerable target. I watched him place the bulbous head right up against the lady's tightly clenched anus. Then he lunged, but the battering ram caused the tiny gate to tighten instinctively, and it refused to yield to his assault even though he poked repeatedly, bearing down with grim determination. Turhan cursed roundly, hauled back, and slapped the offending ass, getting a roaring laugh from his sovereign. He smacked her again, a stinging slap that sent her mounds wobbling, and he lunged forward, fully prepared to ravage his way in when the King stopped him.

"No, wait, my friend. There should be no need to work so hard at the task. Indeed, she must learn to yield to you willingly. A concubine must be taught that nothing she has can be denied to her Master. My chamberlain has devised some clever methods he uses in training the women. Come, let me show you. Uzack!"

Instantly, that worthy appeared at the King's elbow. The chamberlain was responsible for the royal household, as well as keeping the King's constantly squabbling women in line. I didn't envy him his task, yet Uzack, a thin, balding man with an effeminate manner, seemed to quite enjoy himself, especially when he could exercise his authority as disciplinarian of that brood of unruly females. It was widely rumored that while he might occasionally relieve his lust with one of the concubines, he was more enamored of pretty boys, and thus more or less impervious to female blandishments and feminine tearful pleas for mercy.

"This woman's asshole is uncooperative," the King declared, pointing to the well-positioned and waiting rear end. "There is need of considerable improvement there," the King declared. "I think it calls for the methods used with Maya. Show the general," he commanded.

With a sly grin, Uzack nodded his balding head and beckoned to Maya, another of the King's concubines who sat watching from the sidelines. She rose at the summons and came toward us. Like all the King's women, Maya was tall and long-limbed, with long strands of pale brown hair that parted in the middle, draped either side of her long oval face in soft even folds that hung down to tease across her shoulders.

The open-fronted dress she wore was the color of burgundy wine, and it left exposed a lovely pair of breasts, low-slung pendants with russet-colored nipples that tilted upward. The thin dress followed her narrow lines, clinging to her slim midriff and shaping the trim hips as it fell in long, soft folds. I notice a certain stiffness in the way she walked, taking tiny mincing steps as she crossed the room on her high heels. She came to stand before her master and bowed with due deference, letting her long hair fall forward to partially shield her face as she waited with head lowered in docile servitude.

Rahn studied the tilted head and grunted in acknowledgment of the woman's obsequious greeting. Then he turned to his chamberlain.

"Have her show us what she's wearing."

Uzack flashed a truly evil grin at the general and urged Maya to stand with her back to the King and his companion. Her hands came back to obey his injunction to raise her dress up to her waist. She grabbed handfuls of the generous skirt and hauled it upward, exposing stockinged legs, gartered thighs and a pleasingly shaped bare bottom. Now we saw the cause of her discomfort and the curious gait she'd adopted. Under the dress, Maya wore a tight belt that encircled her waist just above the hips. And from the center of the belt a narrow strip ran straight down, disappearing between her fleshy rearcheeks. Embedded in the valley of her rearfurrow, the narrow leather strip ran between her legs and rose up in front to be attached to the center of the belt.

Turhan studied the curious belt with interest, looking to Uzack with a quizzical expression. The chamberlain now proceeded to enlighten the general about the belt's true purpose. He had the concubine lean over, bracing herself with hands on her thighs so that her ass jutted back. Then he placed his slender hands on her cheeks, extended thumbs pressing inward toward the center. He opened her like a ripened peach, to reveal the knobbed end of an ebony shaft whose length was lodged deep in the girl's ass. The belt passed through a slot in the base

THE FALL OF THE ICE QUEEN

of the shaft and thus held it in place so that the evil intruder could not be expelled easily. Indeed, there was a rule that once the chamberlain had secured the rod in place, only he could remove it. It was rumored that some of the girls had to wear the beastly reminder for hours at a time.

Now, like some bizarre impresario, the grinning chamberlain pinched the end of the offending butt plug delicately between thumb and forefinger and jiggled it, causing Maya to jerk upward and wriggle her shoulders, although she held her position in spite of the sudden twinge of discomfort deep in her bowels. The King smiled approvingly as Uzack let the straining mounds snap shut around the capped end of the plug.

Throughout this performance, Alea had not moved, so that the men were now confronted with two nicely displayed feminine bottoms: one plugged, the other soon to be.

Uzack clapped his hands and a slave appeared at his elbow, the same girl who had anointed Alea before. Along with the pot of ointment, she now held a slim, tapering ebony rod and a tangle of leather straps.

The chamberlain went to work. Meticulous, all businesslike, he passed the sturdy leather belt around Alea's waist and tugged on the end to tighten it down through the buckle. The vertical strip hung down in front dangling between her legs. Next, he greased the shaft thoroughly. Then, as his assistant held Alea's rearcheeks open, he set the head of the shaft on the puckered anus and pressed slowly, inexorably, until the tiny gate was breached and the head was buried in Alea's asshole. We watched fascinated as he slowly twisted the rod, screwing it up the girl's ass while she craned back and clenched her jaws against the burning stab of pain. Once past the clinging opening, the shaft slid in with remarkable smoothness. A long steady push soon had it buried deep up the anal canal.

Alea was uttering tight-lipped grunting sounds as Uzack inched it in still farther till only the knobbed end peeked out between her pliant asscheeks. Now satisfied that she was well and truly plugged, the wicked chamberlain threaded the strip through the slotted head and tugged upward, getting a deep grunt from the impaled female as the rude phallus was jiggled and forced in even farther. The strip was pulled taut and then secured in pace through a buckle at the center, that allowed it to be pulled tightly, fitted snugly into her love-cove, then to disappear between her clenching rearcheeks.

Once belted in place, Rahn made Alea turn around, with her dress still raised, so he could point out to his commander how the narrow strip bisected the blond triangle in front and indented the soft flesh of her vagina, pulled as it was high up into the underarch. The pouting netherlips bulged on either side of the snugly ensconced strip as it passed between the legs. Then, with an airy wave of his hand, the King dismissed his newest concubine.

The big blonde let her dress fall back into place. She winced, but otherwise held herself perfectly erect as she shuffled back to her place at the low side table. The only evidence that she wore the phallus was the same stiff gait as Maya's.

"Andur's woman will be quite suitable in a day or two, my friend. Meanwhile, use Maya here to soothe your aching stiffness. You will find her quite a bit more accommodating, since her backside has been well exercised using Uzack's ingenious toys."

And so, at the invitation of his gracious sovereign, the commander of the King's eastern armies fucked the royal concubine up the ass, thrusting into her with savage abandon, holding himself deep in her, buried to the hilt, while he wriggled and shuddered with delight at the exquisite feelings of the snug well-lubricated sheath that gripped his terrible sword and tightened spasmodically, milking him of his male essence.

CHAPTER FOUR

Only a few days after that triumphant celebration, I discovered the reason for General Turhan's presence at court. For some time now there had been rumors that the war was not going very well. Our armies had clashed with those of the evil King of Tarzia, who was forging alliances with the eastern clans, putting up a determined resistance to our expansion. The King was not at all pleased with the military situation, and it was said that he might take to the field to lead our glorious troops to victory.

Within days of Turhan's arrival, other high-ranking officers began to show up at court, thundering in on exhausted horses whose trembling flanks were beaded with sweat. The army had been ordered to stand down and take up defensive positions. They were to await further orders. Meanwhile the top commanders were summoned to a hurriedly called war council at Thralkild.

The secret council lasted three days. When the generals emerged from the meeting, orders went out immediately. Preparations were to be made; the King was going to war!

Now I must confess that while I welcomed the news that our grand and glorious warrior King would once again sweep a vile enemy of the people from the face of the earth, I was less enthusiastic about actually accompanying him to witness yet another heroic victory. Of course, like all male citizens, I had served my ten years in the army, beginning them at the age of sixteen. But that was long ago, and over the years I had found the more comfortable life at court to be a good deal more congenial than a hard camp bed and a drafty tent pitched on some desolate plain and shared with three or four miserable scribes. Rahn seemed to enjoy such hardships, or at least to be indifferent to them; but I much preferred the solid comfort of Thralkild, with its agreeable female companionship.

It really wasn't difficult to arrange things, since Thralkild was a place where "arrangements" were made all the time, and one couldn't help learning a thing or two about how things were done at court. A simple word in the ear of a slave would start the rumor. The story was that Rahn, who used his scribes to write the orders that kept him in touch with the court, was contemplating an additional role for at least one of them. He wished a written record to be kept of his achievements in this campaign. Moreover, if the King was pleased with this account of his heroic deeds, it was predicted confidently that he would reward the fortunate scribe who produced the historic volume with royal favors.

Everyone at court knew Rahn could be quite a generous monarch, especially if he was in his cups, celebrating after bashing in a few heads. It took less than a day till my fellow scribes got wind of this latest rumor. Soon they were lining up, begging the King to be taken along, devastated lest they should be unable to be there to witness and record his glorious triumph over the villainous King of Tarzia. Of course, someone should have to be left behind to manage the correspondence; and as I was the last to approach the royal chamberlain with my modest request, begging humbly that I be allowed to accompany my King, I was disappointed to learn that I was the one chosen to remain at court. I protested—but not too strongly.

Two days later, I stood at the battlements, adding my shouts of encouragement to the wildly cheering throng as our invincible warrior King rode forth to battle at the head of the imperial guard. Colorful banners flew, armor flashed in the sun, as the helmeted warriors rode purposely through the palace gates. The King was in the lead, tall in the saddle, his muscular body clad lightly in a sleeveless leather jerkin and short warrior's kilt, his only armor the iron helmet and the burnished metal breastplate; the familiar broadsword hung at his side. The King preferred this stout weapon for he was what was known in army parlance as a "gut fighter." He relished getting in close to grapple with his opponents man to man.

Once the riders had disappeared in a cloud of dust, I turned from the battlements and headed straight for the baths, congratulating myself at having escaped the long forced march to the bleak frontier and anticipating with much pleasure the opportunity to soak away my cares in the gentle warmth of those perfumed waters while being ministered to by the solicitous hands of a dozen pretty young slaves.

There were numerous baths within the palace, fed by an ingenious series of springs and aqueducts, with the water being gently heated before it was allowed to flow into the sunken tubs. As it was a pleasant summer's day, I headed for the outdoor baths, which were located in a delightful enclosed garden complete with flowering bushes, trees, fountains and statues, the whole surrounded by a colonnaded promenade that provided protection from the midday sun.

I stepped down into the sunken garden to find a surprising number of people already there. These slackers must have slipped away from the crowd even before the King and his retinue had passed through the gates. With so many of the men having gone off to war, the crowd bidding them farewell had been mostly women and children, and now I found myself well outnumbered by bathing females. Ladies and mistresses, concubines and whores, in various stages of undress, were lounging about beside the pools. Slack-limbed and indolent, they

The Fall of the Ice Queen

lay in the sun, their well-oiled naked bodies being pampered by the attending slaves.

I noticed a few sly glances cast my way from under hooded eyes as I strolled down the broad walkway. There was a something in the look of these healthy young women as they eyed me up and down and contemplated the prospect of long months without their men that sent a twinge of excitement through me.

I quickly surveyed the lineup of waiting slaves, lovely girls and eager young lads, all collared, dressed in nothing more than skimpy leather skirts or brief kilts that barely covered the tops of their youthful thighs. A slim girl with a shock of white blond hair, straight sinewy limbs, and narrow pointy tits caught my eye and I beckoned to her. Then I pointed to a second girl—smaller in stature but pleasingly curved, with sparkling dark eyes, cropped brown hair and taut gently mounded breasts.

I allowed the slave girls to undress me slowly as I stood poised on one of the topmost of the raised steps that surrounded the pools. Already I sported an erection, only semihard yet, but swollen enough so that my heavy swaying member did not escape the notice of my appreciative fellow bathers.

Once I was naked, I had my fetching escorts drop their skirts and step free of them. Then, with a naked girl at either side, I slung my arms around their bare shoulders, and together we took the three steps down into the largest of the pools. This was the pool of unheated water, and it felt wonderful, cool and bracing. Of course, the shock of the cold had an immediate and predictable effect upon my burgeoning manhood, so I took each girl by the wrist, dipping their hands under water to place them on my masculine equipment so they might revive my flagging fortunes.

The blonde seemed quite knowledgeable about male anatomy. She slid behind me to reach between my legs and fondle my tightened balls, while the brunette, smiling up at me with a devilish gleam in her dark eyes, curled a small soft hand around my loosely sagging manhood and squeezed. The electrifying touch of those amazingly adept feminine fingers sent a bolt of pure lust racing through me, energizing my cock, which stirred in anticipation, uncoiling in the dark-haired girl's cuddling palm.

I ran a hand down the back of the comely brunette, clamping her bottom and drawing her toward me, kissing her, enjoying the feel of her cool, hard body as she squirmed against me, grinding her high-set tits against my chest.

We splashed about happily for only a few minutes, invigorated by the cold water, before I decided that the gentler waters of the heated pool would be a preferable place to dally with my amorous playmates. So, shivering and sputtering, we emerged and hastened to the warmer waters for their welcoming warmth. We stepped into one of the smaller heated pools, one with sunken steps built in so that one could lounge back, half-submerged, and let the cares of the empire drift away. I eased into the welcoming water, slipping down till it came up almost to my neck before sprawling back to rest on my elbows.

The Fall of the Ice Queen

The girls promptly slithered up on either side of me. It was wildly exciting to feel the wet bodies of these two nubile creatures, so warm and soft, their faces wet, hair drenched and plastered to their heads as they snuggled against me, rubbing their eager little tits all over my extended body and exploring it with sly, impertinent hands, till I had to grab a wrist and caution the overly eager blonde lest her toying fingers end this tantalizing pleasure all too soon.

Emerging once again, this time with my prick fully erect, glowing with the heat and faintly pulsating, I went to a massage table while the girls toweled me off quickly. Now I climbed up on the padded leather table that was deliciously warm from the sun, and immediately turned over on my belly, pressing my stiffened rod into the warm leather, purposely denying my eager slave girls access to my passion.

Offering them my back, I turned my head and laid it down on folded arms, legs parted loosely, letting my eyes close to savor the feel of the sun on my shoulders while the slaves set about their work, each taking up the duties of a well-trained masseuse. I felt the trickle of oil along my back and shoulders, the small hands rubbing it in, then the deeper kneading of my back muscles as the girls made their way across my shoulders and down my body, working at either side. I felt the press of their palms along my spine, the deep, slow massage, which lulled me into lethargy, a warm, and pleasant heaviness that I let overtake me.

Now the fleshy heels of deep rubbing palms were

moving the muscles of my lower back, digging into the shallow dip and then inexorably feeling their way up the twin slopes of my butt. The warm oily hands clasped my butt, fingers tightened, squeezed me, massaged my ass, till I couldn't help letting out a long satisfied moan. An impertinent finger slithered into my rearcrack, the bold sally electrifying me with a stabbing shock of pleasure that had me wriggling my hips.

Then the hands were working over the muscles of my thighs, sliding down my legs, holding my slack legs, rubbing them lovingly, clasping my ankles, massaging my feet. Only when every inch was well oiled did I turn over to offer them my front and my aching prick, which stood proudly erect and throbbing in the warm sun. I cupped my hands behind my head, eased back, and let my eyelids fall half-closed. I watched through narrowed eyes as the girls let twin streams of oil slash down on my chest and then began to use their fingers to work it into the matted hair. They were smiling and giggling as they played with my chest hair, creating little swirls, pinching tufts of oily hair, tugging playfully, pressing into my pectorals, fingering my nipples.

Their languid hands were warmly seductive as they worked their way downward. The blonde positioned herself on my left, the brunette on my right. They sent their hands down along my flanks, working back and forth from hips to the center of my belly, where they met, sliding under and carefully avoiding my all-too-ready prick. Nimble fingers pressed into my belly flesh and edged down into pubic hair before abandoning that line of inquiry and starting over at the tops of my thighs. My prick was avoided, for these experienced girls realized that the slightest brushing of a feminine hand would set me off. They knew instinctively that that most exquisite moment must be delayed till the last possible ounce of pleasure had been wrung out of me through the magic of the full-body massage.

So they worked patiently on my hairy thighs, kneading the muscles, clenching pliant flesh in small hands, smoothing and stroking and caressing as they moved down my loosely parted legs. Only when they finished at my toes, and my laid-out body glistened with oil (but for the most telling omission), did they take up positions standing by my hips and rubbing oil into their hands, impish grins spreading across their lips.

Now they attacked my manhood: the brunette sliding a cupped hand under my scrotum to cuddle my balls, while the blonde took hold of my shaft in a loose grip and oiled the entire length of my throbbing member. The delicious feel of their clever hands was heavenly. I could do nothing more than close my eyes and sigh. I luxuriated in the delicate touch of those soft feminine hands as fluttery fingers explored lightly, became more insistent, firmer, harder in the grip of passion. My balls were being rolled in someone's palm, squeezed lightly in a clenching rhythm. Fingers coiled around my shaft and tightened to stroke me marvelously, gently but firmly, until I threw back my head and whimpered.

The pumping fist tightened still more, the fingers squeezing into my malleable shaft. Then the fist yanked with surprising vehemence. A roar of surging lust powered through me and the merciless hand jerked harder, pumping away till the inevitable eruption welled up from my loins in a single bolt of pleasure. My hips thrust upward, arching up to strain high up off the leather as I tightened my butt against that piercing thrill that fired me into an earth-shattering climax. Now my prick exploded, erupting in gobs of semen which splattered my naked playmate and dribbled over her still-moving fist.

The girls dabbed up my spendings dutifully and, quite sensibly, left me alone to recover my equilibrium, kneeling beside me, sitting back on their heels, deferential, waiting to be of further service. After a few minutes, I floated back to earth and let my eyes flutter open to discover that a number of my fellow bathers had been watching the sensual massage and were studying me with definite interest in their eyes.

Two naked girls who lay on the other side of the pool, attended by some male slaves, smiled at me as our eyes met. It was a warm and not unwelcome invitation. For a moment I considered taking them up on their invitation and joining them. But, as I looked down at the kneeling blonde another idea struck me. Beckoning the slave girls to their feet, I had them stand before me. Then I reached for the vial of oil and poured some onto my hands, rubbing them thoroughly.

I started with the blonde, clamping my slick hands on her naked shoulders, turning her so that she stood with back toward me. I began by rubbing the floating planes of her shoulder blades, pressing and squeezing, and moving the muscles in a slow deliberate massage, leaving a slick sheen of oil as I followed the sinuous lines of her narrow back and lingered lovingly on her solid, high-set butt. Renewing the oil in my hands, I worked the back of her trim thighs, my hands molding her shapely leg muscles, her calves, the hollows behind her knees, up and down her slim, shapely legs. I paused to inspect the results, then had the well-oiled blonde turn around.

She watched me with half-lidded eyes while I poured a fresh supply of oil and gripped her shoulders, sliding them down the soft slopes and along her arms, moving them up the sinuous curves of her slender form, my hands moving over her flanks and hips and loins.

Now I began again at the top of her body, running my slick hands along her shoulders, tracing along the ridges of her collarbones, moving back and forth to meet at the top of her soft chest, and there letting my hands linger slowly before dropping down to those slight conical tits, holding them, letting the pointy shapes rest for a moment in my curved hands, the stiffened nipples pressing like tiny pebbles against my palms. I spent some time playing with her delicate tits, squeezing those slippery cones, toying with them, while the slave girl closed her eyes under the growing heat of my unrelenting stimulation. I savored the pleasure of her young blond body, freely fondling her slick boobs with their pointy tips, while the increasingly excited girl swayed drunkenly before me.

Sliding my hands down her taut breasts, I splayed my

fingers and let my hands blindly follow her form, like a sculptor appreciating her lithe sweeping torso, her midriff, the delicate traces of her rib cage, the taut skin of her belly, tight and smooth, and below, the damp curlings of pubic hair, whose very edge I skirted.

Taking a handful of oil, I slapped my palm abruptly to the girl's pubes, clamping her sex and palming her fleshy mound, making the young slave gasp. Now I played with her pussy, oiling the tiny curlings of her lightly furred sex.

The poor girl was trying to stand still, but she had a put a hand on my shoulders to steady herself, as I lightly fingered her vagina. But I didn't want her to peak too soon so I slid my hand just once between her legs, making a quick, teasing pass—one that electrified her. I pulled back instantly to crouch down on one knee and use both hands to work over the front of her thighs and legs.

Now I had the glistening blonde stand to one side while I turned my attentions to the waiting brunette. I beckoned to the lively dark-haired girl, and she stepped up with a sparkle in her eye and a slyly seductive smile playing across her pouting lips.

I couldn't help smiling with delight as my eyes caressed the girl's softly rounded contours, the firm mounds of her breasts that were full high-set disks with taut wide-capped nipples; a body that was smoothly curved, with tapering sinuous legs. I took her by the shoulders, fully intending to oil up her entire body from head to toe, just as I had the first slave, working the same route down her gently contoured feminine lines.

The Fall of the Ice Queen

Working her over with both hands, I soon had the healthy young brunette squirming hotly under my slick caresses, particularly when I clasped her firm little tits and squeezed, and she murmured something in a strange tongue and fell against me, pressing her loins against mine as passion flooded in her. Despite my growing urgency, I clenched her slick boobs and rotated them slowly while the girl moaned softly in my ear, whispering little entreaties in words I didn't understand. Moving quickly now, I let my hands drop lower, exploring the flaring cradle of her hips, the taut-skinned midriff, passing my slippery fingers through her damp tuft of pubic curls before proceeding down the front of her nicely tapered legs.

After coating her front thoroughly, I turned her around and did her neck, shoulder blades, and back. The brunette's bottom was two nicely curved domes, pert and firm with a deep, thin centerline. I ran an oily finger straight up her rearfurrow, inserting it quite deliberately between the rubbery mounds, shocking the girl so that her hips bucked in surprised reaction, and she clenched her rearcheeks on the impertinent intruder. Finally, I knelt behind her to massage the backs of her thighs and her sleekly muscled calves.

Now that I was well satisfied that both girls had been oiled up thoroughly, I beckoned them closer. I drew the slim blonde to me, clutching her slick, writhing form. The feel of her naked body pressed to mine rejuvenated my spent cock immediately. It swelled and stirred, answering the call to duty once more, if only halfheartedly.

I urged the blonde to climb up on the massage table and sprawl out on her belly, legs set close together. Now I kneeled behind her, straddling her hips. I lay along the length of her oil-slicked body, bringing my hardening prick right up along her rearfurrow, letting it lie there on the crease while I slid my hips up so that my loins were pressed firmly against the twin domes of her hard, symmetrical ass. Once in place, I had the fun-loving brunette climb up behind me to drape her body over mine, pressing me down more firmly on the blonde while squirming to give me the full feel of her oily breasts rubbing over me, burning into my back. I could even feel the hard nubs of her nipples as they moved over my back, pressing into me with hungry urgency.

With fiery impatience, I ordered them both to move. The blonde wriggled her hips and worked her ass, tightening her butt muscles under me, while the brunette twisted and writhed in sensual abandon. The fantastic thrill of those warm, slick bodies sliding and squirming against me, brought me to the peak in an instant. The pleasure was unbearable as I lunged forward, sliding my prick up the blond girl's rearfurrow. An unbelievable bolt of pleasure surged through me, and I exploded in a tremendous climax that went on and on, in powerful earth-shattering pulsations.

Thus passed the first delightful afternoon in a parade of idle days that I would spend in leisurely dalliance at the baths, while my King was busy smiting his enemies in his tireless defense of the Two Lands.

CHAPTER FIVE

As was his wont, the King left his concubines behind, taking with him only a few male slaves. While it was said that certain eastern tribes allowed whores to accompany their armies, Rahn considered women on the battlefront to be a distraction and insisted that they be kept far away from combat. He also considered this to be a wise precaution, since he was fiercely protective, and it was a point of manly honor with him that none of his women should ever be ravished at the hands of his enemies. As a result, the concubines were left behind at Thralkild, left very much to their own devices, although they were under the watchful eye of the chamberlain.

Since I had quite a bit of time on my hands and the concubines found themselves in a similar situation, it was only natural that I should consider all possible means of alleviating the mutual boredom. The House of Women beckoned to me.

Now, Rahn had some curious notions about the girls he kept. For example, fucking one of the King's concubines without his express permission was punishable by death. Still, for some reason, the prohibition did not extend to other forms of sexual enjoyment; for example, one could use those lovely girls freely, like pretty boys. One was equally free to indulge oneself with the sweet caresses of their lips and tongues and mouths. It was perfectly permissible to dally for long hours exploring their feminine charms, savoring each curve and contour of those soft, desirable bodies—playing, toying, discovering, holding, caressing, kissing, stroking, and petting. Spanking, and even a bit of paddling were allowed, should one be so inclined to pursue those particular diversions, and neither the indifferent monarch nor the indulgent chamberlain would take the least notice. The law was clear: Fucking was strictly prohibited!

After the King's absence, I found myself spending more time with those few court officials who had remained behind, Uzack being the first among them. The faithful chamberlain religiously saw to his duties in keeping the royal household running, even though our master was far away. With his usual thoroughness, he supervised each aspect of the women's daily routine, setting the rules, arbitrating disputes, and generally ruling the household with an iron hand. The slaves were terrified when his hawklike shadow fell upon them. The concubines, less terrified, perhaps, remained wary, for his efforts to instill obedience were legendary. The often bizarre and humiliating methods he devised were dreaded by all who, at the King's pleasure, were privileged to dwell in the House of Women.

On several occasions I had witnessed these punishments he meted out regularly, often, I thought, on the flimsiest of pretexts. I was convinced that the dissolute rascal found a great deal of perverse pleasure in contriving the most ingenious punishments for these pretty girls, and that his desire to carry them out so had very little to do with correcting his charges' behavior or, for that matter, punishing their "infractions."

Discipline sessions were conducted in a special chamber superbly equipped for just that purpose. Although in some aspects the room resembled the more sinister torture chamber of the King's dungeons, the resemblance was no more than superficial. It would have cost the chamberlain his head had one of the King's girls been injured seriously during some overzealous discipline session.

Of course, some minor discomfort—and even a hint of teasing pain—were things a girl would have to learn to tolerate. Still, one must know when to stop, as the chamberlain himself once explained to me with a conspiratorial wink. His eyes were large and heavily lidded, his nose curved and beaklike. He was much in his cups at the time, his bald head nodding sagely at the profundity of his own words. The two of us were alone in his quarters, sampling a selection of the finest wines from the King's cellars, and our witty and increasingly brilliant conversation was of sexual matters, as it often was when we shared a few bottles.

As a result of our enforced companionship over those many months, we had discovered that we were both true connoisseurs of sexual indulgence, gentlemen who appreciated the finer points of sensual experience. It was at one such drinking bout that the chamberlain invited me to witness the punishment he had prepared for the following evening.

That night was the first time I had been in that large cavelike room with its beamed ceilings. Elaborate carved candelabra cast weird shadows on the walls from the frames and the racks and stocks used to display the forms of the unfortunate girls who had been singled out for punishment. Chains and pulleys with various rope arrangements hung from the massive beams, lending their menacing shadows to the bizarre scene. The chamber was well stocked with various paraphernalia used to bind, restrict, and otherwise restrain the miscreants who found themselves at the tender mercies of the chamberlain.

Wooden shelves lined two sides of the room, and these held a wide array of instruments of pain and pleasure: light switches and whips, rapier-thin rods, straps and paddles of leather and wood. The phallus was well represented with examples in wood, ivory, and ebony. They seemed to sprout forth like exotic plants in an astonishing variety of shapes and sizes with various textured surfaces. There were brushes, delicate fronds, feathers, and beads. One entire shelf was devoted to pots of ointments and salves; amphorae of fine oils and perfumes, and mysterious potions said to rejuvenate and prolong endurance.

When we got there slaves were already at work, preparing the haughty young women selected by the lecherous chamberlain to be displayed for special treatment. It was almost steamy in that cavernous chamber; hundreds of candles added their heat to the warmth from the massive fireplace. Smoke from the candles, the scent of wax and the perfumed smell of sandalwood all mingled in the warm, moist air. Perspiration covered the half-naked bodies of the male slaves who went about bare-chested, wearing collars and strapped sandals with leather thongs that spiraled up their sturdy calves. Loose leather kilts swirled about their robust thighs as they went about their duties.

The first to be displayed was a small dark-haired girl. Bound and gagged, her arms had been tied behind her, with her wrists together, before being drawn up in back to be suspended from the ceiling beams with a single thin chain. This chain had been pulled taut, raising the young woman's wrists behind her so that she was forced to lean forward from the hips with lowered head and shoulders. Her soft breasts dangled heavily from her bowed torso, the dark, succulent nipples pointing straight down.

She might have been able to keep her balance better and thus relieve the strain on her arms had she been allowed to widen her stance, but that was denied to her—her legs had been tightly bound, held pressed together by thin leather straps that looped them at her ankles, just above her knees, and across her naked thighs. On her bare feet she wore a pair of open high-heeled sandals, and her slim, nude body was banded by a tightly laced waist cincher of supple black leather.

That position had the effect of stretching the skin of her smoothly rounded bottom—a choice bottom that even now was receiving the full attention of a powerfully built slave who stood behind her brandishing a long, thin rod. With this weapon he kept up a light but steady tapping of her well-placed bottom. I watched him whipping the girl's behind using short choppy strokes—not hitting hard; but using no more than sharp flicks of the wrists he soon had her twisting her hips at each slap and mewing into her gag.

The slave paid not the slightest attention to her muffled protests, but went about his business methodically, his simple face expressionless, although from the bulge in the tented kilt he wore, it was obvious he took some degree of pleasure in his work. The rod bit into the girl's pliant rearcheeks repeatedly, the crisp *Thwack!... Thwack!... Thwack!* a steady tattoo that left a crisscross of angry pink welts across the juddering mounds.

My host led me past the tethered brunette to the center of the room where two sleek, elegant girls were about to be punished together for some misdemeanor for which, presumably, they shared equal responsibility. As we came upon the scene, they were being prepared by the burly slaves the chamberlain employed because they could easily manhandle any unruly female who might take it into her head to struggle against her fate.

Now, as I watched, the two miscreants were undressed, gagged, and then bound, their slender bodies banded by narrow straps that pulled their arms tightly against their sides. They were then placed facing each other on opposite sides of an erect hardwood pole, perhaps eight feet high and six inches in diameter.

They were tall girls, of about the same height, with similar builds. Both had small pendant breasts, clear gray eyes, and the same pale brown hair. They might easily pass for sisters. The slaves were busy encircling them with wide belts, passing the straps around both bodies and cinching them in place, thus binding the girls, breasts pressed against breasts with the pole sandwiched between them. Other slaves lent a hand and the pole was tilted over and picked up. The trussed-up pair was carried to a set of stanchions upon which the girls were set up at the proper distance to cradle the suspended pole.

The whole arrangement reminded one of a spit that might be found turning over an open fire. To complete the resemblance, a handle was attached to one end of the pole. It could be turned to rotate the two bound bodies. I soon saw that the purpose was to present a stretched-out girl's bottom for punishment, and as the shaft was turned, rotating the pair, the other girl's behind was presented in turn.

The well-trained slaves took their places, one on either side of the sandwiched pair, each armed with a thin, pliant wooden lath. Now a third slave began to turn the crank, serving up the first attractive derriere. Framed by the leather belts that encircled waist and thighs, the plump mounds were presented quite appealingly, and each slave took full advantage of the opportunity by promptly spanking the rearcheek that appeared in front of them. Three rapid shots rang out: *Whap!... Whap!... Whap!* Then the spit was turned, offering up the complementary behind for similar treatment.

Again there was the repeated *Whap!... Whap!... Whap!* as the flexible lath splattered the vulnerable rearmounds, sending them jiggling as the muffled cries echoed each slap, and the butt tightened and clenched in fearful reaction. The girls' high-pitched yelps were effectively stoppered by the ballgags each had been made to wear. Under the circumstances, there was very little else the victims could do to express their fiery agitation as their spasming bottoms were peppered liberally with the steady blows.

We stood rooted to the spot. I was mesmerized by the unfolding drama, but my host, eager to show me more, urged me to move on to the far side of the room to confront still another bizarre display he had arranged. A girl with a luxurious auburn mane had been placed standing up against a padded trestle set at hip height. She had been bent over the padded crossbar, the rich mane of hair allowed to tumble down around her face, while her outstretched arms were pulled down the far side till she was drawn up high on her toes. Then her

The Fall of the Ice Queen

wrists were secured in place by cords that ran from wrist cuffs to staples set in the floor.

She watched anxiously over her shoulder, peering through the curtain of hair as a slave brought out a hand bellows. He smiled down at her, sizing up her small, compact bottom as he oiled the tip of the instrument. Grinning broadly, he stepped up and, without ceremony, rudely introduced the tip between the girl's cringing bottomcheeks. I watched him insert the nozzle carefully, threading it into her rectum, as she twisted her shoulders in growing dismay. The girl was gagged of course, so she could do no more than shake her head and watch in alarm as the bellows were pumped three or four times, sending a surge of warm water flooding into her innards.

With a wild toss of her head, she flung her hair back, allowing me to see the lines of distress that shot across her face. Her large green eyes widened with sudden alarm, and her surprised expression told of her growing discomfort. She clenched her jaw against the aching need she felt to heed nature's call, but this was to be denied her until her punishment was otherwise complete. She crossed her legs anxiously, pressing one knee behind the other, struggling with the sense of urgency that was overtaking her. Under such duress, she would be made to undergo her final punishment—a smart spanking, a dose of ten of the best laid quite deliberately on her vulnerable upturned bottom.

I watched the attending slave, a squat, barrel-chested fellow, taking his time, hefting a short-handled wooden paddle, tapping the flexible blade against his palm, as he took up his position behind and just to the side of her nicely proffered ass.

We saw him bring back his hand in a small arc to get the proper measure of his target. The girl waited tensely, her butt and leg muscles taut with strain. Then the slave hauled back and struck.

Whack! A solid smack resounded as the wooden blade bit into the malleable rearcheeks, flattening them and driving the girl even higher up on her toes as she recoiled from the shock. She shrieked her outrage into her gag; but before she could recover, he struck again, and again.

Whack!... Whack!... Whack!... Whack! The slave delivered a set of solid blows centered directly across the pert domes, sending the soft mounds undulating while the girl's pale skin darkened with the forming welt.

Uzack took my arm and led me on, while behind me the steady spanking continued, punctuated by the girl's muffled moans.

As we completed our tour of these bizarre scenes, Uzack led me to the very end of the room, where the curving walls enclosed a raised platform that dominated the far corner. A single wooden column, perhaps three feet in diameter, took up the small stage. At the top of the column, a crossbeam had been centered to form a sturdy T, and backed up against the column stood the splendidly nude figure of a royal concubine.

She was a beautiful girl of pleasing proportions with a long, tapering torso, narrow hips, and perfectly formed breasts. Her pose was exquisite. Her arms were lifted as in surrender, raised up and held in place on either side of her head by a set of thin chains which ran from the crossbar to leather straps banding each wrist. Similar bands had been affixed around each ankle just above the straps of her high-heeled sandals. From those bands, short chains ran to either side of the base of the column, so that her legs were drawn back around the girth of the column and kept well parted, splayed thighs forcing her mount of Venus forward in brazen display. Her pubic hair was pale, soft, and inviting; I felt certain I had seen it before.

Although I couldn't be sure, I thought I recognized that superb blond body, the sculpted thighs and sleek loins, the perfectly formed breasts with their wide nipples of soft pink. This had to be the Lady Alea, yet there was a reason that I couldn't be sure. The figure with the upraised arms was hooded! A leather sack had been placed over her head.

She waited motionless in her dark world, her head hanging weakly, slumped between her suspended arms. Did she know that she was about to undergo one of Uzack's infamous "endurance tests"—one of those amusing little diversions that he sometimes staged for the King's benefit? The chamberlain well knew his King; knew that Rahn found perverse delight in testing the sexual stamina of his various concubines, his captives, and slaves of both sexes. And it was the chamberlain's privilege to arrange such performances for his master.

This was the ordeal that the sex-crazed Uzack had

now planned for the Lady Alea. The crafty chamberlain winked at me, put a finger to his lips, and gestured for me to follow him silently. Together we crept up on the unsuspecting woman. She must have sensed our nearness for now she raised her head alertly, her body stiffening in anticipation.

Now that I was so close to her, I, too, felt a tingle of simmering anticipation. A wave of lust passed over me and weakened my knees; my hands itched to sample this mouth-watering treat, those lovely breasts that undulated lightly, moving with her shallow breathing, rising and falling just inches from my nervous fingers. My eager prick, which had hardened the moment I stepped into that intense sexual atmosphere, now pressed demandingly against the front of my breeches, forming a prominent bulge.

The young woman might well have been pleased to see this tribute to her beauty, had she been able to return our scrutiny. But she could only wait there in her darkness, chin raised, motionless. Was she aware that there were two randy men standing before her letting their eyes devour every inch of her vulnerable body?

Uzack had explained his strategy to me beforehand. We would excite her slowly and methodically, raising her passions to a fever pitch while she hung helplessly spread out before us, totally exposed and open, unable to resist the onslaught of unrelenting pleasure we would induce in her responsive body.

Because each of us knew his role, there was no need of words between us; we quietly took up our positions in front of her and at either side. We would work her over in silence, arousing her with slow caresses and bold excursions that explored each curve and contour freely, following each mounded rise and probing every crevice of that delicious strung-out body. She would be played like a fine instrument, our hands touching and withdrawing so that her excitement ebbed and flowed till she resonated with vibrant passion.

At a nod from Uzack, a slave handed each of us a single delicate feather, the plumage of some giant bird, I thought. The flimsy shafts were exquisitely long, with a slight, graceful curve. They sprouted wispy fronds of silvery gray. Alea jerked upright as though she had been burned at the first tentative touch of the soft vanes as they kissed her shoulders. Following Uzack's lead, I let the delicate tips play back and forth across the top of Alea's bare chest. A shiver of excitement shot through her shoulders; she twisted her arms, shaking the chains, as the feathers explored the hollows under her upraised arms and followed a path down her sides over the delicate tracings of her rib cage. We heard a whimper, abrupt and tight-lipped as it escaped from under the open bottom of her hood.

Now we brought the devilish feathers up to the top of her magnificent breasts, sliding down the seductive curve of the slopes, nosing impertinently into her cleavage, tracing over the rich swells of her gently mounded breasts so uplifted by the raised arms that they sat poised proudly before our eyes. The feathers caressed those firm mounds lightly, sweeping under the pert curves, slithering over the soft pink nipples. A long shivering sigh came from under the loose hood; her breasts settled with the gradual release of tension.

We drew the wispy tips methodically back and forth over Alea's sensate nipples, stirring them till they blossomed and grew taut with excitement. The aureoles tightened and expanded before our very eyes, the tiny stems swelling into prominence to thrust out boldly after only a few playful passes. Alea was unable to suppress the plaintive moan that escaped her lips as we delicately teased the protruding nubs of her brash, fully erect nipples.

With some reluctance, I followed the expert lead of that consummate sexual connoisseur as he quit those quivering breasts and played his feather down the front of her tense body, causing her belly to tighten reflexively as the maddening tip made its ticklish way down a line to the very top edge of her triangle. Without a pause, the feather skipped over her jutting blond pubes, and came to rest at one hip before sliding down to kiss her loins. Then, ever so lightly, he was brushing up and down a heavenly thigh.

I mirrored his movements on her other thigh, tickling my way from the knee to the top of the leg while working around, till the tantalizing tip was caressing the smooth flesh of the inner thigh and probing high up in the crease between the top of her leg and the very edge of her distended pussy. Pressing the end of the feather into her splayed underarch, we tickled our way along the folds of the netherlips. Alea squirmed her hips and moaned, as a shudder ran through her body and her shoulders wriggled in involuntary delight.

Uzack turned to me with a truly wicked grin on his thin bloodless lips. He gestured me to follow his lead and, with delicate precision, he placed two fingers on Alea's gaping pussy and forced back the fleshy lips, exposing the pink inner folds of her vagina. He couldn't resist toying with her, pausing to finger her cunt before pressing back the plump lips and inviting me to play the feather lightly over the delicate folds of her pink rose. Quite slowly, I placed the feathery tip along the center of her cleft and caressed the pinkish brown flesh of the slick folds. As Alea's hips bucked uncontrollably she squirmed in her bonds, but Uzack held her open with his body pressed against hers to immobilize her still further. I drew the wicked tip up and down, watching the delicate fronds damped with passion-dew gathered from the glistening inner flesh while the agitated woman quivered and shook as much as she could. Because of the way Uzack had her pinned, her hip movements were reduced to tiny spasms. I was merciless! Up and down the damp feather slid till the tormented woman was whimpering with mounting urgency.

I squatted down before her to guide the feather more closely. The smell of cunt was in the air, that heavy musky scent of a woman in heat. My aim was to lay the devilish tip at the apex of the steepled folds and probe softly till I found the pearl of her clit peeking out from beneath its hood of soft inner flesh.

The sudden shock of pleasure thrilled the tantalized

woman, who couldn't help bucking her powerful loins against the restraining hand of the chamberlain. She shook wildly, rattling her chains. Her whimpering rose in intensity till she was yelping like a hurt animal. I twirled the thin shaft between my fingers and sent her careering over the edge. Every sinew of her body tightened, the tendons of her thighs stood out rigidly. A wrenching convulsion tore through her body, once, twice, then there was a low earthy moan, long and shivering, that came out from under the hood. She fell back to hang limply in her chains.

Uzack smiled his congratulations to me, nodding his silent approval of my efforts. I gazed at my thoroughly depleted victim. Her body was slack, hanging from the chains suspending her wrists. She was sweating from the warmth of the room and the even greater heat of sexual arousal she had been subjected to. Her undulating breasts glistened with perspiration, nipples still taut, though even now lapsing back into quiescence. The edging of pussyfur between her legs was damp, and a slick veneer of feminine spendings glistened on her slack inner thighs.

Even as I contemplated her spent form, Uzack was busy with preparations for her next trial. The slave was bringing forth the large furry gloves we would use on her. The shattering climax this brought on was even more spectacular than the first. The glove treatment was followed by a most thorough massage laid on by oily hands that roamed freely over that marvelous body while the half-crazed Alea squirmed hotly under our masculine hands. A most satisfactory climax to those efforts followed that. It became harder to arouse her, so we concentrated on her well-lubricated cunt. Her honey was flowing copiously from her throbbing sex. At the raging height of her terrible need, a hard rubber phallus was stuffed into her hungry cunt. This was to be followed, in turn, by a long bowed phallus made of ivory, and later a squat rounded shaft of smooth African hardwood. With these tools we took turns fucking the strung-out woman into mindless oblivion.

Finally we undid our breeches and rubbed our stiff, aching pricks all over her sweaty, oil-slicked loins, so we might find for ourselves the blessed release we so richly deserved after all our labors. We left our spendings mingling with the oil down the front her thighs. Only then was the exhausted woman released and led off to be taken to her bed.

In all, Alea had been subjected to five orgasms that night. Well, more accurately, we could say there were four, for Uzack and I debated about the fifth. It had been a little tremor—more of an aftershock, perhaps— the last weak gasps of a satiated body from which every once of pleasure had been thoroughly drained. This final orgasm would be the cause of vigorous debate for the rest of the night as we toasted the fair Alea repeatedly, and congratulated ourselves on a job well done.

CHAPTER SIX

Now, when one reads *The Chronicles of the Kings*, one is left with the impression that every battle we fought was a victory, every skirmish a glorious triumph for our invincible warrior, King Rahn. Nowhere will you find mention of our forces being outfought, outmaneuvered, or even outnumbered on the battlefield. There is not a single word of the stalemates, withdrawals and, yes, if the truth be known, even our occasional defeats.

For although, on the whole, our armies have been so successful that the Kingdom of the Two Lands has been extended to the far-flung corners of the earth, I can assure you we have had our share of setbacks. So it is with a grain of salt, dear reader, that you must approach Plunar's fawning commentary on Rahn's campaign against Ur of Tarzia, if indeed that hopelessly dull chapter of the chronicles somehow manages to survive the ages, which I very much doubt. Plunar is such a dolt!

I caution you thus because I myself have read that account. And, knowing King Rahn as I do, I think I can discern what took place even through the muddled morass of Plunar's plodding prose. It appears that Rahn had gathered three field armies into a single powerful force and amassed his troops behind the hills that guarded the plains of Tuslog.

A word about Ur, the King of Tarzia, is probably in order. Our spies had kept us informed about this vile schemer who was, at one time, an ally of our gracious sovereign. He was a crafty, sly princeling who had persuaded a few of the more gullible chieftains of the frontier tribes that our power was waning and a quick, decisive blow would send our armies reeling back to Thralkild. He spread the word that the years of luxury at Thralkild had softened Rahn, and that he no longer had the stomach for a good fight. That was a fatal mistake!

When studying the chronicles, it is on the matter of numbers that you must be quite skeptical, dear reader. Plunar would have you believe that our legions outnumbered the foe greatly, so that the crushing defeat was inevitable. In fact, just the opposite was the case! The armies of Ur and his eastern allies were vast, our own legions relatively few, although all of them were seasoned fighting troops.

Like most of those petty eastern potentates, Ur liked

to travel in grand style. And unlike Rahn, who was always impatient and hated to be encumbered by civilians, Ur went to war accompanied by his entire retinue, taking with him not only his entire court and treasury, but also his family, the royal household, retainers, concubines and slaves, all of whom followed behind in a long baggage train whose dust could be seen for miles.

The resulting army was a mighty host when on the move. Slow, massive and plodding, it would overcome anything in its path. Still, when one examined the serpentine columns more closely and eliminated the commissary, baggage trains, camp followers, families of aristocrats, prostitutes, entertainers, and assorted hangers-on, perhaps no more than one-fifth of that massive host were actually fighting men.

This host moved gradually to meet the armies of our King, somewhere beyond the Yrgos Mountains. It soon became evident that both armies had to traverse some foothills and the two opposing forces would be funnelled into a narrow defile that ran between high craggy hills. Should Ur get through this bottleneck, the fertile plains of Tuslog would be at his feet. Surrounded by low rolling hills, these grassy flatlands were the ideal place for a clash of mighty hosts.

Undoubtedly, Ur had expected Rahn to hasten to take this strategic pass, placing troops on the steep banks at either side of the defile. But Rahn had neglected to do this for some reason. Instead, the army was comfortably encamped, spread out on the wide plains beyond. Ur was elated, but cautious. Suspecting a trap, he sent a squad of cavalry to scour the guarding heights, which they found deserted.

From those heights they could look down on the armies of the Two Lands. By counting their campfires, tents, men and horses they concluded that the King of the Two Lands was weak, and could muster barely enough troops to meet the threat. What they didn't know was that Rahn had taken a gamble by not sending all of his troops forward. He held a considerable contingent in reserve and these he hid behind the hill on the right, concealing their positions behind the low hills so they were out of view from the valley below.

The army that lay hidden behind the hills was led by a strong contingent of cavalry, seasoned shock troops trained for quick, determined assaults. Turhan would command this army while the King settled himself in the center of the main group. He took his place in plain sight, his standard proudly flying in the breeze; the royal pavilion raised prominently. Turhan's troops were forbidden to show a single campfire. Horses were muzzled. The men camped in silence. On the other hand, the main body were ordered to light hundreds of fires and to hold a very public and noisy feast to propitiate of the gods of war.

When Ur learned from his scouts that the enemy was feasting, and had failed to secure the guarding heights, he couldn't believe his good luck! If he hurried, it might just be possible to sweep through the pass, catch Rahn's encampment by complete surprise, and destroy the unsuspecting enemy with a single mighty blow.

The Fall of the Ice Queen

The impetuous King sniffed victory in the air. There was only one nagging problem. When word had reached him about the strength and disposition of the enemy, Ur had halted the column. He was waiting nervously for the arrival of the army designated to hold his left flank once the battle was joined—a large but undisciplined group led by Baron Ing. But he was troubled because he had yet to hear news of Ing's progress. Ing was notoriously tardy; so Ur, impatient with further delay and seeing a golden opportunity slipping through his fingers, decided not to wait. He spurred his horses onward, forcing the march toward Tuslog, trusting that Ing would rendezvous with him before the decisive battle.

Ur's forces were still some distance from Tuslog, but if his troops marched all day, they would be in place late that afternoon. Surely the tardy Lord of Ing would be at his side by that time.

Ur didn't know that Rahn had sent an emissary to Ing with a secret proposal, an offer he would find quite tempting. Nothing was asked of Baron Ing but that he proceed very leisurely, to delay his arrival. In return, he was offered nothing less than the throne of Tarzia, provided he agreed to serve as a vassal of the great King of the Two Lands. He would merely exchange one overlord for another, and in the process gain the immense wealth of Tarzia as his own. It was an offer he couldn't refuse. The consummate betrayer had been betrayed!

As to the battle of Tuslog, Plunar has described the day as bright and glorious, one in which the heavens were filled with wondrous signs and strange omens, and the sun god smiled benevolently down upon our King. Typical of his overblown prose! I have learned from the veterans who were there that the day was misty. A light, steady drizzle made the ground damp and soft, and all but obscured visibility.

Although his troops were tired after their long enforced march, their spirits quickened as they sensed the nearness of battle and the promise of booty in the offing. Ur maneuvered the unwieldy mass into place like a giant arrow pointed at the defile. He placed his cavalry in the lead to assure a lighting charge and total surprise. A strong contingent of foot soldiers and archers were on his right; a somewhat diminished, but still-respectable force on his left. His scouts reported that the encamped foe seemed unaware of the danger about to befall them. The feasting and revelry had been going on all day, and the carousing enemy soldiers were drunk and disorganized.

Once his troops were drawn up, Ur galloped to the point of the arrow and thundered on through the front ranks, leading the charge with his sword waving in the air. Rahn's well-trained army quickly fell into defensive positions and began to fall back before the charging horsemen. The battle line caved in, bowing before the charging might; it bent, but it did not break. Instead, even as the first ranks clashed, the horns were sounded for a covered retreat, and our army drew back, letting the King of Tarzia rush forward onto the plain. Now the forces were fully engaged, the fighting steady along the lines. It appeared as though the superior numbers of the enemy were bending our lines still farther backward.

The Fall of the Ice Queen

However, it wasn't immediately apparent that the slow retreat was describing a gradual sweep to the left which would place the pursuing left flank of the enemy between our men and the hills behind them. As our troops fell back toward the hills, a great shout went up from Ur's spearmen as they drove the foot soldiers back and broke into a run. Their cavalry became tangled with their infantry as, eager as they were to get in on the pursuit, they charged, determined to finish off the job and hoping to cause a rout.

Now they were at their most vulnerable. As they made the sweeping turn to bear down on the main body, Turhan's troops appeared over the crest of hill at their side. Before they could turn to meet this unexpected threat, Turhan's men were on them, thundering down the slopes, swords slashing left and right.

It was a brilliant maneuver, and it caught the enemy completely off guard. As he fought his way to a hillock, Ur was astonished to see his left wing crumbling, rolled up between the two arms of Rahn's army. Now the horns sounded throughout Rahn's army, and his ranks turned and held their ground. A mighty roar went up as the enemy's left flank collapsed and our troops, sensing victory, surged forward toward the King of Tarzia's standard. They redoubled their efforts, and their counterattack caved in the main force of the enemy and brought our assault wave closer to the King and his standard.

As usual, Rahn was in the thick of things, using his sword like a battle-ax to cut his way through the swarming horde who desperately wanted only to flee from his terrible wrath. Hacking and slashing, he drove toward Ur, who sized up the situation quickly, turned on his heel, and headed south, leaving the field and all his possessions behind. By this time the battle had degenerated into a disorderly rout.

Rahn, his blood fired by the heat of battle, roared his frustration, and pointed his sword toward his fleeing foe. Rallying his guards around him, he set off in hot pursuit.

All that evening the killing went on, as our triumphant troops ran down the bedraggled remnants of Ur's horde, much of which seemed to have melted away magically. Rahn and his escort returned empty-handed, and he was in a foul mood, bitter at having his foe escape his clutches. However, his spirits improved when word came that the King's household and treasure had been taken. Of course, Rahn dashed off to the scene.

Even as he left, a squad of cavalry who had been sent on a mopping up operation found Ur hiding in a nearby marsh. He was disguised as a woman and, when unmasked, he fled across the swampy ground, only to flounder in the muddy waters from which he emerged stinking and covered in slime. They grabbed him and would have slapped him in irons, but he kept struggling and with superhuman effort somehow managed to tear himself from his captors and make one last desperate attempt toward freedom. He was cut down as he ran, his head dispatched to the King of the Two Lands.

Meanwhile, Rahn rode up to the large ornate wagon used by the King's family. At a sign from him, the

THE FALL OF THE ICE QUEEN

soldiers threw back the canvas opening and ordered the occupants out. Three women emerged, followed by two frightened slaves. There was no sign of the Queen.

The two younger girls huddled together on the ground, holding each other, terrified of the muddy, blood-splattered giant who peered down at them with a fierce scowl, his booted feet set in a widened stance, his hands on his hips. But the oldest girl was made of sterner stuff. This was the Princess Lohr! She rose to her full height to stand protectively with her back to her cringing sisters, facing the grim, battle-stained monarch. She stood motionless before him, meeting his fearsome gaze with composure, her lips drawn, the blood drained from her face. Proud, tall, and unbending, she stood firm, fully prepared to die.

The girl stood straight as a willow, long-limbed, with pale, almost luminous skin. Some said that her alabaster pallor was the reason she was later called the Ice Queen, but we at the court knew the real reason—it was her total lack of human emotions. The cool, crisp features that met Rahn's craggy face so evenly were framed by smooth black hair that was swept straight back to fall over her shoulders in a thick, shimmering mantle.

Of course, Rahn knew of Ur's daughters, the three princesses. He had heard that the oldest was said to be quite a beauty, but he was unprepared for the icy reserve, that frosty regal demeanor she turned on him, seemingly indifferent to the threat he posed, even though he might take her life as easily as slicing the blossom off a flower.

I must admit that Lohr did have an arresting beauty about her, but it was an odd, singular sort of beauty. She had not the welcoming attractiveness of the comely Alea, that graceful feminine beauty. Nor did she have the innocent prettiness of a fetching young maiden like Gwin, although they were about the same age. Hers was a different kind of beauty: cold, remote, austere, and brittle. Those who were there said that the King could only stare at her, taken by her implacable defiance, the cold fire that blazed in her hard black eyes.

As he stared at this pale apparition, a blood-curdling scream came from somewhere behind him. Rahn spun around and saw a half-crazed woman rushing at him from out of the bushes, a dagger held high over her head, lunging to strike. His guards leapt forward, but Rahn was equal to the threat. He merely stepped aside and drew his sword, lifting it at an angle so that the onrushing woman impaled herself on the end of his blade. The girls shrieked to see their mother crumple softly to the earth, for this maddened woman was the Queen of Tarzia, making her last desperate stand.

Rahn nudged the corpse with the toe of his boot and pulled out his bloody sword. Blood welled out to stain the fine silk dress and form a slowly expanding puddle in the mud. For a moment, he regarded Princess Lohr, who had weakened and recoiled at the at the swift, violent murder of her mother. She was clearly shaken, but her young body stiffened and she bit down on her curled lip, while her fists clenched in silent rage. Those were the only signs of her inner turmoil. Otherwise, she kept her rigid control, confronting the King of the Two Lands with cold hatred in her dark eyes. The young woman had a will of iron, and she was determined not to show her fear.

"Bring them!" the King ordered, turning swiftly to mount up and riding off without a look back. The girls were bound hand and foot and tossed over saddles like so many sacks of grain. Then the party galloped off after their sovereign, heading for the smoking plains of Tuslog, where the victory celebration was well under way.

If you have never seen a victorious army raping, plundering, and looting their way across fields strewn with corpses and the spoils of war, then it may be difficult to imagine the hellish scene that follows battle. It was pandemonium. By this time the wildly excited soldiers, exhilarated at having faced death and won, crazed with the smell of blood, and drunk on the thrill of victory and the free-flowing wine, had become a raging mob that was totally out of control. The officers stood by indulgently and turned to their own celebrations while their frenzied men looted the corpses of the fallen enemy, hacking away and scavenging for the possessions of the King and his nobles, jewelry, prized gems and baubles, robes of fine silks and satin, snatched up and fought over till the gleeful victors could rush off and stash their newly won plunder in some secret hiding place.

The prisoners were rounded up. The enemy wounded were slaughtered; the able-bodied enslaved. A few of the nobles might be held for ransom, but their wives, daughters, and mistresses were fair game, especially prized by the randy soldiers who had been deprived of female companionship for long months on the campaign trail. The captured women were taken to the camp, there to be shared freely among the tents. A similar fate befell the whores whom Ur had supplied so generously, although they were considerably more accustomed to such usage at the rough hands of lusty soldiers.

I believe King Rahn was happiest when in the masculine company of the field army, carousing with old cronies and reliving past campaigns. It gave him the chance for a loose informality, an easy comradeship that he relished; one that would never be possible at Thralkild, given the rigid protocol that prevailed at the court.

By the time Rahn arrived, the feasting had already begun. His generals, who waited to greet him, had doffed swords and armor, washed the blood from their hands, and changed into fresh tunics. Tired but exuberant, their faces flushed with victory, they ate as though famished and drained cups of wine greedily while a parade of slaves brought forth huge plates of roasted meat and generous flagons of wine.

They cheered their battle-stained King when he entered the tent. Even as a slave helped Rahn remove his armor, a cup was thrust into his hands and his glorious victory was saluted in a stirring chorus. When he was told that Ur's head had been taken, he was elated, his triumph complete. With a lusty roar, he ordered more wine. He settled back onto a low couch and ordered that Ur's daughters be brought to him.

The three sisters were brought to the entrance of the

King's tent, still wearing the finery in which they had been taken. We found out later that Ur was so confident of victory, he had arranged that the royal family might picnic on the slopes overlooking the battlefield so they could witness his glorious deeds! The girls were still dressed as for a day in the country, although their party dresses were stained and splattered with mud from their unceremonious journey to the camp, trussed up and flung over the backs of warhorses.

Now in the light of the torches, Rahn got his first good look at his prized captives as they were hauled before him. Anxious and clearly frightened, the three young women were a sorry lot indeed: bedraggled, dresses torn and disheveled, hair mussed and faces flushed. Their eyes were red and swollen, and stained with dried tears that they had been unable to wipe away as their hands were still tied behind them.

Rahn, who had an eye for such matters, instantly judged his captives to be of marrying age. The rumors must have been true. It was said that Ur, while jealously guarding his daughters, was actively engaged in scheming and conniving with an assortment of petty princes and tin-pot potentates so as to marry them off to his best advantage.

"Release them!" the King ordered. The prisoners' hands were untied, and they were pushed into the tent.

"So these are the famous daughters of Ur?" he began in his leering manner, grinning broadly at the terrified girls. He beckoned to the guards, ordering that they be brought closer so he might better inspect them.

Now he took his time, slowly eyeing them up and down. The smallest girl, with straight boyish limbs and a slight figure, shrunk back in terror, leaning against the guard who held her by the arms. The middle girl was also short, but her girlish figure was decidedly more feminine, with small plump breasts peeking out of the top of her party dress. She stood wide-eyed, staring at him silently, paralyzed with fear. Only Lohr squirmed angrily to twist free of her guards. She pulled herself up to her full height before him.

Rahn was amusing himself. "It's said these girls had trouble finding husbands. Now, that's a pity. Surely we must be able to find a few gentlemen willing to serve—at least for an evening or so, eh?"

There was a ripple of laughter from the King's appreciative male audience in which the King joined, savoring his own little joke.

"My Lord!" The words rang out with imperial clarity, cutting the laughter short. Rahn turned slowly to face the Princess Lohr, for it was she who had spoken out so boldly. Casting an eye on her with renewed interest, he arched a quizzical brow.

"If I may be permitted to speak?" the princess said slowly and precisely, enunciating each word, her anger barely controlled. Rahn pursed his lips as if considering the request and nodded slowly.

"I must remind you, my Lord, that we are the daughters of a King. We expect—we demand—to be treated with respect." She nearly spat out the last word. Her small chin quivered, but she held it high, dark eyes blazing her defiance. Plunar maintains that Lohr was at her most beautiful when she was angry, and in that he was surely right.

She continued undaunted, her clear voice gathering strength. "We are your prisoners, it is true, but of course we will be ransomed. Until then, we are under your protection. We expect to be treated as you might treat any other guest of royal blood."

The room was stunned into silence by the girl's audacity; all eyes shifted to the King. But Rahn gave no hint of his reaction. His jaw was set, eyes studying the girl with a new look of shrewd appraisal. For a moment, no one spoke. Then the King got to his feet and stepped closer to the young woman, who flinched just slightly at his threatening approach.

"Get undressed," he said. His voice was cold, and he looked into her eyes to let her see his implacable will.

CHAPTER SEVEN

They stood facing each other, their gaze unwavering, locked in a silent battle of wills. The universe had narrowed to just the two of them; no one else mattered. At last the girl bit her curled lip and shook her head in mute refusal.

With his eyes still holding hers, Rahn raised a hand and gestured, summoning the captain of the guard. He whispered his instructions in the captain's ear and that obedient soldier unsheathed his sword and raised it over the head of the recalcitrant girl. She didn't flinch as the iron blade was raised on high. She stood proud and aloof, boldly facing the tyrant she despised.

But in spite of her disobedience, the sword did not fall on her, though a flick of the wrist might strike her down easily. Instead, while the guard behind her held her fast by the arms, the captain used his weapon to slit her shoulder straps carefully and tear the dress down the girl's struggling form.

The straps of her breast halter had been severed with the same sure strokes, and now the captain grabbed a fistful of that sagging undergarment and ripped it off savagely, exposing the girl's breasts, a pair of narrow pointy tits, taut, and snowy white, with neatly centered nipples that stuck straight out in front. Now she was reduced to her shoes and stockings and the short white underskirt that swirled around her thrashing thighs. The men edged closer. Lohr, who twisted and squirmed in a futile struggle to wrench herself free from the guard who held her by the arms, suddenly went rigid as the deadly tip of the sword approached her belly.

"*No!*" she shrieked in desperation.

The captain ignored her, inserting the blade neatly under the waistband of her underskirt so that, with the slightest flick of his wrist, her sole remaining undergarment was cut loose to drop straight down her stockinged legs. Now, for the first time, Lohr's cold, hard body was revealed to the men of the Two Lands, a body that was lithe as a panther's, with the cool beauty of a fine marble statue. Rahn let his appreciative gaze fall down over her sleek, streamlined flanks, the sweeping lines of a willowy torso that tapered to a subtle flare at the girl's modest hips, savoring the pure white smoothness of those twisting loins accented by a narrow triangle of rich black curls.

Rahn stepped up closer to her struggling body and

scanned her face, looking into her angry eyes. Then he let his gaze fall pointedly to the slight hard tits that rose and fell with her labored breathing.

"On your knees, girl!" he spat out, his eyes narrowing with determination.

Lohr was clearly frightened, but somehow she found the inner strength to swallow her fear and she shook her head in mute refusal. Her bloodless lips were drawn and set grimly with equal determination.

The King grunted and waved a hand at the guard, who tightened his grip on her arms so strongly that she cried out as he shoved her down onto her knees.

Now Rahn stood over her, looking down at his naked captive, who knelt with huddled shoulders heaving raggedly, her bowed head just inches from his crotch.

"So you would be treated like a princess, eh? And why should I? Even if you were called 'Princess' once, you certainly are not one now," he growled in cold fury. "You are nothing! A mere slave. A sex slave who, if she is allowed to live at all, lives at the pleasure of the King. And if I let you live…it will be only as long as you please me. You make no demands here; you live only to obey."

With that fateful sentence he reached for her, ran his fingers through her rich black mane, and grabbed a fistful of thick hair. Then he twisted his hand and yanked the girl's head back by the hair till she was looking straight up at him, pain welling up in her eyes.

"What we have here are not princesses," he spat in disgust. "We have three spoiled brats who grew up ill-mannered in the disreputable house of a ludicrous so-called King. No wonder you have no manners. But we will teach you. You will begin by learning how to approach your King...on your knees!"

Abruptly, the King called the captain of the guard to receive his whispered instructions, while the King's officers crowded around, smiling and eager for their chance to savor the lovely spoils of war.

As the guards moved to carry out the King's orders, the horrified girls began to scream in helpless indignation. Lohr was a hellcat, shrieking her fiery protests, and spitting her curses at the soldiers who manhandled her, while her two sisters wailed and pleaded for mercy. In order to stop the infernal racket, Rahn ordered them gagged. The guards subdued the struggling captives easily and soon had them prepared according to the King's instructions.

A space had been cleared in the center of the tent, and sets of stakes driven into the ground. Now the three princesses lay beside each other, spread out on the ground before the King and his riotous comrades. Stripped of their finery and spread-eagled, the captives had been placed on their bellies, their supple limbs stretched out and attached to the stakes with strips of leather.

Even a casual observer would have noted the family resemblance. All three girls had similar features, the same pale skin and shiny ink-black hair. Lohr was the prettiest of the sisters, with her lean, pleasingly proportioned body, but the other two were also quite attractive and especially enticing when their taut naked bodies were spread out to be admired freely and feasted upon by the greedy eyes of the sex-starved soldiers. Rahn stretched back on a couch while his officers sprawled about on rugs and carpets, taking in the blood-stirring sight of the three young women so enticingly displayed.

The youngest twisted and tugged on her bonds, struggling anxiously, unreasonably, overcome with helpless desperation. Her narrow, sinewy limbs pulled against her restraining straps, while her small, tight buttocks wriggled and clenched most appealingly.

The middle girl lay rigid and fearful. There was a tension in the muscles of her well-parted legs as she strained to pull them together, drawing the tendons so that they stood out along her inner thighs. From where Rahn sat, he could look up between the converging lines of her shapely feminine legs to the gaping vagina set in its nest of black curls. This girl's bottom was more rounded, fleshier than her sister's; two firm, meaty mounds, high-set, proud, seductive curves that invited the hand.

Then there was Princess Lohr. She lay sullen and still, as if prepared to yield to her fate: her long-limbed body taut, the sinuous lines of her nude form narrowing to the compact hips and sweeping up behind to form a set of long ovals. Rahn's lusty gaze fell on the elongated mounds of Lohr's ass, two sleek domes separated by a narrow dark slit.

Now the captain of the guards returned with three slaves, each of whom held a slim whippy rod, long and thin as a reed, wickedly stiff yet pliant. The slaves took their positions, kneeling next to each of the staked-out girls.

Rahn squatted down beside Lohr, close to her resting head, bending his knees and bouncing lightly on the balls of his feet. He was in a jovial mood.

"We're going to teach you to mind your manners, 'Princess,'" he sneered. "You see, most gracious lady, these slaves have been summoned to attend to your royal bottom. In short, they are here to whip your insolent ass. Then, if you are lucky, I shall invite these gentlemen here to bestow their favors on you, should they choose to do so. In fact, if I am so inclined, I might even fuck you myself. I'll wager you've never been fucked by a King before, unless that old reprobate of a father of yours went in for that sort of thing," he added with a lewd chuckle.

Tied and gagged as she was, Lohr could do little to fend off these insults. But she turned her head away from her leering captor, pressing her cheek against the hard earthen floor of the tent. This brought her eyes close to the loins of the waiting slave who knelt beside her, sitting back on his heels. Obviously, he anticipated his task eagerly, as his kilt was tented most suggestively.

Rahn noted where her eyes had landed and smiled to himself.

"And maybe, when we're done with you, we'll give you to the slaves for a bit of sport. They'd like that, I think," Rahn purred, lifting the slave's kilt delicately to reveal to Lohr's eyes a lust-swollen member that quivered in proud salute to the bare bottom upon which the man had been invited to beat a wild tattoo.

The Fall of the Ice Queen

Now the King resumed his seat, stretching back on the divan, one hand flung back, holding the cup negligently so that a waiting slave sprang forth to fill it to the brim. A wave of his other hand set the kneeling slaves in motion.

The whippy rods rose and fell in sharp, choppy strokes, beginning a light but steady rapping on the exposed butts that immediately had the girls squirming and yelping into their gags. The slaves moved with mechanical precision; each snap of the wrist sent a whippy rod biting into the firm but yielding flesh of a well-placed feminine bottom with a single sharp retort: *Thwack!... Thwack!... Thwack!... Thwack!*

Each clear, precise slap of the wood splattering flesh was followed inevitably by a tiny yelp, muted but audible. Their combined response rose in muffled chorus from the howling victims.

His eyes drawn to the middle girl, Rahn watched her soft, malleable mounds being crisscrossed with a set of pink welts as she jerked in her bonds and clenched her rearcheeks reflexively against the steady rain of blows. She wriggled her hips furiously, shifting them from side to side in fiery agitation, in a futile attempt to ward off the methodical slaps of the stinging rod peppering her dancing behind.

At the first few strokes, Lohr had not moved. Except for tightening her small fists, she held herself rigidly still. The sullen, carefully controlled princess was grimly determined to merely absorb the punishment in silence. She was resolved to deny her captor the pleasure of seeing her squirm. But even her iron will could not long resist the light-but-methodical spanking. Her resolve to to endure the punishment silently crumbled quickly. Soon she was joining her sisters in the lively dance, mewing into her gag along with the others, wriggling her loins, even as she tried to steel herself against the repeated blows. Rahn smiled to see the way she was working her ass, tightening the hardened muscles of her coiled butt till supple shallows formed at the sides of her cheeks and the deep division between her rearmounds was reduced to a narrow slit.

The men were talking and laughing excitedly, enjoying the dance of the juddering rearmounds that shook beneath the steady rain of punishing strokes, joking and pointing out features of the amusing spectacle to each other as the spanking went on in its relentless rhythm, the whippy rods splattering the resilient softness of those tenderized mounds till the upturned bottoms took on a rosy hue. Finally Rahn called a halt to the proceedings by raising his right hand. The slaves held their blows immediately, but stayed kneeling in place, rods held erect before them.

Rahn rose and slowly strode over to where the bedraggled Princess Lohr lay spread out and depleted, her blushing ass throbbing with a deep, dull ache. The King stepped between her splayed legs and—quite deliberately—placed a booted toe squarely on the center of Princess Lohr's well-punished bottom, pressing into the yielding flesh, squashing the bulging mounds till she screamed into her gag and threw back her head, craning backward while the persistent toe dug into her rearfurrow and nudged her there.

Once again the King squatted down beside his royal prisoner. He couldn't resist those lovely rearmounds that were smarting and throbbing so temptingly at hand. Hauling back, he gave the girl a final smack, striking her ass with his curved hand and getting a muted shriek in response. Giving her no time to recover, he grabbed her by the hair and snapped her head around so she was forced to look into his eyes as he addressed her. But the face that met his startled him.

The eyes that met his above the wide leather gag were big and dark and wet with tears. But what surprised him was that the hard anger had melted away; her gaze had softened, the flinty hardness replaced by a curious, almost seductive look.

He looked into her eyes, questioning what he saw there, saying not a word. Then he let her head flop down, and stood up to undo his kilt and free his terrible sword that stood solidly erect, throbbing with desire. Now he stepped around behind her, dropping to his knees between Lohr's outstretched legs, where he knelt, gazing down on the object of his affection. With a generous wave he beckoned Gan and Turhan to join him, inviting each to take a sister in a similar manner.

He laid a possessive hand on her still-warm behind, watched the sensitive skin flinch at his touch. Her butt muscles clenched, then relaxed, assuming their soft, rich fullness when he ran his hand down to cup the twin curves. Lohr felt his large masculine hand curve to comfortably fit the contour of her aching ass; felt him grip her, hold her. Then she felt his fingers slip between her legs, probing the lips of her vagina. She realized she was actually wet. The sudden realization sent a throb of lust welling up in her, and she felt her womb quiver with excitement. Then she felt his prick—long, hard, and demanding. He guided it up between her buttocks. She couldn't help squeezing it. Rahn grunted as she tightened his prick in a viselike grip.

Prying back her rearcheeks, he pressed into the narrow valley, and holding her open with his thumbs, Rahn wiggled his hips, burying his prick deep between those heavenly pillows. Savoring the warm smoothness of her solid rearmounds he slithered up over the princess's pinioned form, rubbing up and down in the moist valley, grinding his loins over her ass. She squirmed beneath him, and he groaned helplessly in her ear.

Then he was fumbling with her slick pussylips, blindly seeking the opening toward which he was guiding the head of his straining prick. He drew back his hips and lunged forward, driving into her with a sudden stab. Lohr's groan was muffled by the gag as she threw back her head, craning back at the breathtaking suddenness of the savage penetration. The King's prick slid in smoothly, easily; he luxuriated in the sheer delight of Lohr's incredible pussy, a pussy that was small and tight and very, very wet.

He slid his raging manhood right up her hot, wet cunt, burying it all the way to the hilt, grinding his hips against her assmounds till he could hear the low, wavering moan that escaped around the gag. Then he drew back his hips quite deliberately, extracting the gleaming shaft slowly till only the head remained enveloped between her clinging labia. Then he fell on her again, letting his weight thrust forward while sliding up and into the slick folds of her cunt in one smooth stroke that had the girl gurgling with delight in spite of herself.

With such slow, measured strokes the Lord of the Two Lands began fucking her, building in power and intensity, his hard-muscled body tensing and relaxing in powerful spasms as he rutted and fucked the beautiful princess thoroughly. The passionate young woman twisted and shook beneath him, her hips bucking with his as he rode her to ecstatic heights. She moaned and quivered as excited tingles coursed through her body, renewed at each repeated stab of pleasure. Rahn grunted like a savage animal and powered into her with determined thrusts of his mighty thighs, clenching his jaw against the surging escalation of wild excitement that ran through his body. He tightened his buttocks and pumped furiously while below him the girl's body stiffened and she jerked convulsively in her bonds. Now she was raging out of control, writhing sensually, caught in a frenzy of excitement.

While Lohr trembled and shook beneath him, Rahn struggled against the inevitable rapture, determined to hold on and drain the last ounce of pleasure before yielding himself. At last he could resist no longer; he surrendered to the undeniable shudder of lust that racked his rigid body, letting the wild tide of excitement well up in him just as he extracted his glistening cock so that he sent the erupting semen arcing up to rain down on Lohr's well-punished ass. Gobs of cream splattered down on the warm pink skin of those taut domes as Rahn guided the head of his pulsating prick, painting her tenderized bottom with his spendings.

He knelt back on his heels as the residue of his issue dribbled from his softening penis. He rubbed the head across the smarting twin domes, smiling to himself all the while. Lohr lay perfectly still. Only the heaving of her shoulders and the occasional twitch of her loins told of her earthshaking orgasm and the slowly receding waves of rapture that flooded through her.

By the end of that long night, all the princesses had been used well and shamelessly: spanked, fucked and sodomized, not once but several times. Only after all the officers had been satiated thoroughly, the last shred of male lust satisfied, were the exhausted princesses finally released. But their ordeal was far from over. Immediately upon being released, they were bound once more, this time hand and foot. Then their limp, depleted bodies were thrown rudely over the back of the divan.

While the King and his officers lounged about, raising their cups to victory, sinking into an oblivion induced by the potent southern wine, the three maidens, naked and trussed up, lay draped over the divan, so that the trio of feminine behinds were exposed lewdly, lined up in a row, hip to hip, their smarting bare buttocks presented openly for the amusement of the boisterous revelers.

The Fall of the Ice Queen

One can only speculate what went through proud Princess Lohr's head as she lay there that night, used and degraded, upended over the divan, a helpless captive in the tent of the King of the Two Lands. For probably the first time in her young life, that strong-willed young woman had faced a man of implacable determination, and, in the end, had been made to yield to him. But she would not be defeated! Lying there, inverted, her naked ass upended, she must have sworn to herself that this would be only the first of many contests.

CHAPTER EIGHT

The next day, as the soldiers were breaking camp, Plunar overheard the sisters talking. Apparently, the two younger girls had been crying, one sobbing gently while the other was bawling openly. But if they expected comfort and sisterly solicitude from their older sister, they were doomed to disappointment. On the contrary, Plunar heard her sternly berating them for showing weakness before the King.

"Stop that sniffling! At least you can act like princesses!" she hissed. "So they treated you roughly—so what of it? What has been injured but your dignity? Have you been tortured? Maimed? Killed? No! You're still alive, aren't you? So you've had your bottom warmed. It's not the first time. As you well remember, that was one of Father's favorite sports. And you've been fucked a few times. You've even taken it up the ass. Well, it's not the first time for that, either, if I am to believe you two. The tales you told me, bragging about all the boys you've had. Or were they all lies?"

One of the distressed lasses demurred, whining for better consideration, but the impatient Lohr scolded her. She would have none of it!

"You must show no weakness before this…King. Always remember he is but a man; and, like all men, he can be made use of. I saw the way he looked at me. I know that look, and I know what he wants. And he will pay dearly for it!"

So Plunar relates the conversation, and I have no reason to doubt it, for it is so like Lohr. She was ruthless. In many ways, she and Rahn were very well matched.

It turned out that what Rahn had in mind for her and her sisters would test all her resolve; he was intent on stripping her of every last shred of dignity. Even as they were breaking camp, the carpenters were put to work constructing three wooden crates that could be carried on open flatbed wagons. The crates would be open and barred cages, large enough so that the captives could stand and even move about a bit, although their movement was otherwise restricted in that each girl would be collared; a thin chain would tether her to the side of the cage. The chains were quite unnecessary, of course, but such symbolism was not lost on Princess Lohr, nor on the army. In this manner the captives would be hauled naked through the streets of Thralkild.

The Fall of the Ice Queen

For it was the King's pleasure that they should enter Thralkild thus displayed, naked and in chains. They were no more than the spoils of war, to be shown along with the other booty that was drawn in the train behind him as the King rode in glorious triumph through the streets of the city. The cheering citizens of Thralkild would thus get their first look at the pale, slender girl who would someday be their Queen, and that proud young beauty would never forget the humiliation she had been made to endure at that most ignominious entrance.

Of course I knew nothing of this. We had received word of Rahn's great victory and the total rout of the enemy before our glorious forces; but, as I have said, one learns to be skeptical of such reports from the battlefield. We could only await the return of the army and, in the meantime, pass the time as pleasantly as possible.

Now it so happened that I found my thoughts turning increasingly to the fair Alea. From time to time I would catch sight of her, splendidly nude at the baths or in the House of Women, where she went about barebreasted and graceful, moving with such dignity so that I found myself drawn to the irresistible allure of her calm beauty.

The reader may remember that at His Majesty's command, her rear portal was to be exercised so that it might be visited at some future time by his most favored general, the illustrious Turhan. The hastily arranged departure of King Rahn and his general had kept that visitation from taking place. But even so, the edict stood, and poor Alea was made to bear the discomfort of wearing the belt with the intrusive penetrator up her behind for several hours each day. Uzack always carried out his duties most conscientiously. The thought of that attractive young blonde going about naked and impaled under one of her long, thin gowns made my cock twitch with desire.

While mindful of the royal prohibition about fucking the King's concubines, I became obsessed with the possibility of taking Alea up the ass, which was surely allowed. The mere thought of it sent a thrill of excitement racing through my veins. My obsession grew, fired by new lust each time I saw the blond beauty. Finally I decided I had to act. Driven by an intense longing that was almost palpable, I sent for her.

The audience took place in my private chambers, and she must have known what was in the offing, for concubines were seldom summoned to the bedrooms of court officials. But if she sensed the possibilities—felt the least twinge of anticipation of sex in the air—she didn't show it.

At her knock on my door, I hurriedly took a seat facing the door and called for her to enter. She came to me, calm and composed, dressed in one of her open-fronted court gowns: a creamy satin dress that left her breasts freely exposed and clung to her narrow waist, flaring out to cover her svelte hips softly before falling to her ankles in long pleats.

By now Alea had grown totally indifferent to being bare-breasted before the men at court. That was the way with concubines, who learned to accept their nudity casually, since they spent so much time naked or very nearly so, and quickly grew quite used to letting their healthy, well-toned bodies be admired freely—by both sexes. It was more than acceptance of their condition; for if the truth be known, those girls found it quite pleasant to be warmed in the glow of that adulation.

Now Alea stood before me, her blond head tilted down, her eyes lowered.

"Welcome, Alea," I began in a friendly voice, for I meant to win her affections. "Come closer."

She took two steps closer to me. I looked her up and down from the crown of her golden hair to the firm, slightly flattened cones of her splendid breasts with their distinctive nipples, uptilted rather impertinently, I thought, and then on down the sweeping lines of her narrow pleated dress to the open toes of her delicate high-heeled sandals.

"I understand it is the King's desire that your bottom be exercised by an anal penetrator. Is that so?" I asked innocently, but with a tone of solicitous concern in my voice.

"Yes, my lord." She addressed me thus, even though I was not of royal blood. This was the manner of address used by the women of the court when dealing with court officials. It was a subtle admission of their status and ours, yet it didn't tell the whole story; for there was the occasional concubine who became more powerful that the highest court official, even though her influence over our mercurial King might be tenuous.

"And are you wearing it now?" I asked with a disingenuous smile, full well knowing the answer.

"Yes, my lord," the lovely lady whispered, her eyes still studying the floor. A quiver of excitement ran through me.

I nodded approvingly. "It's probably a wise precaution. A concubine should always be accessible, you know. Don't you agree?"

I waited till I saw the blond head give a tiny nod before I went on, chatty and friendly.

"It will prepare you so that when the King decides to take you up the ass, it will be a less trying experience, especially the first time. His Majesty can be rather brutal at times." I took a chance in commenting on Rahn's manners, but I wanted her to feel I would take her into my confidence. She held herself expressionless. "But surely, Alea, that would not be a novel experience for you, would it? I mean, your husband must have visited the reargate from time to time. Didn't he?"

For the first time, her head rose, and she regarded me with those penetrating blue eyes—eyes that she used with such deadly effectiveness. Her look held me captive.

"Yes...he did," she admitted in a hushed whisper, letting her eyes flutter closed.

I smiled to myself.

"Turn around now and lift up your dress. I want to see," I managed to get out, though my mouth was dry and I could barely control my sense of excitement.

Alea turned her back to me slowly and reached down obediently behind her to gather up handfuls of the long silken gown. She drew up the hem slowly, uncovering the back of her legs, her thighs, and then her bare ass as she gathered the dress up around her waist. Like all concubines, she was naked under the thin dress, although her elegant legs were sheathed in fine stockings that were sheer and milky white, the top bands accented with lacy white garters. The snug leather belt constricted the soft flesh of her waist; the thin center strip bisecting her behind disappeared as it ran deep between those choice rearmounds.

I let my eyes adore the seductive lines of those pleasing contours, appreciating their sinuous sweep, the way the backs of her thighs tapered gently into the long feminine contours of her stockinged legs, as she stood straight and tall, her heels set close together. My penis surged in hopeful anticipation. How I had longed to savor the shape and feel of her beautiful ass!

"Go over to the worktable; step up against it." This was a sturdy oak table. It was normally strewn with scrolls and correspondence, but I had cleared it of my work so that I could use it for just this purpose.

Still holding her dress up behind her, the obedient concubine walked over to the table. I watched the smooth, even sway of her naked buttocks and felt a deep throb of desire well up in me once more. Now she stood in place against the table; the edge of the tabletop crossed her at mid-thigh.

"Lean down...on the table," I commanded in a voice that was suddenly strained and choked with emotion.

Alea lowered herself, leaning over the table propped up on her elbows. Her breasts swayed heavily under her, hanging full and rich, the thick nipples barely touching the tabletop. In assuming the position, she had allowed the dress to fall back into place and now I set things right again by stepping up to pluck up her slippery skirt and drape it over her lower back, completely exposing her lush bottom.

"Spread your legs!" My words came out in a hoarse whisper.

The big blonde shifted obligingly, setting her heels apart in a widened stance, thighs pressed up against the table, leaning all the way over so that she rested on her forearms, her bottom jutting back in tempting invitation. I gazed at the subtle feminine contours of her long stockinged legs, their elegant lines elongated by the high heels that kept her up on her toes. Between her rigidly set legs, I could see the soft purse of her vulva, lightly shaded with its pale wispy pussyfur.

I reached under her with trembling hands, finding the belt and following the encircling band around her waist. I felt blindly for the buckle, which I worked open, while my favorite concubine stood stock-still, waiting patiently. Once the buckle was undone, I peeled the clinging strip out from between her clenching rearcheeks and let the loosened belt fall to her feet.

Now, with my hardened prick making its pressing demand on the front of my breeches, I stepped up behind Alea and placed my open hands on her splendid ass for the first time. Thrilled to touch her at last, I shaped my fingers so they fitted those smooth silken contours and drew them down slowly, savoring those twin curves, till my widely splayed fingers spanned Alea's bare bottom, my extended thumbs pointing inward toward her rearcleft. Slowly, I tightened my grip on her soft bottom, digging my fingers into the sculpted sides of her rearmounds, pressing my thumbs into her bottomcrease till I pried back the pliant mounds to expose the flaring base of the well-embedded buttplug.

Holding the girl's rubbery cheeks open with one splayed hand, I dug clawed fingers into the soft flesh around the protruding shaft to get a grip on the rod's base and draw it out. Alea uttered a tight little grunt with every inch that was extracted. I withdrew the smooth thin taper slowly from the clinging anus that seemed to suck onto the withdrawing rod till it popped free and the little orifice snapped shut. Alea's groan of relief was low and breathy.

I left her rearcheeks snap back in place and went to get a pot of ointment while Alea closed her eyes and sighed. Her shoulders dropped and a quiver ran through her as she settled in. Once more, I gripped her ass to pry the pillows back and this time I paused to examine the dimpled rosette, watching the little vortex spasm in anticipation. Holding her straining cheeks apart with one hand, I dipped the middle finger of the other in the pot of ointment and placed a dab of it squarely on Alea's clenching anus, causing that sensitive portal to tighten anxiously at the first feel of my inquisitive fingertip.

I worked the ointment in a little, smearing the puckered entrance generously, pressing tentatively, testing the tightly closed gate that instinctively refused to yield to me. When I had her rear entrance well greased, I drew back. It was time to get rid of some clothes. I slipped off my sandals and shoved my breeches down, pulling them off in a frenzied rush, for by now I was burning with eagerness, half-maddened in my eagerness to sample Alea's lovely ass.

As for the woman herself, she folded her arms beneath her and turned her head, lowering it to rest on folded arms, to wait with eyes closed. I thought I could detect just the trace of a smile on her lips as she slid down farther on the table so that her ass stuck up even more provocatively.

Meanwhile, my liberated prick was taut and aching with need. I dipped my fingers in the ointment and began applying the amber gel to my lust-swollen penis, pulling on it slowly, but not too hard, for I meant to prolong my pleasure till I had fully savored that splendid ass that was jutting back at me in lewd invitation.

Although still wearing my tunic, I was now naked from the hips down, my prick standing proudly before me as I approached the bent-over woman. Now I draped myself over her, slithering a hand down between us, sliding my middle finger down her valley to give her a friendly tickle on her cringing asshole, as I ground my hips against her solid rearmounds and buried my face in her hair, luxuriating in its scented softness.

When Alea felt the press of my finger in that most intimate spot, she squirmed excitedly, twisting her shoulders like a skewered fish.

"Relax," I breathed, my lips placed close to her ear.

I felt Alea quiver beneath me and sensed her anxious

tension melt away as she expelled a long, shivering breath. I felt the weakening of her instinctive resistance and seized that moment to stab abruptly, driving my stiffened finger through the fleshy ring of muscle that spasmed one final time and then yielded, so that I suddenly entered her with miraculous ease.

A gurgling sound was coming from deep in Alea's throat. I worked my finger up her ass, twisting my hand, screwing my stiffened finger into her to lubricate the squeezing rectal sleeve, while Alea grunted through her clenched jaws. When I pulled my finger out, she gasped and uttered a moan so soft it was almost a whimper.

But her sense of relief at having expelled my probing digit gave only temporary respite, for I was about to replace that rude visitor by an even more demanding masculine presence.

Splaying the fingers of the hand I held between us, I pressed her pliant mounds apart. I wiggled against her joyfully, letting Alea feel the swollen head of my prick as I nuzzled up her exposed rearvalley.

I grabbed my trusty weapon and poked impertinently between her cheeks, feeling blindly for my target. And when I found her clenching anus I settled in, pressing lightly at first, and then with greater urgency, applying steady pressure against the tiny gate.

Alea threw her head back, and sucked in a shivering breath. Suddenly her sphincter muscle gave way under my determined assault, and I slid into her with one swift, powerful lunge. Alea whimpered and bit her lip to keep from crying out at the stabbing pain of the assault. She arched up on her elbows, craning backward, her eyes clenched shut.

I clamped her swaying hips and pressed forward with steady, unrelenting pressure till all shreds of resistance melted away and I was suddenly through the tight ring of muscle, and my entire length was sliding up her in a single smooth penetration. I paused with half my swollen length buried up the concubine's nicely rounded bottom.

Alea gurgled from deep in her throat and, as I inched my prick farther up her anus. She couldn't help wriggling her shoulders, shivering with delight. I heard her long wavering sigh, a helpless moan, low and throaty when, with a thrust of my loins, I lunged the rest of the way into her, burying my sword to the hilt. The smooth tightness that now held my prick in a viselike grip was incredible. I wriggled my hips letting her get the feel of me, giving her time to accommodate to the masculine presence up her ass.

My hips movements, brought an immediate reaction from Alea, who thrust her ass back against me in happy response. After the first twinge of discomfort, the well-drilled concubine was definitely enjoying herself. Now I began to fuck her, moving slowly, sliding in and out in steady, even strokes as I tightened my grip on her.

Wave after wave of delight coursed through my body. I gritted my teeth, determined to hold on against the incredible rush of pleasure. I let myself savor the slick smoothness of her rearchannel; the tightness, the warmth, the reflexive spasms of her sphincter that tried instinctively to expel me from her depths. I knew I could not bear the repeated thrills much longer, and I slowed my pace, pulling back and driving in a slow, even, measured pace till I got a low groan of deep-seated pleasure from the impaled woman.

Then, when I was in all the way, my loins grinding against the full curves of her solid butt, I clamped her flanks and moved my hips, tickling her innards with my prick. Alea's moan was a plea of plaintive surrender, quivering with the beginning tremors of a deep-seated orgasm. The surging climax threatened to overtake her, so close that she teetered on the edge.

The blond woman raised herself up on her elbows and craned back, arching her back in a deep curve and thrusting her naked bottom back at me.

"Oh... Yes... Yes... Yes... *Yes!*" she babbled breathlessly as I withdrew slowly till only the bulbous head remained buried up her churning ass.

I threw back my head and tightened my buttocks. With a single brutal thrust, I slammed into her, burying myself in her, then fucked her furiously to send the twisting, squirming, passionate woman, raging out of control.

The rising tremors welled up in her body to become a prolonged quivering, the definite convulsions of a tremendous orgasm that overtook her and shook her to the core. I felt the onrush of a massive surge of pure pleasure, the inevitability of the rising sperm, the singular ecstatic thrill of the pulsating eruptions that sent thick wads of my sperm deep into the fair Alea's twisting, thrashing bottom.

CHAPTER NINE

Those few months spent in pleasant dalliance with the girls at court were among the happiest days I ever spent in service of King Rahn. They were over all too soon with the return of the King, who arrived that fall with his latest prize in tow.

I well remember the day that I first laid eyes on the caged beauty who would one day become our Queen. Rahn rode in triumph through the gates, serene and imperturbable, accepting—as no more than his due—the thunderous applause of the assembled multitudes. Behind him rode his generals, resplendent in polished armor that gleamed in the sun; all banners flying, their warhorses bedecked with colorful trappings. They were followed by an array of staff officers, then squad after squad of mounted cavalry. Next came the ranks of our victorious soldiers, archers, spearmen and foot soldiers, trudging along and beaming with pleasure as they acknowledged the adulation of the crowd while marching through the streets of Thralkild. Captured nobles were placed next in the parade, shuffling along with hands bound before them, looking defeated and forlorn. They would bring a pretty ransom.

Behind these, wagon after wagon rolled by, piled high with loot, the riches of the east rolling by on endless display. Next marched the slaves, naked and collared, manacled and led in chains into uncertain captivity. Among these former soldiers of the fallen King were many strong and handsome men who would make good slaves, and I noticed the many gentlewomen in the crowd eyeing them, critically examining the dusty, sweating bodies of those muscular naked men with the thought of purchase clearly in mind.

Finally, the three wagons at the rear rolled by slowly, each containing a naked princess. Two of the girls were huddled in corners, making themselves small, to expose as little of their nudity as possible to the ogling crowd. But Princess Lohr would not cower before them! She stood alone, facing those who mocked and jeered at her. She was splendid in her nudity, a pale, solitary, dark-haired figure standing with legs parted slightly to absorb the rolling gait of the wagon and maintain her erect pose.

She stood with her arms folded across her chest just under her small, hard breasts. One couldn't help being impressed with her proud beauty, the gentle slope of her shoulders, her long neck, her slender chest with taut pointy breasts that stuck out firm and hard, with precise nipples that were bold and insolent. One couldn't help being struck by the sweeping lines of her torso, the slight ridges of her compact hips, the sinuous lines of her choice young loins. One couldn't help appraising the marvelous curves of her gently tapered thighs, the smooth contours that beckoned the hand. One couldn't help staring at the brazen set of her legs, one leg thrust forward defiantly, the richly furred womanhood on display boldly, uncaringly, as she stood with legs parted, proud and unflinching, impervious to the catcalls of the rabble.

But if it was her naked body that first drew one's attention, it was the girl's eyes that were the most startling. Her face was neutral: no flicker of emotion crossed her brow, and yet her eyes had narrowed, almost imperceptibly. There was tightness there, a deep resolve along with cold, implacable hatred. And if one of those jeering louts got too close, and his bleary-eyed gaze came into contact with her hard black eyes, he would recoil as though he had been hit by an arrow—taken aback, not quite sure why.

It didn't take long for those of us who knew the King to realize that his manner toward the haughty princess was different from the way he treated his other women. For one thing, he never carried out his threat to have her relegated to the ranks of the sex slaves. Not only did he spare her that ultimate humiliation, instead he installed her directly into the House of Women, a sure sign of favor.

Once there, the demanding princess immediately set about ordering special gowns to be made for her. They were long dresses cut in the traditional style of the concubines, but they were made of a gleaming silver fabric. The slippery dresses hung straight on her spare frame, layering her slight hips and flowing down her sleek lines like molten metal. At court she dressed all in silver. Uzack took to calling her "the silver girl."

But we had another name for her. Behind her back, she was known as the "Ice Queen." It was not her silvery raiment, nor the translucent quality of her pale good looks that earned her that epithet. Rather it was the total lack of human emotion. For under that carefully controlled surface, Lohr was the coldest, most bloodless female I had ever met, selfish and totally indifferent to the joys or pains of others. She might seethe with anger inside, but outside she always maintained her icy control. Only the fire of her eyes told of the rage within.

For some reason Rahn became fascinated with the cool aloofness of the Ice Queen, so much so that he seemed blind to the dangerous game she was playing. For beneath that icy exterior, Lohr burned with ambition, and she was at least as ruthless as our merciless King. She sensed what it was the man wanted from her, needed from her; and she schemed to use those very qualities to attract him and bind him to her, even as she plotted ceaselessly against him.

Like King Rahn, Lohr, too, had dreams of conquest.

The Fall of the Ice Queen

Even at the lowest depths of her degradation, when she was paraded as a naked captive before the gawking crowd by the man who had subjugated her, even then, she kept alive a dream of conquest. And she swore to herself, with that implacable will of hers, that someday she would be their Queen.

Now, jealousy and ambition were hardly foreign to life among the concubines, and no one was surprised when it became obvious that Lohr was maneuvering to be the first among them, for there were always those who strove to become the King's favorite. Those of us at court knew she would stop at nothing. Not content with being the first among equals, she plotted to become the King's consort. Then, after destroying, banishing, or accepting the subservience of her rivals, she would be Queen!

What we didn't know then—what no one knew—was that she dreamed of even greater power. At some point, Lohr got it into her head that she could rule supreme, having disposed of the inconvenient King whom she hated. That was Lohr's way with men: They would be kept close to her while they were useful, then discarded when no longer needed. It didn't matter to her whether the man was a slave, a strategically placed minister, a fawning noble, or a powerful King.

Now, the notion of a woman as absolute ruler was unknown in the history of the Two Lands. We had been ruled by a long, illustrious line of Kings. If the throne became vacant, a male regent would be appointed as a temporary expedient. The people of the Two Lands had never been ruled by a woman. Lohr knew this, but tradition was of no importance to our single-minded Queen. She would stop at nothing once she had set her sights on the throne. She would be supreme ruler, the first female monarch of the Two Lands!

Only years later, I came to see that Lohr had planned her attack on two fronts. The ambitious young princess knew she could never hope to succeed without the support of certain men: the rich and powerful, certain members of the aristocracy, the key court officials. She needed their goodwill if she were to succeed. So she set about studying the men around the King in that cold, calculating way of hers, to see who might best be useful to her, separating out those who might prove valuable as allies, those who should be tolerated, those who might be safely ignored or spurned. The ones she judged as being of some use to her would find themselves flattered, bribed, otherwise pleased, and seduced shamelessly. For the wily princess would offer her feminine charms freely in whatever way was necessary to entice a man into doing her bidding.

I was never quite sure just where I stood in her scheme of things, but she invited me to her bedchamber once. It was an offer that a gentleman could hardly refuse. I remember with fondness those sleek heavenly thighs. Although she could be quite cruel and spiteful to those who were of no use to her, she was inevitably charming to those from whom she sought to curry favor. Lohr well knew how to please a man!

But if Lohr was masterly in the way she played male

egos, drawing from men their strength, and exploiting their weaknesses, I don't think she ever had quite the same understanding of her own sex, although she well knew the more subtle influence that women had on the affairs of the kingdom. So on this front, too, she began to lay her plans.

Cautiously, patiently, she moved to establish strategic friendships among the women of the court, carefully selecting the favored women of the court's most influential officials. Wives and mistresses, concubines, and slaves were flattered and cajoled, and promises were made amidst pacts sealed with kisses of sisterly affection. It was said that more than kisses were exchanged in a few cases, and that idea is not surprising given that women, too, found Lohr's cool beauty strangely attractive. Still she seemed especially wary and suspicious, never really at ease with the women at court, except for her sisters who now served the King. Perhaps because she felt less sure of herself among other women, Lohr gave special care to cultivating this web of feminine alliances.

Thus Lohr insinuated herself at the court. Her power and influence grew quietly behind the scenes, while publicly it was acknowledged that she was becoming the King's current favorite. Now, when Rahn surveyed the girls around him, she was the one he would most often invite to sit at his side at affairs of state, just as he was likely to turn to her at the revelries and feasts when he felt the urge for female companionship.

As Lohr became more sure of herself, she became

more difficult and demanding. She might even, on occasion, be sharp with the King, although there she was always very careful, checking her tongue before she went too far.

Rahn was certainly not a patient man, yet he seemed to tolerate her bitchiness to a point, and he might even smile on her indulgently. Yet it was equally possible that he would suddenly turn on her and release that royal wrath that made mere mortals tremble. For months at a time, he might banish her from his presence, but in the end he would relent. One day she would simply be there, seated in her customary place at the left side of the King, serene and unperturbed as though he noticed neither her presence nor her absence.

We were not surprised when Rahn named Lohr his Queen. Many have remarked what a curious pair they were: the crude, earthy King, brooding and mercurial, with his fiery temper; and the haughty and beautiful Queen, controlled, wrapped in her icy reserve.

But if they were in many ways different, they also were much alike. Both were ruthless and cruel and entirely self-centered, so I think they understood each other well. And it turned out that Lohr, like Rahn, had a voracious sexual appetite. It didn't take long for the word to get out—she was insatiable; her lustful demands knew no bounds. The two of them shared in the most outrageous sexual indulgence, reveling in the licentious decadence of the court they created at Thralkild. However, here, too, there were subtle differences.

The King was crude and bawdy in his greedy sexual

appetite, Lohr's tastes were altogether more exquisitely refined, her manner cool and detached, even in the midst of passion. The Queen was totally dissolute; combining a lustful imagination with a carefully cultivated sense of debasement. Her icy elegance was made all the more shocking by the unbridled enthusiasm with which she pursued the most bizarre and degrading sexual acts imaginable. Then, there was her cruel streak. For some reason, Lohr had discovered that a bit of suffering lent piquancy to her simmering lust, thrilling her in new and unexpected ways.

Most often it was her sex slaves with who bore the brunt of her cold, sadistic fury. Like the King, Lohr kept a retinue of favored slaves around her, young girls and pretty lads who were kept on hand to attend her in her bath and in her bedchamber. She would select a favorite to curl up naked to sleep at the foot of her bed. And, if she was inclined have him service her, the lad might be summoned to pleasure her with lips and tongue; or perhaps, if he was especially favored, he might even be permitted to enter between those aristocratic thighs and dip his wick in the royal honeypot before the night was through. It was said that Queen Lohr occasionally indulged a similar passion for fair young girls, and I have no reason to discount that rumor.

If the slaves weren't quick enough, eager enough, or obedient enough, if there was detected a lack of zeal in carrying out their sexual duties, in their willingness to offer their bodies, in the enthusiasm they showed in servicing masters and mistresses with hands or lips or mouth or tongue, if they displeased a finicky courtier for even the slightest reason, swift punishment followed inevitably. Some of the most bizarre sexual punishments were devised by the Queen, who, for some reason, took it into her head to see to it personally that discipline was administered to those slaves who fell into royal disfavor.

As she increased her circle of female friends, Lohr used these occasions to entertain them. Of course I was not invited to these feminine gatherings, but wild rumors of what went on at these sessions abounded. Naturally, I was curious.

The invaluable Uzack supplied a way to satisfy my curiosity. We shared an abiding interest in sex, and at our frequent get-togethers over wine, the subject of the Queen's soirees naturally came up. When I mentioned that I would love to be privy to one of those events, he surprised me, telling me that it would be no problem. He, who knew every nook and cranny of the meandering palace, informed me that there was a secret passage that ran along the upper floor. From a certain vantage point, one could look down and watch the proceedings completely unobserved.

The crafty chamberlain assured me that I could see everything that went on! With that intriguing promise, I found myself following him one night when we knew one of the Queen's dissolute revelries was to be held. I made my way cautiously through darkened attics, across rafters, following his single candle and feeling my way through the shadows till we came to an opening that looked down into one of the rooms of the Queen's

THE FALL OF THE ICE QUEEN

chambers. There was Lohr, radiant in her lustrous silvery garments, seated as on a throne, a group of her intimates lounging around her on scattered pillows.

Although we could not make out their words, it appeared that two slave girls, barely out of their teens, were about to be punished for some minor infraction. The two penitents, their heads hung low, were led forward to present themselves to the stern Queen. She spoke a few words and gestured curtly, and immediately they slipped off the short white tunics that were their sole garments. I admired the spare, clean lines of their small-breasted bodies, unbroken save by the high collars and the skimpy trace of pubic fuzz. Lean and sinewy, with their straight limbs, close-cropped hair and small, neat buttocks, they shared a fawnlike grace and trim youthful lines.

It sometimes amused Lohr to order the slaves to punish one another, and this was to be the arrangement she had decided on for tonight. The naked girls were ordered down on all fours, placed side by side and turned so that they were arranged head to tail. Each girl was now given a small wooden paddle, and since her partner's bottom was conveniently within reach, it was not difficult for her to impart a smart slap to the other girl's behind, even as her own tail was receiving similar treatment. At the command from their imperious mistress, the girls started to lay soft, tentative taps on each other.

With her eyes on the bizarre performance, she made a gesture to a male slave who stood by her side. (Lohr was always thus attended by at least one young man.) I didn't know this one. He might have been one of the new slaves recently acquired, for Lohr liked to personally introduce each new man to her circle of women friends. He was a handsome lad, with a well-muscled, wiry body, a tightly knit torso with long, tapering waist, compact hips, and straight, strong legs. He was barechested. Wrapped around his loins was a brief linen kilt, which, at a gesture from his mistress he peeled away nonchalantly so that he stood beside her, his exposed sex hanging heavy and slightly swollen.

Lohr contemplated the drooping prick that sprouted from the tuft of soft brown pubic hair and turned to say something amusing to her friends, who laughed and eyed the masculine equipment with interest. His mistress reached out a slender hand lovingly, as though she were about to stroke a favorite pet.

At the touch of her cool fingers, the young man's penis jumped with excitement. She lifted his languid cock with her fingers, studied it, let it drop again. She examine his balls, lightly furred with silvery brown hair. She cupped them in her palm and lifted them, as if weighing them in her open hand. Then, using just the pads of her fingers, she brushed up the underside of the shaft, letting her teasing fingers slither playfully up to the head. The reaction was immediate! She only had to stroke him once or twice till she had the lad's highly responsive manhood fully erect, standing swollen in a flush of full-blown masculine pride.

We watched the smiling Queen hike up her gown

quite deliberately, open her knees, and point to her lap. Her obedient slave knew what his mistress wanted. He moved forward to lay himself down across her silver-stockinged legs, offering his bare ass to her hand while his hard, slightly curved prick was pressed between his belly and the heavenly softness of the Queen's slightly spread thighs. It amused Lohr to have a male in this position. She would make a point of forbidding the poor fellow to come, an edict clearly impossible to obey, what with his hard erection rubbing up and down her smooth thighs as he twisted his hips, squirming helplessly under her punishing hand.

Now the Queen drew on a pair of long gloves, finely made of the same silvery fabric she much favored. She paused to caress the masculine butt that sat exposed before her, tracing over the coiled muscles, the slightly hollowed sides of his sculpted buttocks. She let her gloved hand stroke the slave's rearmounds while she turned her attention to the two girls on their hands and knees before her.

Meanwhile, the slave girls were twitching to the soft staccato of wood rapping their flesh, as the gentle beating went on. But their efforts were entirely too restrained to satisfy the sadistic Queen.

"Harder!" she shouted, so loud that we heard the command plainly from our perch in the rafters. Immediately, the slaps became crisper, louder, delivered with more vigor.

As if to emphasize the point, she drew her hand back and delivered a stinging slap to her slave's handily placed butt. The young fellow absorbed the blow and lay silent while Lohr ran a gloved hand over the crest of his hard ass.

Her lips curled back in an evil grin and she leaned forward to attack that masculine behind with enthusiasm, hauling back to swing in a wide arc, delivering ringing slaps with the flat of her gloved hand, alternating between his tightened buttocks as the young man grunted and twisted in her lap.

Whap!... Whap!... Whap!... Whap!

We could hear each shot clearly as the dull thuds of the spanking echoed among the rafters, punctuated by the sharp retorts of the paddles on the bottoms of the two slaves, who were beginning to warm to their work. By now Lohr was all but ignoring the action on the floor, so engaged was she in smacking the solid, muscular butt of the slave who squirmed in her lap. Her face was set, lips curled with glee. The lusty Queen's eyes shone with excitement as she struck with the vicious fury of an obsessed woman, hair flying, hand pounding down in a maddened blur. The other girls watched on, paralyzed in rapt silence to see the maniacal Queen so caught up in passion that she was oblivious to all else.

Suddenly the punishing rain of smacks stopped, and Lohr shuddered. Her shoulders shivered as she gulped a deep breath, and ran a hand over the slave's well-warmed butt. I watched her clench her fingers into a claw and dug viciously into the meaty buttocks. The pain of this new attack made him throw back his head and arch his back. Then she extended her stiffened middle finger and rammed it between the poor fellow's rearcheeks, working that gloved finger up his ass while he twisted and moaned in sweet agony. At that point, the poor fellow lost the struggle to hold back the orgasmic surge and the inevitable triumph of pleasure took place, just as any sane person knew it would. The skewered slave let out a groan as his issue erupted to splatter the Queen's silver-stockinged thighs.

Lohr became indignant immediately; her manner expressed mock outrage. She had the lad slide down to his knees; forced him to lick her thighs, to lap up all his own spendings to the great amusement of the salacious party. Once he had licked clean his mistress's thighs dutifully and run his tongue along the stockinged columns where his spendings had dribbled, Lohr opened her legs to her slave. Still on his knees he inched forward while the Queen draped her slack stockinged legs over his shoulders, clamped his face and drew his lips to her hot, needy core. For a moment, the onlooking women, tense and excited, watched their Queen being serviced, and then they turned in surprise as a half-dozen male pages entered the room. The pages still wore their short tunics, but their tights had been removed, leaving them quite naked from the hips down.

Ever thoughtful of her guests, Lohr had seen to it that her randy friends would not leave unsatisfied.

As the newly appointed Queen gained power and influence over the King, even those concubines who occasionally fell from grace found themselves in her clutches. And for those unfortunate ladies she reserved the most exquisite and refined punishments imaginable.

Now that she was ensconced in her own quarters in the palace, she most enjoyed publicly humiliating those girls with whom she had once shared the House of Women. Often she arranged to have their punishment witnessed at a feast or other widely attended celebration. So it was with the ingenious humiliation she arranged for Ana.

Ana was a well-built girl with fully curved medium-sized breasts, a stocky but curvaceous body, generous hips, and a full, rich ass. She was well known for her sharp tongue. Like many of the concubines, she tended to be haughty and conceited (although in the end none of them were as imperious as the Ice Queen came to be). Still she was not popular at court, so her punishment was witnessed by some of us with gleeful—if hidden—satisfaction.

Ana also had the dubious distinction of being not too bright. She was so forthright in her speech that she possessed a dangerous combination of traits that was bound to get her in trouble, for by that time Lohr had spies everywhere. Some indiscreet remark she had made had reached the ears of the Queen, and now Ana found herself in the middle of the banquet hall, her wrists and neck clamped into the standing stocks, head and hands extending through the cut circles in the hinged boards, while behind the rest of her body was exposed in a particularly ingenious way. For our vengeful Queen had arranged that Ana's long dress be cut out in back so as to leave her nether regions displayed openly: the plump ass and full thighs banded near the top by the garters of the long hose that sheathed her glamorous legs all the way down to her high-heeled sandals. Her lush, meaty bottom peeked out between the parted folds of the draping fabric in a blatantly lurid invitation.

But what made the arrangement particularly interesting was that a short-handled paddle had been attached by a thin chain to the upright side of the tall stocks. The royal guests were invited to use the convenient paddle to warm the loudmouthed concubine's bare bottom as they passed by. To be sure, there would be no unseemly protests; Ana had been gagged. Restrained as she was, the poor woman never knew when some playful guest of the King's might be tempted to come up behind her and deliver a sharp, stinging smack that would send her hopping from foot to foot. I noticed the women took particular delight in trying their hand in this amusing diversion.

CHAPTER TEN

I never envied Uzack his job in trying to keep the peace in the fractious House of Women. While there were frequent spats and constant outbreaks of petty jealousy, by the time Lohr was named Queen, she seemed well above the fray. No cutting remarks were aimed her way—at least, not with the experience of the unfortunate Ana fresh in everyone's memory. Having banished all her rivals, Lohr had the field all to herself. Her place at the King's side seemed secure, with possibly one disturbing exception: No one could fail to notice the way Rahn's eyes lit up when the fair Alea came into the room. That appreciative gleam certainly did not escape Lohr's attention, and it was inevitable that she would campaign to discredit the one woman whose beauty might rival her own.

I studied the three of them at one of those drunken orgies, fascinated to see the drama unfold. Rahn was sprawled naked on thick silken pillows while Lohr, her short white underskirt rucked up shamelessly around her waist, lay stretched out beside him in front of the low tables. His eyes were heavy, and he wore the smug, self-satisfied smile of the slightly drunk. Propped up on one elbow, he surveyed the room regally while one hand absently stroked his Queen's sleek lines as if she were a piece of prized sculpture, running a hand idly up and down the smooth contours of her naked haunches. Inevitably, his roaming gaze fell on the row of attending concubines, and he smiled to himself, pleased that their beauty decorated his court. Then his adoring hand paused abruptly as his gaze fell on Alea kneeling there, sitting back on her heels, her attractive features composed serenely, her manner deferential as she waited to be of service to her King.

Lohr tensed under Rahn's caressing hand, sensing the pregnant pause, alert to the threat. Those terrible, wonderful eyes shot up to his face, but he ignored her inquisitive look and generously beckoned for the blonde to join them. Alea came to him and, at his nod, peeled the narrow straps down her shoulders, letting the thin dress slither down her streamlined form to collapse into a puddle of silk around her ankles, leaving her standing in skimpy underskirt, garters, and stockings. She stretched out where the King pointed, lying on the other side of him, but inverted so that her head lay toward Lohr's feet. Now he knelt between them and, obviously pleased with the arrangement, began to enjoy both superb feminine bodies.

Lohr said nothing, but she gave him a hard look. He must have seen the spiteful envy in her expressive eyes for he grinned hugely at her, amused at her humiliation. He smacked her playfully and ran a hand down over her hip, even as he kept up his deliberate stroking of Alea's long flanks, sliding his hand from her stockinged knee up the sheer fabric and over the gartered ridge of the stockings to delve under the little skirt, pushing it up with his burrowing hand while his fingers explored the silken flesh of the blonde's naked loins.

This sort of simultaneous attention to both young women was a sport Rahn loved to engage in, particularly when he found out how incensed Lohr became when he taunted her by comparing her publicly to her rival. I remember how once, in a drunken revelry, he had made the comparison even more explicit by having the two of them stand next to each other with their backs to him, raise up their dresses in back and bend over, so that he and some of his drunken cronies could compare their exposed assets: Lohr's twin swells, sleek and elongated, with a deep, narrow division between her well-proportioned rearcheeks; and Alea's inviting ass, more perfectly rounded, the taut, symmetrical domes, well defined, with hollowed dimples at the sides.

Perhaps Rahn was remembering that pleasant picture now, as with a half-smile plastered on his lips, he slid his hand in to explore between Alea's legs. She shifted uneasily, letting her eyes flutter closed as she spread her thighs to allow her master easier access to her blond sex. The King let his fingers dabble in the blond curls of soft pussyfur, sampling a tuft of fine pubic hair, rubbing it between his fingers, tugging gently. He looked directly at Lohr as he played with Alea's womanhood, his eager fingers cupping and squeezing the golden-furred mount of Venus. He let a smile play over his lips as he fingered Alea's delicate pussy. The healthy young woman couldn't keep her body from responding. Soon he had her slithering sensually, writhing with the heat of lust he kindled in her moistened loins.

Now the Monarch of the Two Lands curled his joined fingers, dipped them deep into Alea's honeypot, and jiggled his hand so that she grunted and twitched and arched her back, seeking more of his pleasuring hand. When he extracted them, his fingers glistened with her copious spendings. Now he brought his fingers, still wet and redolent of Alea's pussy, to Lohr's face, holding them just below her nose, offering them to her. She wrinkled up her nose and turned away in disgust, but he held her jaw in a viselike grip, laughing, as he rubbed his sticky fingers all over her tightly pressed lips and mouth and cheeks.

The wanton King shouted to his guests, cheerfully inviting them to witness the Queen's debasement. She was ordered to lick his fingers clean, forced to taste the other woman's spendings. Roaring with laughter, Rahn took great delight in the degradation of his haughty consort. He pressed insistently against the taut line of her lips and forced her set teeth apart. He slid his hooked fingers into her mouth and had her suck on them. That was too much for the Ice Queen, who lowered her pretty lashes and shut her eyes to hold in her rage, even as she hollowed her cheeks obediently and sucked her rival's juices from the fingers of the King.

After Lohr's latest humiliation, things became even more contentious between the two women, with Rahn taking perverse delight in fanning the fires of their smoldering jealousy whenever the opportunity might arise. The King's bawdy jokes and mocking treatment infuriated the proud Queen!

Things came to a climax one memorable night when the two women were forced to square off before the King and his nobles. It was at one of the drinking bouts he sometimes held with a small group of his more dissolute lords, the sort of all-male gatherings where the King was certain to provide some amusing entertainment for his guests. Rahn, who disapproved of revenge being wreaked in the more subtle ways of women, decreed that his two favorites should engage in a fair and open fight. There was to be a wrestling match!

A space was cleared hurriedly within the hollow square formed by the tables, and thick rugs laid down in layers. At a nod from the King, the doors were thrown back. The two rivals entered the room, splendid in their naked beauty, walking with heads held high, wrapped in a calm dignity that placed them well above the crude comments and lecherous ogling of those wine-besotted louts. They had been prepared for their contest: Their nude bodies gleamed with a light sheen of oil. Their hair had been swept back, twisted, and pinned up; they wore no adornment save the metal bands clamping their upper arms, marking them as the King's own.

I marveled at how well they maintained that aristocratic bearing as I sized them up for the contest. Alea, tall and long-limbed, was superbly fit. Her strength was evident in the sleek biceps and robust thighs typical of those hardy northern women. Lohr was also tall and slender, although not quite as tall as Alea. She had thinner shoulders, smaller, jutting breasts, straighter hips and long, narrow thighs; her linear body was strong and wiry.

The two rivals came before their King to make obeisance. Alea's bow was low and deferential, Lohr's not much more than a curt nod. The difference in their manner was not lost on Rahn. The King smirked, then nodded his permission for the match to begin, and the opponents took their places on either side of the rug.

The two crouching women circled each other warily. Alea widened her stance and shifted her weight forward, rising up on the balls of her feet, her body coiled, ready to spring. She was fast, but Lohr was even faster. As the blonde launched herself, reaching out for the wiry brunette, Lohr dove under the outstretched arms and lunged into the stretching blond body, ramming her head in the soft midriff, so that Alea grunted and folded. Now the two grappled, arms wrapped tightly around each other's naked body.

For a moment they struggled upright, matched

evenly. Then Alea managed to wedge a leg between Lohr's thighs and began to overpower her. Using her superior weight, she bent her opponent backward, grinding her ample tits against Lohr's squashed globes till the dark-haired Queen was forced backward inexorably. Lohr stumbled, on the verge of losing her balance. At that moment, Alea pressed her attack, grabbing for Lohr's shoulders. But the agile Queen was able to squirm away, her oil-slicked body too slippery for Alea's grasping fingers.

After this first skirmish, the two wrestlers settled in, slower now, circling cautiously, taking each other's measure, looking shrewdly for openings.

Alea's hair was half-undone, wispy tresses sticking out so she had the look of a wild woman. She was flushed with excitement. Her breasts swung heavily under her as she crouched low and menacing, and scuttled sideways, reaching out with splayed hands held before her. Lohr never took her eyes off the blonde's as she edged around, sinewy limbs taut and ready. Her hair was disheveled and she was breathing heavily. Her small, taut tits rose and fell raggedly.

Again the two opponents closed quickly, grappling with one another, flailing limbs seeking the ultimate hold. Their arms wrapped around each other in tight embrace, and they spun and twisted in a frantic blur.

Aroused by this naked display of raw female aggression, the lusty men roared their approval. Shouting with delight, they cheered for one woman or the other, as the two combatants struggled savagely, emitting animallike grunts, each seeking the advantage, that ultimate hold that would force painful submission.

They were locked in a lover's embrace when Lohr hooked a leg behind Alea's and sent the big blonde tumbling backward. They fell crashing to the floor. The oily bodies twisted and tussled, gyrating in a wild flurry of limbs.

The blonde seemed to gain a momentary advantage as she squirmed on top, her flopping breasts pressed into Lohr's smaller tits while she used her greater weight to pin her rival to the floor. But in a twinkling of an eye, her advantage was lost as they were rolling, over and over again, until finally it was the wiry Queen who ended up on top.

Lohr planted her bottom on her rival's heaving breasts and, wildly excited, began slapping Alea, smacking her face from side to side. This so infuriated the powerful blonde that she let out a fierce cry. With a mighty pelvic thrust, she upended the lighter woman. She leapt immediately on Lohr, who lay momentarily stunned, sprawled on her back. But Lohr recovered instantly and slithered out from under the big blonde to spring lightly to her feet.

Now the two women went at it in a wild, vicious catfight, talons extended, scratching, clawing and pulling hair, struggling to find a grip on those sweaty, oily bodies, as the men applauded and cheered them on. The general mayhem subsided gradually into a contest of raw power. Then the blonde's greater strength began to be felt.

Now she jammed her leg between Lohr's thighs, spun her around, and flung her to the floor with a dull thud. This time there was no escape as Lohr, momentarily winded, lay there panting and gulping for air. The big blonde fell heavily on her, pinning her shoulders. She sat straddling Lohr's hips and pulled her wrists up next to her head to pin them to the rug as she peered down at the Queen with her penetrating blue eyes.

Alea's hair was in glorious disarray, her face flushed with excitement. She was sweating profusely. Perspiration mingled freely with the oil that covered her body. Gasping for air, her shoulders heaving, she looked down in triumph at her defeated rival. Lohr returned the blonde's stare with fire blazing in her eyes, the movement of her heaving breasts subsiding gradually. Her loosened hair floated around her head like a dark halo. From time to time, she gritted her teeth and tossed her head from side to side, straining upward. But she could do no more than squirm helplessly beneath Alea's weight.

"Enough!" Rahn cried. The two women stopped struggling, although Alea made no move to disengage. "Kiss her."

Alea turned to look over her shoulder at her hated consort, as if she wasn't certain she had heard what he said.

"Go on, kiss her!" Rahn repeated.

The blonde reached down and slipped her curving hands behind Lohr's ears. Lifting the Queen's head, cradling it in her hands, she bent down and kissed her opponent full on the lips. Lohr went limp, letting herself be kissed, neither embracing nor protesting what must be, simply allowing it to happen, acquiescing to the will of the all-powerful King.

Rahn watched the girls kissing and turned with a devilish grin to his drinking companions.

"Now I want my favorite girls to kiss and make up," he announced grandly. "Come, let us have a reconciliation. I'm sure my lords would appreciate a proper display of affection."

Now both women turned to look at the King, disbelieving expressions on their wide-eyed faces. But he only sat there, grinning at them, waiting implacably. Alea dismounted and eased on down till she lay next to Lohr on the rug. They turned to face one another and embraced, hugging and kissing in the demonstration of hollow affection that had been ordered by the King.

The two women lay on the floor naked before their lusty all-male audience, limbs intertwined loosely, stroking and petting each other lightly. But their movements were desultory; they were obviously doing no more than going through the motions. Their obvious lack of ardor greatly displeased the King.

"Let's see a little enthusiasm, or we'll warm up your bottoms to get you to move!" he shouted.

The clear threat had the desired effect. Obediently, their caresses became bolder; inquisitive hands exploring curves and crevices, stroking breasts, delving between scissoring legs. And soon the writhing of their loins told of the unmistakable urgency of growing sexual arousal.

The Fall of the Ice Queen

They held each other tightly, legs intertwined, needy pussies rubbing against aching thighs, breasts grinding against yearning breasts.

As the lissome blonde felt the first stirrings of sexual desire, she slid into a sensual lassitude. Meanwhile, Lohr was becoming more excited, her hands more eager, her willowy loins squirming with rising lust. With little fluttering kisses, she teased the blonde's lips, her chin and neck, licking a wet trail along the narrow path between the flattened mounds of those magnificent breasts. Throughout this adoration, the blonde lay perfectly still, sunk in languorous warmth. Her hands came up in a loose caress, and she drew her eager lover closer, till the dark head nuzzled between her tits. Alea's pale lashes fluttered, her eyes slid closed as her amorous playmate used a single finger to trace the slope of a breast and then cupped that gently mounded tit lovingly, squeezing it to force the nipple up toward her hungry mouth.

Alea rolled her head mindlessly from side to side. Her eyes were half-lidded in dreamy reverie; her hips twitched restlessly. She inhaled sharply through clenched teeth as the captive nipple was drawn into the hot, damp cavern, to be thoroughly worked over by greedy lips and lively tongue.

Lohr worried that nipple, clamping the stiffening bud lightly between her teeth and shaking her head from side to side like a playful puppy, gently tugging on the sensate tip. The blonde let out a strangled groan and strained upward, raising her hips, arching her back. And when the wet tip fell free, we could see that the glistening pink nipple was now fully erect, hard, taut with excitement.

Now, with unrestrained enthusiasm, her eager lover slid hot insatiable hands over the rib cage and on down the long, streamlined flanks of the writhing, sensual blonde. Her hands sought to savor every inch of the undulating body before seeking and finding the lightly furred vulva. Alea opened her scissoring thighs, eager to encourage the intimate caress, welcoming the exploring fingers instinctively, urging her lover on with little whimpers of pleasure uttered through tightly pressed lips.

Meanwhile, Lohr cupped and palmed the pale blond mount of Venus, pressing hard, rubbing deeply, till she had the passion-driven blonde moaning in helpless surrender. A that precise moment, she inserted a single finger up Alea's cunt; then two joined fingers; then three, jammed hard up the big blonde's vagina. Alea's eyes widened and her arched brows shot up at the sudden stab of pleasure. Then her eyes shut, and her brow knitted with the sudden intensity of an abrupt flood of sensations as the adept woman caressed her damp sex expertly, the fingers probing, penetrating, exploring her satiny inner recesses. Alea's lips parted in a long, drawn-out sigh, a breathy purr of deep animal satisfaction. The sensual moan and the quiver of arousal spurred her eager paramour to even greater heights, and soon Lohr was thrusting her stiffened fingers vigorously in and out of the blonde's quivering cunt.

The rhythmic squishing sounds broke the stillness of the room. The passion-soaked blonde was squirming in sensual abandon now, tossing her head from side to side, driven by lust; flailing the carpet with her long silken strands. Through moans and sighs, she urged her lesbian lover on, till she was responding to the frenzied finger-fucking by a series of high-pitched cries, repeated with mounting urgency. Driven by demonic fury, Lohr fucked her rival with pounding thrusts of her hand. Then, with a sharp cry, we saw the thrashing body stop; her limbs stiffened and she arched her back, suddenly going rigid from head to toes, as she clung there, poised on the ragged edge of a rampaging orgasm.

With exquisite timing, Lohr plunged her hand up the straining cunt, burying her fingers as deeply as she could and jamming her knuckles solidly against the underarch at the precise moment the straining blonde hit her peak. Alea moaned and her body trembled. Then, with a tiny whimper, she slipped almost imperceptibly over the top and collapsed in a spent heap.

Now, as the languid blonde basked in the afterglow, Lohr leaned over to whisper in her ear. Alea nodded weakly and, in a moment, she stirred herself, pulling herself to her knees, while the agile brunette took her place, lying flat on the carpet, her arms at her sides. Next, the lissome blonde swung a leg over the reclining form, to kneel straddling Lohr's narrow hips, facing her feet. Then Alea let herself fall forward onto all fours and backed up, squatting slightly to bring the soft, dew-moistened folds of her underarch right down on the pretty face of the supine Queen. Resting on her elbows, she lowered her head till her pursed lips grazed the proffered tangle of ebony curls below her. Now, in the position of mutual love, the women began to pleasure each other with the obviously practiced skill of well-trained courtesans.

I saw Alea's tongue slither out to lovingly lap the perimeter of her partner's triangle. The blond head burrowed between thrashing white legs, licking at the smooth flesh of the inner thighs, silky strands of blond hair spilling down over long pale thighs. She placed a hand on each thigh eagerly, prying open her lover still farther, increasing her lover's vulnerability, laying her open to the probing tongue.

Now Alea switched tactics, flattening her tongue and lapping up and down the ragged slot in long, broad strokes, till she had Lohr whimpering in delight. Swollen and distended, the yawning netherlips had darkened with infused passion, and to those heavenly gates Alea now turned her entire attention. Lohr's hips bucked up in instinctive reaction as she strained to clamp down and force the tantalizing tongue in deeper. Meanwhile, Alea had pried open the petals of that dark orchard. She held Lohr open, stiffened her tongue, and plunged in, bobbing up and down furiously.

Lohr responded by arching upward and clamping her spasming thighs on the attractive blonde, seeking to draw her lover with even deeper pleasure into her hot, welcoming snatch. Lohr's thighs were quivering, the tendons straining rigidly as they tightened on the blond head. Then, with hips bucking furiously and legs thrashing, the slim, dark-haired Queen bounded to a roaring climax.

Panting heavily, Alea drew herself up on her elbows and sat back to reveal a face glistening with love-nectar. As she straightened, her hands went to her dangling tits. She cupped her breasts and inched backward on her knees till she could perch with her wet, splayed sex plastered squarely on the brunette's face. She held herself, let her half-lidded eyes slide closed, and slowly began to fondle her breasts. I saw a smile broaden across her blissful countenance and her hardworking partner, half-smothered, struggled to bring her to a second shattering orgasm.

This time, when the blonde came, her body arched. She threw back her head and strained upward, the tendons on her neck rigid, her eyes clenched shut as she held herself at the peak. A delicious quiver ran through her as the soaring rapture overtook her. With a wild cry, she flung out her arms and tumbled forward. The two depleted females lay in a heap, their breath ragged as they sprawled exhausted on the rug, basking in the warmth of the afterglow as the lapping waves of pleasure receded slowly.

The all-male audience roared its approval and broke into cheers and hearty sustained applause.

CHAPTER ELEVEN

After her humiliating contest with her chief rival, Lohr became even more secretive. When she was not at her place at Rahn's side at court, she schemed and manipulated behind the scenes, seeking constantly to further her own nefarious ends. There were rumors of intrigues and plots being hatched at the secretive all-female meetings she held in her quarters.

At about this time, the Queen began to show an unexpected interest in our religion. She approached the chief priest with the humble request that she be instructed in the ways of the ancient gods. Of course, Druz was pleased at this sudden conversion; he found the young Queen a surprisingly apt and eager pupil. Rahn paid little attention to this newfound interest of his consort even when he learned she was forming her own circle of young women dedicated to serving the gods. Just as the men had their ceremony of the Crimson Moon, she had explained to the chief priest, she felt that women might best serve the gods in certain rites performed by their own dedicated sisterhood. Theirs was to be a cult of Venus.

Rahn might have put a stop to it right then and there, but he didn't. He was tolerant in religious matters, mostly because the crafty King saw little value in religion, except insofar as it served his interests. To the King's surprise, only Druz objected. But his objections were on theological grounds, and Rahn found them largely incomprehensible. So the cult of Venus was allowed to be born and flourish, and soon Lohr had invested herself as high priestess of that weird sisterhood.

Now the meetings she held in the entrance hall of her quarters took on a religious air. The society was closed and secretive. New girls were carefully chosen to be inducted into this strange sect through an initiation process that it was forbidden to reveal. There were rumors of bizarre rites and outrageous hedonistic rituals, all conducted in the name of the goddess of love.

For a while the adherents of Sappho threatened to take over this women's movement. Some of the more extreme would go so far as to ban all males from the inner sanctum. But Lohr would not allow that. Even though she welcomed them into the fold, and was herself quite capable of appreciating the delights of a well-made feminine body, Lohr's lusty appetite was insatiable and her loins craved more than what her sisters could offer. And so there was often a masculine presence in the sanctuary—male slaves who would be used shamelessly in the pursuit of lewdness. They were the handsomest young men, selected solely for their attributes and their ability to pleasure the lascivious ladies of the cult.

In those days, there were spies everywhere. The court abounded in rumors, whispered hints, intrigues, the gossip of slaves, the idle chatter of concubines, the subtle machinations of nobles, all of which found their way to the ear of the King, by way of the ubiquitous chamberlain. The King had a full network of spies, although it was rumored that the Queen's was even more extensive. Once again Uzack was to prove invaluable to his King, as he gathered reports from the household slaves of the strange goings-on of the cult of Venus.

The tales that intrigued Rahn were those of slaves being used in bizarre sexual experiments. It was common knowledge that our Queen was studying ancient texts, pouring over obscure works that held secrets on how to concoct powders, potions, and elixirs of strange and wondrous powers. It was said that she came to possess certain books, rare, hidden volumes that held the lore of arcane arts of alchemists—secrets of their magic that had passed through holy priesthoods from generation to generation.

It was rumored that the Queen had learned the

secrets of an ancient potion designed to arouse and sustain the sexual appetite. A woman who drank this strange brew would experience a tremendous surge of arousal, her desire escalating wildly till it reached a fever pitch. And there she would be held, a helpless victim of her own raging lust, driven frantic with an insatiable sexual hunger, an aching in her loins that could never be satisfied, and would lessen only when the effects of the devilish potion wore off.

According to the rumors, a novice about to be initiated into Lohr's bizarre sisterhood was given a draught of this mixture. She would then be allowed various means to satisfy the raging desire welling up in her. It was whispered that each new girl had to service the high priestess while in the throes of this burning lust.

Now, Uzack had learned, the high priestess was testing a similar compound for male potency. This magic elixir was said to cause an incredible erection to blossom forth. The man would find himself in possession of a prick so taut it was almost painful, harder then it had ever been before. And, most wondrous of all, his powerful tool might be used over and over again without the slightest hint of flagging. This remarkable endurance resulted in sexual marathons which surpassed anything yet seen at the most lascivious court on earth. Naturally, Rahn took quite an interest in these rumors. He was eager to learn the truth of such incredible accounts.

Ordered to learn firsthand about these strange rituals, Uzack and I were sent on a spying mission. Once again we carefully made our way through the attics, clambering over the rafters to find our secret perch high above the reception hall in the Queen's inner sanctum. Below us were banks of candles and the all-enveloping haze of a scented reddish mist that arose from a dish of burnt offerings placed on a marble altar dominating one corner of the room. On a pedestal behind the altar stood a gilded statue of the goddess, depicted in a lewd pose, standing with legs spread. Her hands were at her arch, fingers spreading her inner thighs so that she held back the petals of her heavenly flower. A gigantic phallus stood erect before her, just inches from where she held her sex splayed open.

On the top step, just before the altar, knelt the goddess's high priestess flanked by six acolytes, who knelt in two rows of three behind her on the lower steps. Like her sisters, the priestess was bare-breasted, and dressed all in black. But although their robes were of a sheer dull black fabric, hers was opaque, and it shone with a satiny luster, the gleaming ebony folds draping her slender form.

I looked down on the dazzling white skin of those taut breasts that jutted out so defiantly and the long black hair that formed a silken mantle cascading down to curtain those pale, thin shoulders. There was no doubt that the young woman who knelt erect before the altar was our Queen, yet she looked somehow…different. Her eyes held a vacant stare and she walked with slow, solemn dignity, her movements liquid and dreamlike.

Perhaps she was under the influence of some mysterious potion. She had been made up heavily; her pale features were enhanced by black kohl, which shadowed her eyelids and formed the dark grooves that outlined the hollows of those large, expressionless eyes under their thickened black lashes. A purplish tint had been applied to her lips, and the same tint had been used to darken her exposed nipples so that they gleamed seductively in the soft candlelight.

Scarcely daring to breathe, we watched the strange religious ritual begin to unfold. As the smoke rose, the women chanted and swayed, muttering repeated prayers to the goddess. When the chanting ceased, the smoldering dish was removed from the altar and the marble slab was cleared.

Then, from a hidden passageway behind the altar, a naked slave was led into the room. His fair features were somewhat obscured by a blindfold, but we could tell he was young and his body was well-tanned, slim, and hard-muscled. Like all slaves, he was clean-shaven; a thin blond stubble had been left on his head. The tangle of pale down on his chest thinned into a trickle running down the center of his belly before spreading out to form a thicket of blond pubic hair. His masculine equipment hung heavy between his legs; the dormant penis dangled, limp but substantial; pendulous balls swayed in their lightly furred pouch.

His hands had been tied behind his back, a thin lead attached to his slave's collar. By this leash, a young acolyte led the blindfolded slave to the altar steps. There he was ordered to kneel. Now more chanting followed. Then a silver vial was handed to the priestess, who poured its contents into a shallow cup. This cup was now held before the bowed head of the slave, and he was urged to drink. It was awkward for him without the use of his hands, but he dipped his face in the elixir and drank greedily.

When he finished, two of the black-robed girls came up to take him by the arms and raise him up. His escorts led him up to the altar and helped him onto the slab where they laid him down on his back. They arranged him spread-eagled, his arms raised over his head, his legs spread out so he could be tied down by leather straps that ran from his wrists and ankles down to the base of the altar. Although the girls had been careful to avoid touching his manhood as they stretched out his body, his organ was already responsive, lengthening and uncurling in its first awakening. By the time he was on his back, it had already swelled into a substantial erection. I marveled at the speed of the magic elixir; by the time the last line had been affixed, the young man sported a massive hard-on that sprang out from the root and curved so the burgeoning head was arching back toward his belly.

Next, one of the girls was sent to prepare him. She had an amphora of some oil—holy oil, I suppose—to anoint his erect member. She poured the oil over her hands, wrapped her fingers lightly around the hard, slightly bowed shaft, and ran her small hand up and down, rubbing over a tumescent head that was flushed purple with passion, then down the thickening length, finally pausing to lift and fondle his balls. A shivering moan escaped the slave's lips at the feel of those delicate fingers toying with his swollen member. It was obvious that the young man didn't need such preparation, but it seemed that the girl chosen for this job took her duties very seriously and she was determined to see that his male apparatus was well oiled.

By now his upright prick had stiffened into full prominence. It stood proudly, vibrant with sexual power, glistening in the golden light. The inspiring sight of that incredibly hard phallus blossoming forth in the full glory of masculine pride must have induced pangs of urgency in the loins of those healthy young girls, who stood with hungry eyes openly devouring the blatantly ready male.

Lohr came forward, took the first of her followers by the hand, and led the girl up to the altar. Every muscle in the slave's naked body tensed expectantly as they climbed the steps, as though he sensed their approach. He tried to rise against his bonds, straining up, twisting his blindfolded head. The high priestess ignored him and helped her acolyte out of her robe. The girl stood before her stark naked but for the long black stockings she wore. She was a tall, thin girl whose rich tawny tresses hung to her lanky shoulders. Her lithe body was long waisted, and she had loose dangling breasts. Lohr helped her up onto the altar so that the girl knelt straddling the hips of the tethered man.

At a nod from the priestess, the girl bent forward

and lowered herself down till the tips of her narrow breasts brushed the man's chest. Then she inched her way down his body while the priestess held the straining cock between her fingers and guided the burgeoning head toward the girl's splayed sex. The penetration was smooth and slick. The girl settled in with the prick ensconced up her cunt. She shook back her thick hair with a quick toss of her head, and wriggled her shoulders in a shiver of unrestrained delight.

The circle of women joined hands, closed in on the altar, and chanted something in a strange shrill tongue. Then the girl began to move. She placed her hands on the man's chest to brace herself, closed her eyes, and started a gentle rocking. The movement that began as a rhythmic nodding of her head rippled down to head and shoulders. Soon her lean body was undulating, her slight tits bouncing merrily, as she rode her male mount with growing excitement.

Of course the helpless male could do nothing as the girl fucked herself on him, riding his phallus. Nevertheless, the exquisite pleasure of that slick, enveloping cunt sliding up and down his shaft soon had him snapping his head from side to side and grunting as she bore down on him repeatedly. By now she was hunched well forward, tits jiggling, hips bucking vigorously as her long haunches strained under the power of those sinewy thighs each time she fucked herself on his rigid pole. She shook and trembled, raging in a frenzy of excitement; the others watched her with wide eyes, holding hands, not saying a word.

As she neared her peak, she arched her back and, plunging up and down like a madwoman, she threw back her head and cried out. A deep convulsion ran though her rigid body as she teetered on the pinnacle of pleasure. Then she fell forward, collapsing on the man, holding onto him as aftershocks of pleasure coursed through her narrow body.

They gave her a few minutes to rest there, a blissful smile curling her lips, eyes closed to the world. Her breathing slowly evened out. Two of then came forward to help her to dismount. As she was lifted free, the man did not move. Incredibly, his straining erection remained perfectly intact. The rumors were true!

The spent girl let herself be taken away and, weak-kneed, she was led away to collapse in a nearby chair. Her legs were parted, and I noticed that the inner surfaces of her thighs glistened with sexual spendings that saturated her bush of tawny pubic hair.

Now the next girl was brought forth. She was slim, slightly built, with caramel-colored hair that was swept back from her small face, pinned up behind the ears, while the rest fell down her gently sloping shoulders. She let herself be undressed, standing perfectly still while the high priestess slipped the robe from her and let it drop to slither down her nude body.

The naked girl was helped to mount the jutting prick, which gleamed with a sheen of nectar from her sister's loins. Once more we were treated to the sight of a randy young girl pleasuring herself on that indomitable phallus. She bounded up and down, her smoothly undulating hips churning with growing passion till she was thrashing about in erotic frenzy, tossing her head wildly and moaning as repeated paroxysms of lust racked her eager young body.

And so the parade continued: each girl taking her turn, mounting up to be serviced by the slave with the iron cock. Throughout his ordeal, the helpless man could do no more than squirm and turn his head from side to side, groaning as climax after climax was wrenched from his pleasure-racked body. Only after the sixth girl had been well and thoroughly satisfied did the Queen herself step forward.

The young man was untied, but his relief was short-lived. They turned him over onto his belly immediately and once more tied him down over the altar. He groaned as he was flopped over onto his solid prick which, still erect, was now pressed between his belly and the cool, smooth slab of marble. Now two girls came forward to divest the Queen of her robe, allowing me to once more appreciate her taut, lithe body, splendidly nude but for the black stockings that sheathed the smoothly tapering lines of her slender legs.

I watched with growing curiosity as one of her handmaidens brought forth a strange device, a sort of phallus with a tangle of leather belts attached. Uzack and I exchanged looks and then watched in amazement as the Queen drew on this strange contraption, tied one belt around her waist, while hitching up two others that ran from the crotch around her rearcheeks to meet the first belt. Finally, one of the girls who was helping her pulled up on the narrow center strip that hung down directly behind, bisecting her rearcheeks. This was hitched up a few notches and secured in place. When she turned, we saw the full consequences. Now our illustrious Queen sported a huge swaying phallus that seemed to sprout from between her legs.

It was a strange sight indeed to see our Queen striding about like a man, the artificial phallus bobbing and weaving as she moved before the altar. Now, as her newly acquired member was oiled to assure smooth penetration, Uzack and I realized that she meant to use the male slave in the way some men use other men! It was a bizarre—but fascinating—notion, and we leaned forward eager to better see what was about to follow.

Naturally, her blindfolded victim knew nothing of what was to come. He rested on his still-hard cock, savoring the cool feel of the marble, no doubt profoundly grateful that his ordeal seemed to be over and his hard-driven penis would be allowed a brief respite. Imagine his surprise when he felt someone climbing up between his spread legs, kneeling behind him; felt the thrill of those slim feminine hands on his butt; realized with sudden alarm that his cheeks were being grasped and pried apart.

His head and shoulders shot upright, and he howled when that diabolical tool first touched his anus. Lohr, kneeling behind him and holding her odd appurtenance as a man might hold his cock, placed the head squarely on her target and drove forward. Her victim groaned and twisted helplessly, as she bore down on him, powering in with a hard pelvic thrust while an evil grin broadened on her tight-set lips.

Fascinated, scarcely daring to breathe, we watched the unnatural phallus disappear up the ravaged asshole as the slave twisted and cried out in dismay. Of course it could hardly have been a novel experience for him. At one time or another, most of our male slaves had been used by those at court who fancied men and boys. Still, the feel of that foreign intruder penetrating his bowels must have shocked him, for it could hardly have been expected!

He cried out in his anguish while Lohr ignored his pleas and drove into him, pumping her hips, and thrusting deep into his innards with all the power of her straining thighs, fucking ruthlessly, as though she were a man. Her pretty face was contorted, the hard eyes narrowed, jaw clenched in vicious determination as she ravaged him, fucking with deep, angry thrusts.

Uzack and I had seen quite enough. We left them at it, the Queen engaged in this bizarre parody before her admiring followers who stood gaping, awestruck, marveling to see a man thus used.

The next day we reported to Rahn all that we had seen. He insisted on knowing all the details, and was most intrigued by the astonishing success of the Queen's experiment with the male-potency drug. But when we came to recount her use of her slave in the manner of men, he had a curious reaction. His expression changed from disbelief to curiosity to finally settle into that tight narrowing around the eyes that I recognized as smoldering anger.

I never could quite figure out exactly why Rahn resented what the Queen did since he himself had been known to dally with men and boys himself in a similar manner. Though rare, the practice was hardly unknown at the court of Thralkild. Still there was something about this particular variation, with the Queen mounting the man and breaking him, forcing his submission. It was the act that Rahn found deeply disturbing.

While Rahn used to laugh off or airily dismiss those who warned him to be beware of his consort, our account of that nefarious act we had witnessed brought about a subtle change toward his Queen. His suspicions regarding her began to deepen. There were other disturbing trends that began to trouble him about this time.

Druz, who kept an eye on the growing power of the Queen's sect, was convinced that her motives were less than purely religious. He felt certain she meant to use the sect as a base of political power. This women's movement might speak of high ideals, but it was concerned only with power. That was the message he whispered in Rahn's ear. And where once he would have been dismissed, he now found a more receptive audience.

There were strange goings-on at court, and I watched the brow of the King darken with increased concern. His attitude toward his consort took on a certain distant coolness.

CHAPTER TWELVE

One could sense the subtle difference in Rahn's attitude toward his Queen. He became warier, the wily old gut fighter falling back on his instinctive caution. He watched her…and he waited. An experienced observer could see the difference when they sat enthroned before the court. There they sat, proudly erect in all their splendid majesty, eyes forward, properly oblivious to the courtiers around them. But just occasionally, Rahn would glance out of the corner of his eye to study his consort, as if taking her measure for the first time. If she felt that appraising gaze, Lohr seemed to take no notice of it. She remained, cool and imperturbable, the regal Queen secure on her throne, supremely confident; a woman content in her place at the side of her most revered monarch.

Things might well have continued this way, with that simmering uneasiness growing, had not Rahn's sudden illness hastened the events that were to follow.

One day our King, who had the constitution of a warhorse, began to complain of weakness and dizziness. At first the army doctors were called in, but, of course, they were useless before such a mysterious illness, or indeed any physical complaint that could not be directly attributed to a sword wound. With or without their help, Rahn seemed to worsen daily. Soon he was racked with chills, even as his brow burned with fever. He had no choice but to take to bed.

At that point, Druz was summoned. It was a measure of how sick the King was that he should call on his chief priest, for he knew him to be a fraud, as indeed we all did. Still, he might have something in his prayers and magic that would ward off the strange ailment, and Rahn, who lay tossing and turning, consumed by fever, was growing desperate.

Druz took one look at the King and declared that he was the victim of a spell. Magic from sorcery so terrible as to befall a mighty monarch must be very strong indeed. It could only be witchcraft!

Druz swore he was up against another magic, and he was sure he knew the source of that magic. Dressed in his full regalia, the priest denounced superstitions and false gods and announced publicly that the gods would allow the King to fall ill only because they were displeased with sacrilegious rites being conducted in "certain quarters" of the court. He alone, he reminded us, had been anointed to serve the true gods in the prescribed manner; all else was blasphemy. Throughout his tirade he never mentioned the Queen by name. Yet many of us realized his true target. We kept silent and waited to see what would unfold. As it turned out the priest was right about the source of the King's discomfort, but wrong about the means.

It was not divine wrath, nor some nefarious spell that had been cast, but rather a slow-acting poison placed in the King's food that had caused him to fall ill. It was Uzack who discovered the plot and probably saved his monarch's life.

In any case, certain arrests were quietly made among the kitchen slaves, and in few days, the King's health began to improve. Soon he was on his feet and roaring for food and wine. His recovery seemed miraculous, and Rahn, in typical fashion, ordered a feast to be held in celebration.

The day before the feast, the full truth came to light. Rahn was holding court, Lohr at his side, when Uzack burst into the room with a concerned look on his face. He looked for permission to approach the throne, and Rahn nodded. He rushed up to whisper in our monarch's ear. For a moment a flicker of anger crossed the royal brow, but Rahn kept his iron composure.

He began in the ringing voice he used from the throne. "I wish to announce that we have discovered the reason for our recent bout of...indigestion. It appears that someone has been dropping certain powders in the royal meals."

There was a shocked gasp of surprise from the audience; a deathly silence descended on the room. All eyes were on the King. No one moved.

"We have captured those who committed this dastardly deed. I have just been informed that after a bit of 'persuasion' in the torture chambers, they have confessed freely. It seems there was a plot to take the throne!" The King let this sink in. One could feel everyone in the room tense in dread expectation. Even the innocent—and no one in that room could be called totally innocent—had plenty of reason to fear Rahn's wrath, more than one blameless man had died at the hands of the royal executioners because of Rahn's rages.

"These slaves were employed by someone at the court," he went on, after a meaningful pause, clearly relishing their discomfort, "Someone very high up at the court. Indeed, that someone who supplied the evil powder was none other than a handmaiden of our Queen. She has confessed all. It was her mistress who gave her the powders and sent her on her mission."

He turned his head slowly to behold the woman at his side. "Is this true?" he asked, a simple question raised in a voice that was cool, detached, unemotional.

For the first time since I laid eyes on her, I saw Queen Lohr struck speechless, taken aback. Color rose to her cheeks, just beneath the ridge of those high cheekbones. Her lips parted, but no words came out.

The King never moved a muscle. He waited, sitting erect with his back perfectly straight. His hands tightened their grip on the arms of the throne. Although he addressed his consort, who sat at his side, his even gaze remained in front of him as he sat looking down on the assembled courtiers.

At last Lohr recovered enough to reply. Swallowing to gain control of her agitated voice, she gave the only answer she could. It would do no good to deny it. Once someone had been accused by the King, one was guilty. In any case, it was not in her proud nature to beg for mercy.

She rose to her feet and turned to face the seated King.

"Yes, it's true," she admitted in a barely audible whisper. Her hands became fists that she held rigidly at her sides, but otherwise she showed no emotion. "I have done what I had to. Now I ask only to be executed swiftly. You owe me that." Now her voice showed the first strains as though she realized from the King's expression that a swift death might be denied to her. Like any sane person Lohr feared the King's torture chambers. When Rahn didn't move, she went on, a trace of desperation in her voice.

"You owe me that!" she repeated. And then, summoning back her old dignity: "Let me remind you I am of royal blood, and I am…your Queen."

Rahn turned to the rigid woman, who held herself tightly in control, more beautiful than ever, I thought. But even her icy resolve weakened and she seemed to quiver when his cold, angry eyes bored into hers. With a barely perceptible shiver, she straightened and stood facing her accuser. He smiled, but he said not a word. Then, to his guards: "Take her away!"

In spite of the Queen's downfall, or maybe because of it, the feast was held as planned the following day. The smaller chair that had once stood next to the King's had been removed. Once again, only one throne stood at the top of the stairs in the palace at Thralkild.

The partygoers celebrated the King's joyful return to full health with their usual enthusiasm, reveling in the licentious decadence that surrounded King Rahn. It was a feast to be remembered, one of those occasions that pressed the outer fringes of sensual pleasure.

The great hall had been decorated for the event. At one end of the hall, an altar had been erected to Priapus, a symbol of the King's gratitude to the old gods. Atop the altar was a marble likeness of the god, his divine member hugely erect. Nude young men and women, their bodies gilded, stood in alcoves that lined the room, striking poses like living statues, their golden bodies to be freely admired by those lewd and lascivious pleasure seekers. Attractive pages wearing only their short tunics were fondled shamelessly; naked sex slaves were freely sampled by guests of both sexes. Lusty courtiers shed their clothing till they lounged about in the natural state. Except for the cropped hair and leather collars, it would have been impossible to tell slaves from guests in the tangle of nude bodies that littered the carpeted floors.

As the evening's festivities followed their inevitable descent into wild debauchery, ingenious games and sexual contests were held with prizes awarded to both men and women who showed the greatest endurance.

The Fall of the Ice Queen

When the feast had begun, the King was not present. This was not unusual for Rahn often made a late entrance, forcing everyone to stop doing what he or she was doing, catching and holding them *in flagrante delicto*, as it were, while he made his royal entrance.

As he entered, the guests pulled themselves together as best they could. Bare-breasted women, flushed and bedraggled, scrambled to their feet to curtsy; naked slaves pressed their foreheads to the floor; men with members still half-swollen with lust, stood at attention to make obeisance, as the King of the Two Lands passed through the room and took his place at the head table. A hush descended on the room.

Now the King motioned to his guards. The doors at the far end of the hall were flung back to admit our erstwhile Queen accompanied by two burly guards. Even as a captive, Lohr was magnificent! She had been dressed in the open-fronted dress of a concubine; but instead of the metal band on her upper arm, she wore a high leather collar around her neck, the significance of which was not lost on the assembled courtiers. Still she was as regal as ever, still the Ice Queen, even though she had lost the crown. She stood perfectly erect, shoulders back, with those small taut breasts jutting forward like white marble. She looked neither right nor left, but ignored the degenerate mob as she strode forward, magnificent in her high heels, head held high in that proud regal bearing, as she walked to face her Lord and King.

Rahn watched her, shifting in his chair, leaning forward as she came to him. Once at the bottom step of the throne, she lowered herself to her knees and, without a word, bowed her head in abject submission. Rahn nodded, and eased forward, opening his knees and sprawling back so that he sat in a rather dissolute manner. I noticed the thin kilt he wore was tented slightly, and it came to me that our Monarch was aroused by the sight of the Ice Queen on her knees! She never ceased to fascinate Rahn. I wondered if he would take her right then and there, forcing her to service him before the court by taking the royal instrument in her mouth. But if Rahn considered that intriguing possibility, he soon rejected it, for he had other plans for her.

Now as he sat staring down at his erstwhile Queen, contemplating the shiny black hair at the top of her bowed head, he motioned for a slave, who brought forth a shallow cup. The slave held the cup before our former Queen, who with head still tilted looked up at the grinning King with questioning dark eyes. Did he mean for her to drink the poison she had plotted to use on him? It would be so like Rahn to devise such a fitting revenge!

She took the cup in both her hands and brought it to her lips. Rahn's gaze never left her face as she drank humbly what was offered to her. Then, resigned to her fate, she closed her eyes to wait for the poison to take its deadly effect. The room was perfectly quiet; time seemed to stand still. All eyes were on the slender figure in the long silken gown who knelt erect before the King. She seemed to sway. Then suddenly she tensed. Her head came up. I could see that her eyes flew open wide and a sharp gasp escaped her painted lips.

The Fall of the Ice Queen

A curious look crept over her pretty face, a look of dawning awareness. She bit down on her curled lower lip with a row of small even teeth. She must have felt the first stirrings of lust in her loins, and knew immediately what was in that cup. Instead of poison, she had been given the magic elixir of sexual potency, the potion she herself had devised—the one that was said to have such a marvelous and profound effect on females.

Now we saw the first results as the dark-haired woman threw back her head and closed her eyes, swaying drunkenly, caught up in the first dramatic surge of welling passion. She eased back to settle on her heels and her hands, with a will of their own, came up her folded legs to slide into the silky folds of the dress between her thighs there to find and grip her throbbing sex through the thin fabric. With eyes shut tightly, she pressed her knees together, imprisoning her hands between her clamped thighs while she rubbed her womanhood. A long, shivering moan, low and breathy, escaped from her lips as Lohr bent over and held herself. The moan trailed off into a series of tiny helpless pleas uttered before the raging tide. By now she was consumed by lust, clearly agitated as she hunched over and rubbed the insatiable itch between her thighs.

"Look at me!" Rahn shouted to the kneeling woman who was bobbing down till her forehead almost touched the floor, her features curtained by the fall of sheltering hair.

She lifted her head and tossed back her hair to regard her King through hooded eyes. Her head rolled weakly from side to side, her features slack and flushed with passion. She was panting heavily through moist parted lips, her bosom heaving with the effort. The distended tips of her breasts were taut with excitement; one hand, jammed down hard between her legs, was moving slowly, as her shoulders quivered with ripples of pleasure at the caressing hand induced in her loins.

Rahn opened his knees and looked into those unseeing, passion-soaked eyes as he brushed back his kilt to allow his massive erection to spring free.

"Is this what you want?" he asked with mock innocence.

Caught in the throes of passion, Lohr could only close her eyes and nod. But that was not good enough for the King, who was intent on humiliating her further.

"Go on, say it!" he demanded.

"Yes...yes...I want it!" she muttered in a low voice.

"Say 'I want a big stiff prick,'#" he insisted.

"I want a big stiff *prick!*" the tormented woman hissed with sudden vehemence.

A huge grin broke out on Rahn's craggy features. He beckoned to his guards.

They lifted Lohr's arms, hauling her to her feet and dragging her down the long carpet as she squirmed in their clutches, twisting mindlessly out of control, driven by the all-consuming lust. Without ceremony, they stripped her of her gown and lifted her up to stand on the altar facing the life-sized statue with the enormous phallus. She knew what was expected of her, and the wave of desire that swept over her gave her no choice but to mount it. She threw her arms around the marble god and placed a foot on the steps that had been set at either side. The guards seemed to enjoy their task immensely. One of them hoisted her up with a huge cupped hand fitted to her pert bottom, while the other fiddled with her netherlips, opening her wet, needy sex as she wrapped her stockinged legs around the statue's hips. They let her ease down slowly, impaling herself on the smooth marble phallus.

Although one of the guards now picked up a thin switch and waved it menacingly, Lohr needed no urging. Using the conveniently placed steps as a foothold, she pushed herself up and, embracing the statue like a lover, she lowered herself down. Soon she was bobbing in steady rhythm, fucking herself on the cold, hard phallus while the guard occasionally took a swipe at her bouncing bottom.

The King laughed uproariously, and the obsequious court joined in cheering and laughing and shouting bawdy comments as the former Queen of the Two Lands clutched the marble form of the god of pleasure and rode his jutting member happily till she was thrashing about in erotic frenzy, her body racked with a string of massive, uncontrollable orgasms.

Rahn wasn't content with merely humiliating his former consort before the court; he felt that his people would also rejoice in her downfall. And in that he was certainly right, for the common folk much despised the foreigner who had become their cold, haughty Queen.

And so the young woman's degradation continued the next day, when at high noon the King had her brought forth in her concubine's gown to be secured in the standing stocks at the center of the market square. Since she herself had devised this particular form of punishment, it seemed especially fitting that she should now suffer the humiliation of having her dress lifted up to be pinned in place in back, exposing her bare bottom to the rabble. A small light paddle was supplied, chained to the stocks, and the townspeople were invited to try their hands at peppering their onetime Queen's bottom as she stood helpless and seething with rage. That pretty bottom was reddened and swollen and throbbing with pain by the time the sun fell on that fateful day, as the commoners of Thralkild joyfully took advantage of the entertainment provided by their gracious King.

I had often wondered why Rahn didn't have Lohr executed. I remembered how he had often expressed his notions on war. "If you go to war," he used to say, "be sure you will able to slay your enemy. A weakened enemy is a threat; a wounded enemy bent on revenge, a very lethal danger. No, the first attempt to kill the enemy must be effective, done with a sure, swift hand. Nobles might be held for ransom, wives and concubines enslaved, but a King must die." Lohr found out too late the consequences of a failed attempt on the life of a King.

Did our King spare her life out of leniency? I think not. Rahn had not a shred of mercy, and human kindness would have been unthinkable to him. Somehow he couldn't bear to part with her. Perhaps Druz was right and Rahn had been bewitched by her, held by a powerful spell he could not break. The two of them were bound to each other by their implacable hatred, but also by their endless fascination with one another. And so he let her live, but in such a way as to make her degradation complete, and in such circumstances that he could keep an eye on her.

For the onetime Queen of Thralkild was tossed to the troops, thrown into servitude as a common barracks whore. Dear reader, understand that while King Rahn had prohibited women from accompanying his armies to the field, he had no such ban against their servicing the troops when the soldiers were billeted in winter quarters in and around Thralkild. To the contrary, he saw to it that each barracks was given a generous allotment of slave girls.

Tradition had it that a new girl being pressed into service with the garrison troops had to satisfy all twelve soldiers of her barracks on her initiation night. They say that Rahn ordered a detailed report on Lohr's welcome into her new home.

You've heard of the writers
but didn't know where to find them

Samuel R. Delany • Pat Califia • Carol Queen • Lars Eighner • Felice Picano • Lucy Taylor • Aaron Travis • Michael Lassell • Red Jordan Arobateau • Michael Bronski • Tom Roche • Maxim Jakubowski • Michael Perkins • Camille Paglia • John Preston • Laura Antoniou • Alice Joanou • Cecilia Tan • Michael Perkins • Tuppy Owens • Trish Thomas • Lily Burana • Alison Tyler • Marco Vassi • Susie Bright • Randy Turoff • Allen Ellenzweig • Shar Rednour

You've seen the sexy images
but didn't know where to find them

Robert Chouraqui • Charles Gatewood • Richard Kern • Eric Kroll • Vivienne Maricevic • Housk Randall • Barbara Nitke • Trevor Watson • Mark Avers • Laura Graff • Michele Serchuk • Laurie Leber • John Willie • Sylvia Plachy • Romain Slocombe • Robert Mapplethorpe • Doris Kloster

You can find them all in
Masquerade

a publication designed expressly for the connoisseur of the erotic arts.

ORDER TODAY
SAVE 50%
1 year (6 issues) for $15; 2 years (12 issues) for only $25!

Essential. —*SKIN TWO*

The best newsletter I have ever seen!
—*SECRET INTERNATIONAL*

Very informative and enticing.
—*REDEMPTION*

A professional, insider's look at the world of erotica. —*SCREW*

I recommend a subscription to **MASQUERADE**... It's good stuff.
—*BLACK SHEETS*

MASQUERADE presents some of the best articles on erotica, fetishes, sex clubs, the politics of porn and every conceivable issue of sex and sexuality.
—*FACTSHEET FIVE*

Fabulous. —*TUPPY OWENS*

MASQUERADE is absolutely lovely ... marvelous images.
—*LE BOUDOIR NOIR*

Highly recommended. —*EIDOS*

DIRECT

Masquerade/Direct • DEPT BMMQ27 • 801 Second Avenue • New York, NY 10017 • FAX: 212.986.7355
MC/VISA orders can be placed by calling our toll-free number: 800.375.2356

☐ PLEASE SEND ME A 1-YEAR SUBSCRIPTION FOR $30 *NOW* $15!
☐ PLEASE SEND ME A 2-YEAR SUBSCRIPTION FOR $60 *NOW* $25!

NAME _____

ADDRESS _____

CITY _____ STATE _____ ZIP _____

TEL (___) _____

PAYMENT: ☐ CHECK ☐ MONEY ORDER ☐ VISA ☐ MC

CARD # _____ EXP. DATE _____

No C.O.D. orders. Please make all checks payable to Masquerade/Direct. Payable in U.S. currency only.

MASQUERADE BOOKS

MASQUERADE

GERALD GREY
LONDON GIRLS
$6.50/531-X
In 1875, Samuel Brown arrived in London, determined to take the glorious city by storm. And sure enough, Samuel quickly distinguishes himself as one of the city's most notorious rakehells. Young Mr. Brown knows well the many ways of making a lady weak at the knees—and uses them not only to his delight, but his enormous profit! A rollicking tale of cosmopolitan lust.

OLIVIA M. RAVENSWORTH
THE DESIRES OF REBECCA
$6.50/532-8
A swashbuckling tale of lesbian desire in Merrie Olde England. Beautiful Rebecca follows her passions from the simple love of the girl next door to the relentless lechery of London's most notorious brothel, hoping for the ultimate thrill. Finally, she casts her lot with a crew of sapphic buccaneers, each of whom is more than capable of matching Rebecca lust for lust....

ATAULLAH MARDAAN
KAMA HOURI/DEVA DASI
$7.95/512-3
Two legendary tales of the East in one spectacular volume. *Kama Houri* details the life of a sheltered Western woman who finds herself living within the confines of a harem—where she discovers herself thrilled with the extent of her servitude. *Deva Dasi* is a tale dedicated to the cult of the Dasis—the sacred women of India who devoted their lives to the fulfillment of the senses—while revealing the sexual rites of Shiva.

"...memorable for the author's ability to evoke India present and past.... Mardaan excels in crowding her pages with the sights and smells of India, and her erotic descriptions are convincingly realistic."
—Michael Perkins,
The Secret Record: Modern Erotic Literature

J. P. KANSAS
ANDREA AT THE CENTER
$6.50/498-4
Kidnapped! Lithe and lovely young Andrea is whisked away to a distant retreat. Gradually, she is introduced to the ways of the Center, and soon becomes quite friendly with its other inhabitants—all of whom are learning to abandon restraint in their pursuit of the deepest sexual satisfaction. Soon, Andrea takes her place as one of the Center's greatest success stories—a submissive seductress who answers to any and all! This tale of the ultimate sexual training facility is a nationally bestselling title and a classic of modern erotica.

VISCOUNT LADYWOOD
GYNECOCRACY
$9.95/511-5
An infamous story of female domination returns to print in one huge, completely unexpurgated volume. Julian, whose parents feel he shows just a bit too much spunk, is sent to a very special private school, in hopes that he will learn to discipline his wayward soul. Once there, Julian discovers that his program of study has been devised by the deliciously stern Mademoiselle de Chambonnard. In no time, Julian is learning the many ways of pleasure and pain—under the firm hand of this beautifully demanding headmistress.

CHARLOTTE ROSE, EDITOR
THE 50 BEST PLAYGIRL FANTASIES
$6.50/460-7
A steamy selection of women's fantasies straight from the pages of *Playgirl*—the leading magazine of sexy entertainment for women. These tales of seduction—specially selected by no less an authority than Charlotte Rose, author of such bestselling women's erotica as *Women at Work* and *The Doctor is In*—are sure to set your pulse racing. From the innocent to the insatiable, these women let no fantasy go unexplored.

N. T. MORLEY
THE PARLOR
$6.50/496-8
Lovely Kathryn gives in to the ultimate temptation. The mysterious John and Sarah ask her to be their slave—an idea that turns Kathryn on so much that she can't refuse! But who are these two mysterious strangers? Little by little, Kathryn not only learns to serve, but comes to know the inner secrets of her stunning keepers.

J. A. GUERRA, EDITOR
**COME QUICKLY:
FOR COUPLES ON THE GO**
$6.50/461-5
The increasing pace of daily life is no reason to forgo a little carnal pleasure whenever the mood strikes. Here are over sixty of the hottest fantasies around—all designed to get you going in less time than it takes to dial 976. A super-hot volume especially for modern couples on a hectic modern schedule.

ERICA BRONTE
LUST, INC.
$6.50/467-4
Lust, Inc. explores the extremes of passion that lurk beneath even the coldest, most businesslike exteriors. Join in the sexy escapades of a group of high-powered professionals whose idea of office decorum is like nothing you've ever encountered! Business attire is decidedly not required for this look at high-powered sexual negotiations!

BUY ANY 4 BOOKS & CHOOSE 1 ADDITIONAL BOOK, OF EQUAL OR LESSER VALUE, AS YOUR FREE GIFT

MASQUERADE BOOKS

VANESSA DURIES
THE TIES THAT BIND
$6.50/510-7
The incredible confessions of a thrillingly unconventional woman. From the first page, this chronicle of dominance and submission will keep you gasping with its vivid depictions of sensual abandon. At the hand of Masters Georges, Patrick, Pierre and others, this submissive seductress experiences pleasures she never knew existed....

M. S. VALENTINE
THE CAPTIVITY OF CELIA
$6.50/453-4
Colin is considered the prime suspect in a murder, forcing him to seek refuge with his cousin, Sir Jason Hardwicke. In exchange for Colin's safety, Jason demands Celia's unquestioning submission.... Sexual extortion!

AMANDA WARE
BINDING CONTRACT
$6.50/491-7
Louise was responsible for bringing many prestigious clients into Claremont's salon—so she was more than willing to have her miss a little work in order to pleasure one of his most important customers. But Eleanor Cavendish had her mind set on something more rigorous than a simple wash and set. Sexual slavery!

BOUND TO THE PAST
$6.50/452-6
Anne accepts a research assignment in a Tudor mansion. Upon arriving, she finds herself aroused by James, a descendant of the mansion's owners. Together they uncover the perverse desires of the mansion's long-dead master—desires that bind Anne inexorably to the past—not to mention the bedpost!

SACHI MIZUNO
SHINJUKU NIGHTS
$6.50/493-3
A tour through the lives and libidos of the seductive East. No one is better than Sachi Mizuno at weaving an intricate web of sensual desire, wherein many characters are ensnared and enraptured by the demands of their long-denied carnal natures.

PASSION IN TOKYO
$6.50/454-2
Tokyo—one of Asia's most historic and seductive cities. Come behind the closed doors of its citizens, and witness the many pleasures that await. Lusty men and women from every stratum of Japanese society free themselves of all inhibitions....

MARTINE GLOWINSKI
POINT OF VIEW
$6.50/433-X
With the assistance of her new, unexpectedly kinky lover, she discovers and explores her exhibitionist tendencies—until there is virtually nothing she won't do before the horny audiences her man arranges! Unabashed acting out for the sophisticated voyeur.

RICHARD McGOWAN
A HARLOT OF VENUS
$6.50/425-9
A highly fanciful, epic tale of lust on Mars! Cavortia—the most famous and sought-after courtesan in the cosmopolitan city of Venus—finds love and much more during her adventures with some of the most remarkable characters in recent erotic fiction.

M. ORLANDO
THE ARCHITECTURE OF DESIRE
Introduction by Richard Manton.
$6.50/490-9
Two novels in one special volume! In *The Hotel Justine*, an elite clientele is afforded the opportunity to have any and all desires satisfied. *The Villa Sin* is inherited by a beautiful woman who soon realizes that the legacy of the ancestral estate includes bizarre erotic ceremonies.

CHET ROTHWELL
KISS ME, KATHERINE
$5.95/410-0
Beautiful Katherine can hardly believe her luck. Not only is she married to the charming and oh-so-agreeable Nelson, she's free to live out all her erotic fantasies with other men. Katherine's desires are more than any one man can handle—luckily there are always plenty of men on hand, reading and willing to please her!

MARCO VASSI
THE STONED APOCALYPSE
$5.95/401-1/mass market
"Marco Vassi is our champion sexual energist."—VLS
During his lifetime, Marco Vassi was praised by writers as diverse as Gore Vidal and Norman Mailer, and his reputation was worldwide. *The Stoned Apocalypse* is Vassi's autobiography; chronicling a cross-country trip on America's erotic byways, it offers a rare glimpse of a generation's sexual imagination.

ROBIN WILDE
TABITHA'S TICKLE
$6.50/468-2
Tabitha's back! The story of this vicious vixen—and her torturously tantalizing cohorts—didn't end with *Tabitha's Tease*. Once again, men fall under the spell of scrumptious co-eds and find themselves enslaved to demands and desires they never dreamed existed. Think it's a man's world? Guess again. With Tabitha around, no man gets what he wants until she's completely satisfied—and, maybe, not even then....

MASQUERADE BOOKS

ERICA BRONTE
PIRATE'S SLAVE
$5.95/376-7
Lovely young Erica is stranded in a country where lust knows no bounds. Desperate to escape, she finds herself trading her firm, luscious body to any and all men willing and able to help her. Her adventure has its ups and downs, ins and outs—all to the undeniable pleasure of lusty Erica!

CHARLES G. WOOD
HELLFIRE
$5.95/358-9
A vicious murderer is running amok in New York's sexual underground—and Nick O'Shay, a virile detective with the NYPD, plunges deep into the case. He soon becomes embroiled in an elusive world of fleshly extremes, hunting a madman seeking to purge America with fire and blood sacrifices. Set in New York's infamous sexual underground.

CLAIRE BAEDER, EDITOR
LA DOMME: A DOMINATRIX ANTHOLOGY
$5.95/366-X
A steamy smorgasbord of female domination! Erotic literature has long been filled with heartstopping portraits of domineering women, and now the most memorable have been brought together in one beautifully brutal volume.

CHARISSE VAN DER LYN
SEX ON THE NET
$5.95/399-6
Electrifying erotica from one of the Internet's hottest and most widely read authors. Encounters of all kinds—straight, lesbian, dominant/submissive and all sorts of extreme passions—are explored in thrilling detail.

STANLEY CARTEN
NAUGHTY MESSAGE
$5.95/333-3
Wesley Arthur discovers a lascivious message on his answering machine. Aroused beyond his wildest dreams by the acts described, Wesley becomes obsessed with tracking down the woman behind the seductive voice. His search takes him through strip clubs, sex parlors and no-tell motels—and finally to his randy reward....

AKBAR DEL PIOMBO
DUKE COSIMO
$4.95/3052-0
A kinky romp played out against the boudoirs, bathrooms and ballrooms of the European nobility, who seem to do nothing all day except each other. The lifestyles of the rich and licentious are revealed in all their glory.

A CRUMBLING FAÇADE
$4.95/3043-1
The return of that incorrigible rogue, Henry Pike, who continues his pursuit of sex, fair or otherwise, in the most elegant homes of the most debauched aristocrats.

CAROLE REMY
FANTASY IMPROMPTU
$6.50/513-1
Kidnapped and held in a remote island retreat, Chantal—a renowned erotic writer—finds herself catering to every sexual whim of the mysterious and arousing Bran. Bran is determined to bring Chantal to a full embracing of her sensual nature, even while revealing himself to be something far more than human.....

BEAUTY OF THE BEAST
$5.95/332-5
A shocking tell-all, written from the point-of-view of a prize-winning reporter. And what reporting she does! All the secrets of an uninhibited life are revealed, and each lusty tableau is painted in glowing colors.

DAVID AARON CLARK
THE MARQUIS DE SADE'S JULIETTE
$4.95/240-1
The Marquis de Sade's infamous Juliette returns—and emerges as the most perverse and destructive nightstalker modern New York will ever know. One by one, the innocent are drawn in by Juliette's empty promise of immortality, only to fall prey to her deadly lusts.

ANONYMOUS
NADIA
$5.95/267-1
Follow the delicious but neglected Nadia as she works to wring every drop of pleasure out of life—despite an unhappy marriage. A classic title providing a peek into the secret sexual lives of another time and place.

NIGEL McPARR
THE TRANSFORMATION OF EMILY
$6.50/519-0
The shocking story of Emily Johnson, live-in-domestic. Without warning, Emily finds herself dismissed by her mistress, and sent to serve at Lilac Row—the home of Charles and Harriet Godwin. In no time, Harriet has Emily doing things she'd never dreamed would be required of her—all involving the erotic discipline Harriet imposes with relish.

THE STORY OF A VICTORIAN MAID
$5.95/241-8
What were the Victorians really like? Chances are, no one believes they were as stuffy as their Queen, but who would have imagined such unbridled libertines!

TITIAN BERESFORD
CINDERELLA
$6.50/500-X
Beresford triumphs again with this intoxicating tale, filled with castle dungeons and tightly corseted ladies-in-waiting, naughty viscounts and impossibly cruel masturbatrixes—nearly every conceivable method of erotic torture is explored and described in lush, vivid detail.

BUY ANY 4 BOOKS & CHOOSE 1 ADDITIONAL BOOK, OF EQUAL OR LESSER VALUE, AS YOUR FREE GIFT

MASQUERADE BOOKS

JUDITH BOSTON
$6.50/525-5
Young Edward would have been lucky to get the stodgy old companion he thought his parents had hired for him. Instead, an exquisite woman arrives at his door, and Edward finds his lewd behavior never goes unpunished by the unflinchingly severe Judith Boston! Together they take the downward path to perversion!

NINA FOXTON
$5.95/443-7
An aristocrat finds herself bored by run-of-the-mill amusements for "ladies of good breeding." Instead of taking tea with proper gentlemen, naughty Nina "milks" them of their most private essences. No man ever says "No" to Nina!

P. N. DEDEAUX
THE NOTHING THINGS
$5.95/404-6
Beta Beta Rho—highly exclusive and widely honored—has taken on a new group of pledges. The five women will be put through the most grueling of ordeals, and punished severely for any shortcomings. Before long, all Beta pledges come to crave their punishments—and eagerly await next year's crop!

LYN DAVENPORT
THE GUARDIAN II
$6.50/505-0
The tale of Felicia Brookes—the lovely young woman held in submission by the demanding Sir Rodney Wentworth—continues in this volume of sensual surprises. No sooner has Felicia come to love Rodney than she discovers that she must now accustom herself to the guardianship of the debauched Duke of Smithton. Surely Rodney will rescue her from the domination of this stranger. *Won't he?*

DOVER ISLAND
$5.95/384-8
Dr. David Kelly has planted the seeds of his dream— a Corporal Punishment Resort. Soon, many people from varied walks of life descend upon this isolated retreat, intent on fulfilling their every desire. Including Marcy Harris, the perfect partner for the lustful Doctor....

THE GUARDIAN
$5.95/371-6
Felicia grew up under the tutelage of the lash—and she learned her lessons well. Sir Rodney Wentworth has long searched for a woman capable of fulfilling his cruel desires, and after learning of Felicia's talents, sends for her. Felicia discovers that the "position" offered her is delightfully different than anything she could have expected!

LIZBETH DUSSEAU
THE APPLICANT
$6.50/501-8
"Adventuresome young women who enjoys being submissive sought by married couple in early forties. Expect no limits." Hilary answers an ad, hoping to find someone who can meet her special needs. The beautiful Liza turns out to be a flawless mistress, and together with her husband, Oliver, she trains Hilary to be the perfect servant—much to Hilary's delight and arousal!

ANTHONY BOBARZYNSKI
STASI SLUT
$4.95/3050-4
Adina lives in East Germany, where she can only dream about the freedoms of the West. But then she meets a group of ruthless and corrupt STASI agents. They use her body for their own perverse gratification, while she opts to use her talents in a final bid for total freedom!

JOCELYN JOYCE
PRIVATE LIVES
$4.95/309-0
The lecherous habits of the illustrious make for a sizzling tale of French erotic life. A widow has a craving for a young busboy; he's sleeping with a rich businessman's wife; her husband is minding his sex business elsewhere! Sexual entanglements run through this tale of upper crust lust!

SARAH JACKSON
SANCTUARY
$5.95/318-X
Sanctuary explores both the unspeakable debauchery of court life and the unimaginable privations of monastic solitude, leading the voracious and the virtuous on a collision course that brings history to throbbing life.

THE WILD HEART
$4.95/3007-5
A luxury hotel is the setting for this artful web of sex, desire, and love. A newlywed sees sex as a duty, while her hungry husband tries to awaken her to its tender joys. A Parisian entertains wealthy guests for the love of money. Each episode provides a new variation in this lusty Grand Hotel!

LOUISE BELHAVEL
FRAGRANT ABUSES
$4.95/88-2
The saga of Clara and Iris continues as the now-experienced girls enjoy themselves with a new circle of worldly friends whose imaginations match their own. Perversity follows the lusty ladies around the globe!

SARA H. FRENCH
MASTER OF TIMBERLAND
$5.95/327-9
A tale of sexual slavery at the ultimate paradise resort. One of our bestselling titles, this trek to Timberland has ignited passions the world over—and stands poised to become one of modern erotica's legendary tales.

MARY LOVE
MASTERING MARY SUE
$5.95/351-1
Mary Sue is a rich nymphomaniac whose husband is determined to declare her mentally incompetent and gain control of her fortune. He brings her to a castle where, to Mary Sue's delight, she is unleashed for a veritable sex-fest!

THE BEST OF MARY LOVE
$4.95/3099-7
Mary Love leaves no coupling untried and no extreme unexplored in these scandalous selections from *Mastering Mary Sue, Ecstasy on Fire, Vice Park Place, Wanda,* and *Naughtier at Night.*

MASQUERADE BOOKS

AMARANTHA KNIGHT

THE DARKER PASSIONS: THE PICTURE OF DORIAN GRAY
$6.50/342-2
Amarantha Knight takes on Oscar Wilde, resulting in a fabulously decadent tale of highly personal changes. One young man finds his most secret desires laid bare by a portrait far more revealing than he could have imagined....

THE DARKER PASSIONS READER
$6.50/432-1
The best moments from Knight's phenomenally popular Darker Passions series. Here are the most eerily erotic passages from her acclaimed sexual reworkings of *Dracula*, *Frankenstein*, *Dr. Jekyll & Mr. Hyde* and *The Fall of the House of Usher*.

THE DARKER PASSIONS: FALL OF THE HOUSE OF USHER
$6.50/528-X
The Master and Mistress of the house of Usher indulge in every form of decadence, and initiate their guests into the many pleasures to be found in utter submission.

THE DARKER PASSIONS: DR. JEKYLL AND MR. HYDE
$4.95/227-2
It is a story of incredible transformations achieved through mysterious experiments. Explore the steamy possibilities of a tale where no one is quite who—or what—they seem. Victorian bedrooms explode with hidden demons!

THE DARKER PASSIONS: FRANKENSTEIN
$5.95/248-5
What if you could create a living human? What shocking acts could it be taught to perform, to desire? Find out what pleasures await those who play God....

THE DARKER PASSIONS: DRACULA
$5.95/326-0
The infamous erotic retelling of the Vampire legend.
"Well-written and imaginative, Amarantha Knight gives fresh impetus to this myth, taking us through the sexual and sadistic scenes with details that keep us reading.... A classic in itself has been added to the shelves."
—*Divinity*

THE PAUL LITTLE LIBRARY

PECULIAR PASSIONS OF LADY MEG/ LOVE SLAVE
$8.95/529-8/Trade paperback
Two classics from modern erotica's most popular author! What are the sexy secrets *Lady Meg* hides? What are the appetites that lurk beneath the surface of this irresistible vixen? What does it take to be the perfect instrument of pleasure—or go about acquiring a willing *Love Slave* of one's own? Paul Little spares no detail in these two relentless tales, guaranteed to thrill and shock even the most jaded readers!

THE BEST OF PAUL LITTLE
$6.50/469-0
Known throughout the world for his fantastic portrayals of punishment and pleasure, Little never fails to push readers over the edge of sensual excitement.

ALL THE WAY
$6.95/509-3
Two excruciating novels from Paul Little in one hot volume! *Going All the Way* features an unhappy man who tries to purge himself of the memory of his lover in a series of quirky and uninhibited lovers. *Pushover* tells the story of a serial spanker and his celebrated exploits.

THE DISCIPLINE OF ODETTE
$5.95/334-1
Odette was sure marriage would rescue her from her family's "corrections." To her horror, she discovers that her beloved has also been raised on discipline. A shocking erotic coupling!

THE PRISONER
$5.95/330-9
Judge Black has built a secret room below a penitentiary, where he sentences the prisoners to hours of exhibition and torment while his friends watch. Judge Black's brand of rough justice keeps his lovely young captives on the brink of utter pleasure!

TEARS OF THE INQUISITION
$4.95/146-2
A staggering account of pleasure and punishment. "There was a tickling inside her as her nervous system reminded her she was ready for sex. But before he was...the Inquisitor!"

DOUBLE NOVEL
$4.95/86-6
The Metamorphosis of Lisette Joyaux tells the story of a young woman initiated into an incredible world of lesbian lusts. *The Story of Monique* reveals the twisted sexual rituals that beckon the ripe and willing Monique.

CAPTIVE MAIDENS
$5.95/440-2
Three beautiful young women find themselves powerless against the debauched landowners of 1824 England. They are banished to a sexual slave colony, and corrupted by every imaginable perversion.

SLAVE ISLAND
$5.95/441-0
A leisure cruise is waylaid by Lord Henry Philbrock, a sadistic genius. The ship's passengers are kidnapped and spirited to his island prison, where the women are trained to accommodate the most bizarre sexual cravings of the rich, the famous, the pampered and the perverted.

BUY ANY 4 BOOKS & CHOOSE 1 ADDITIONAL BOOK, OF EQUAL OR LESSER VALUE, AS YOUR FREE GIFT

MASQUERADE BOOKS

ALIZARIN LAKE
SEX ON DOCTOR'S ORDERS
$5.95/402-X
Beth, a nubile young nurse, uses her considerable skills to further medical science by offering incomparable and insatiable assistance in the gathering of important specimens. Soon, an assortment of randy characters is lending a hand in this highly erotic work.

THE EROTIC ADVENTURES OF HARRY TEMPLE
$4.95/127-6
Harry Temple's memoirs chronicle his amorous adventures from his initiation at the hands of insatiable sirens, through his stay at a house of hot repute, to his encounters with a chastity-belted nympho!

JOHN NORMAN
TARNSMAN OF GOR
$6.95/486-0
This controversial series returns! Tarl Cabot is transported to Gor. He must quickly accustom himself to the ways of this world, including the caste system which exalts some as Priest-Kings or Warriors, and debases others as slaves. A spectacular world unfolds in this first volume of John Norman's Gorean series.

OUTLAW OF GOR
$6.95/487-9
In this second volume, Tarl Cabot returns to Gor, where he might reclaim both his woman and his role of Warrior. But upon arriving, he discovers that his name, his city and the names of those he loves have become unspeakable. Cabot has become an outlaw, and must discover his new purpose on this strange planet, where danger stalks the outcast, and even simple answers have their price....

PRIEST-KINGS OF GOR
$6.95/488-7
Tarl Cabot searches for the truth about his lovely wife Talena. Does she live, or was she destroyed by the mysterious, all-powerful Priest-Kings? Cabot is determined to find out—even while knowing that no one who has approached the mountain stronghold of the Priest-Kings has ever returned alive....

NOMADS OF GOR
$6.95/527-1
Another provocative trip to the barbaric and mysterious world of Gor. Norman's heroic Tarnsman finds his way across this Counter-Earth, pledged to serve the Priest-Kings in their quest for survival. Unfortunately for Cabot, his mission leads him to the savage Wagon People—nomads who may very well kill before surrendering any secrets....

RACHEL PEREZ
AFFINITIES
$4.95/113-6
"Kelsy had a liking for cool upper-class blondes, the long-legged girls from Lake Forest and Winnetka who came into the city to cruise the lesbian bars on Halsted, looking for breathless ecstasies...." A scorching tale of lesbian libidos unleashed, from a writer more than capable of exploring every nuance of female passion in vivid detail.

SYDNEY ST. JAMES
RIVE GAUCHE
$5.95/317-1
The Latin Quarter, Paris, circa 1920. Expatriate bohemians couple with abandon—before eventually abandoning their ambitions amidst the intoxicating temptations waiting to be indulged in every bedroom.

GARDEN OF DELIGHT
$4.95/3058-X
A vivid account of sexual awakening that follows an innocent but insatiably curious young woman's journey from the furtive, forbidden joys of dormitory life to the unabashed carnality of the wild world.

DON WINSLOW
THE FALL OF THE ICE QUEEN
$6.50/520-4
She was the most exquisite of his courtiers: the beautiful, aloof woman whom Rahn the Conqueror chose as his Consort. But the regal disregard with which she treated Rahn was not to be endured. It was decided that she would submit to his will, and learn to serve her lord in the fashion he had come to expect. And as so many knew, Rahn's depraved expectations have made his court infamous....

PRIVATE PLEASURES
$6.50/504-2
An assortment of sensual encounters designed to appeal to the most discerning reader. Frantic voyeurs, licentious exhibitionists, and everyday lovers are here displayed in all their wanton glory—proving again that fleshly pleasures have no more apt chronicler than Don Winslow.

THE INSATIABLE MISTRESS OF ROSEDALE
$6.50/494-1
The story of the perfect couple: Edward and Lady Penelope, who reside in beautiful and mysterious Rosedale manor. While Edward is a true connoisseur of sexual perversion, it is Lady Penelope whose mastery of complete sensual pleasure makes their home infamous. Indulging one another's bizarre whims is a way of life for this wicked couple, and none who encounter the extravagances of Rosedale will forget what they've learned....

SECRETS OF CHEATEM MANOR
$6.50/434-8
Edward returns to his late father's estate, to find it being run by the majestic Lady Amanda. Edward can hardly believe his luck—Lady Amanda is assisted by her two beautiful, lonely daughters, Catherine and Prudence. What the randy young man soon comes to realize is the love of discipline that all three beauties share.

KATERINA IN CHARGE
$5.95/409-7
When invited to a country retreat by a mysterious couple, two randy young ladies can hardly resist! But do they have any idea what they're in for? Whatever the case, the imperious Katerina will make her desires known very soon—and demand that they be fulfilled... A thoroughly perverse tale of ultimate sexual innocence subjugated and defiled by one powerful woman.

MASQUERADE BOOKS

THE MANY PLEASURES OF IRONWOOD
$5.95/310-4
Seven lovely young women are employed by The Ironwood Sportsmen's Club, where their natural talents are put to creative use. A small and exclusive club with seven carefully selected sexual connoisseurs, Ironwood is dedicated to the relentless pursuit of sensual pleasure.

CLAIRE'S GIRLS
$5.95/442-9
You knew when she walked by that she was something special. She was one of Claire's girls, a woman carefully dressed and groomed to fill a role, to capture a look, to fit an image crafted by the sophisticated proprietress of an exclusive escort agency. High-class whores blow the roof off in this blow-by-blow account of life behind the closed doors of a sophisticated brothel.

N. WHALLEN

TAU'TEVU
$6.50/426-7
In a mysterious land, the statuesque and beautiful Vivian learns to subject herself to the hand of a mysterious man. He systematically helps her prove her own strength, and brings to life in her an unimagined sensual fire.

COMPLIANCE
$5.95/356-2
Fourteen stories exploring the pleasures of ultimate release. Characters from all walks of life learn to trust in the skills of others, hoping to experience the thrilling liberation of sexual submission. Here are the many joys to be found in some of the most forbidden sexual practices around....

THE CLASSIC COLLECTION

PROTESTS, PLEASURES, RAPTURES
$5.95/400-3
Invited for an allegedly quiet weekend at a country vicarage, a young woman is stunned to find herself surrounded by shocking acts of sexual sadism. Soon, her curiosity is piqued, and she begins to explore her own capacities for cruelty.

THE YELLOW ROOM
$5.95/378-5
The "yellow room" holds the secrets of lust, lechery, and the lash. There, bare-bottomed, spread-eagled, and open to the world, demure Alice Darvell soon learns to love her lickings. In the second tale, hot heiress Rosa Coote and her lusty servants whip up numerous adventures in punishment and pleasure.

SCHOOL DAYS IN PARIS
$5.95/325-2
The rapturous chronicles of a well-spent youth! Few Universities provide the profound and pleasurable lessons one learns in after-hours study—particularly if one is young and available, and lucky enough to have Paris as a playground. A sexy look at the pursuits of young adulthood.

MAN WITH A MAID
$4.95/307-4
The adventures of Jack and Alice have delighted readers for eight decades! A classic of its genre, *Man with a Maid* tells an outrageous tale of desire, revenge, and submission. This tale qualifies as one of the world's most popular adult novels—with over 200,000 copies in print!

CONFESSIONS OF A CONCUBINE III: PLEASURE'S PRISONER
$5.95/357-0
Filled with pulse-pounding excitement—including a daring escape from the harem and an encounter with an unspeakable sadist—*Pleasure's Prisoner* adds an unforgettable chapter to this thrilling confessional.

CLASSIC EROTIC BIOGRAPHIES

JENNIFER
$4.95/107-1
The return of one of the Sexual Revolution's most notorious heroines. From the bedroom of a notoriously insatiable dancer to an uninhibited ashram, *Jennifer* traces the exploits of one thoroughly modern woman.

JENNIFER III
$5.95/292-2
The further adventures of erotica's most daring heroine. Jennifer has a photographer's eye for details—particularly of the masculine variety! One by one, her subjects submit to her demands for sensual pleasure, becoming part of her now-infamous gallery of erotic conquests.

RHINOCEROS

KATHLEEN K.

SWEET TALKERS
$6.95/516-6
Kathleen K. ran a phone-sex company in the late 80s, and she opens up her diary for a very thought provoking peek at the life of a phone-sex operator. Transcripts of actual conversations are included.

"If you enjoy eavesdropping on explicit conversations about sex... this book is for you." —Spectator
Trade /$12.95/192-6

THOMAS S. ROCHE

DARK MATTER
$6.95/484-4
"*Dark Matter* is sure to please gender outlaws, body-mod junkies, goth vampires, boys who wish they were dykes, and anybody who's not to sure where the fine line should be drawn between pleasure and pain. It's a handful." —Pat Califia

"Here is the erotica of the cumming millennium.... You will be deliciously disturbed, but never disappointed." —Poppy Z. Brite

BUY ANY 4 BOOKS & CHOOSE 1 ADDITIONAL BOOK, OF EQUAL OR LESSER VALUE, AS YOUR FREE GIFT

MASQUERADE BOOKS

NOIROTICA: AN ANTHOLOGY OF EROTIC CRIME STORIES
$6.95/390-2

A collection of darkly sexy tales, taking place at the crossroads of the crime and erotic genres. Thomas S. Roche has gathered together some of today's finest writers of sexual fiction, all of whom explore the murky terrain where desire runs irrevocably afoul of the law.

ROMY ROSEN
SPUNK
$6.95/492-5

Casey, a lovely model poised upon the verge of super-celebrity, falls for an insatiable young rock singer—not suspecting that his sexual appetite has led him to experiment with a dangerous new aphrodisiac. Casey becomes an addict, and her craving plunges her into a strange underworld, where the only chance for redemption lies with a shadowy young man with a secret of his own.

MOLLY WEATHERFIELD
CARRIE'S STORY
$6.95/485-2

"I had been Jonathan's slave for about a year when he told me he wanted to sell me at an auction. I wasn't in any condition to respond when he told me this..." Desire and depravity run rampant in this story of uncompromising mastery and irrevocable submission. A unique piece of erotica that is both thoughtful and hot!

"I was stunned by how well it was written and how intensely foreign I found its sexual world.... And, since this is a world I don't frequent... I thoroughly enjoyed the National Geo tour."   —bOING bOING

"Hilarious and harrowing... just when you think things can't get any wilder, they do." —Black Sheets

CYBERSEX CONSORTIUM
CYBERSEX: THE PERV'S GUIDE TO FINDING SEX ON THE INTERNET
$6.95/471-2

You've heard the objections: cyberspace is soaked with sex. Okay—so where is it!? Tracking down the good stuff—the real good stuff—can waste an awful lot of expensive time, and frequently leave you high and dry. The Cybersex Consortium presents an easy-to-use guide for those intrepid adults who know what they want. No horny hacker can afford to pass up this map to the kinkiest rest stops on the Info Superhighway.

AMELIA G, EDITOR
BACKSTAGE PASSES
$6.95/438-0

Amelia G, editor of the goth-sex journal *Blue Blood*, has brought together some of today's most irreverent writers, each of whom has outdone themselves with an edgy, antic tale of modern lust. Punks, metalheads, and grunge-trash roam the pages of *Backstage Passes*, and no one knows their ways better...

GERI NETTICK WITH BETH ELLIOT
MIRRORS: PORTRAIT OF A LESBIAN TRANSSEXUAL
$6.95/435-6

The alternately heartbreaking and empowering story of one woman's long road to full selfhood. Born a male, Geri Nettick knew something just didn't fit. And even after coming to terms with her own gender dysphoria—and taking steps to correct it—she still fought to be accepted by the lesbian feminist community to which she felt she belonged. A fascinating, true tale of struggle and discovery.

DAVID MELTZER
UNDER
$6.95/290-0

The story of a 21st century sex professional living at the bottom of the social heap. After surgeries designed to increase his physical allure, corrupt government forces drive the cyber-gigolo underground—where even more bizarre cultures await him.

ORF
$6.95/110-1

He is the ultimate musician-hero—the idol of thousands, the fevered dream of many more. And like many musicians before him, he is misunderstood, misused—and totally out of control. Every last drop of feeling is squeezed from a modern-day troubadour and his lady love.

LAURA ANTONIOU, EDITOR
NO OTHER TRIBUTE
$6.95/294-9

A collection sure to challenge Political Correctness in a way few have before, with tales of women kept in bondage to their lovers by their deepest passions. Love pushes these women beyond acceptable limits, rendering them helpless to deny anything to the men and women they adore.

SOME WOMEN
$6.95/300-7

Over forty essays written by women actively involved in consensual dominance and submission. Pro doms, lifestyle leatherdykes, titleholders—women from every walk of life lay bare their true feelings about explosive issues.

BY HER SUBDUED
$6.95/281-7

These tales all involve women in control—of their lives, their loves, their men. So much in control that they can remorselessly break rules to become powerful goddesses of the men who sacrifice all to worship at their feet.

TRISTAN TAORMINO & DAVID AARON CLARK, EDITORS
RITUAL SEX
$6.95/391-0

The many contributors to *Ritual Sex* know—and demonstrate—that body and soul share more common ground than society feels comfortable acknowledging. From personal memoirs of ecstatic revelation, to fictional quests to reconcile sex and spirit, *Ritual Sex* provides an unprecedented look at private life.

MASQUERADE BOOKS

TAMMY JO ECKHART
PUNISHMENT FOR THE CRIME
$6.95/427-5
Peopled by characters of rare depth, these stories explore the true meaning of dominance and submission. From an encounter between two of society's most despised individuals, to the explorations of longtime friends, these tales take you where few others have ever dared....

AMARANTHA KNIGHT, EDITOR
SEDUCTIVE SPECTRES
$6.95/464-X
Breathtaking tours through the erotic supernatural via the macabre imaginations of today's best writers. Never before have ghostly encounters been so alluring, thanks to a cast of otherworldly characters well-acquainted with the pleasures of the flesh.

SEX MACABRE
$6.95/392-9
Horror tales designed for dark and sexy nights. Amarantha Knight—the woman behind the Darker Passions series—has gathered together erotic stories sure to make your skin crawl, and heart beat faster.

FLESH FANTASTIC
$6.95/352-X
Humans have long toyed with the idea of "playing God": creating life from nothingness, bringing life to the inanimate. Now Amarantha Knight collects stories exploring not only the act of Creation, but the lust that follows....

GARY BOWEN
DIARY OF A VAMPIRE
$6.95/331-7
"Gifted with a darkly sensual vision and a fresh voice, [Bowen] is a writer to watch for."
—Cecilia Tan

Rafael, a red-blooded male with an insatiable hunger for the same, is the perfect antidote to the effete malcontents haunting bookstores today. The emergence of a bold and brilliant vision, rooted in past and present.

RENÉ MAIZEROY
FLESHLY ATTRACTIONS
$6.95/299-X
Lucien was the son of the wantonly beautiful actress, Marie-Rose Hardanges. When she decides to let a "friend" introduce her son to the pleasures of love, Marie-Rose could not have foretold the excesses that would lead to her own ruin and that of her cherished son.

JEAN STINE
THRILL CITY
$6.95/411-9
Thrill City is the seat of the world's increasing depravity, and this classic novel transports you there with a vivid style you'd be hard pressed to ignore. No writer is better suited to describe the extremes of this modern Babylon.

SEASON OF THE WITCH
$6.95/268-X
"A future in which it is technically possible to transfer the total mind...of a rapist killer into the brain dead but physically living body of his female victim. Remarkable for intense psychological technique. There is eroticism but it is necessary to mark the differences between the sexes and the subtle altering of a man into a woman." —*The Science Fiction Critic*

GRANT ANTREWS
ROGUE'S GALLERY
$6.95/522-0
A stirring evocation of dominant/submissive love. Two doctors meet and slowly fall in love. Once Beth reveals her hidden desires to Jim, the two explore the forbidden acts that will come to define their distinctly exotic affair.

MY DARLING DOMINATRIX
$6.95/447-X
When a man and a woman fall in love, it's supposed to be simple and uncomplicated—unless that woman happens to be a dominatrix. Curiosity gives way to desire in this story of one man's awakening to the joys of willing slavery.

JOHN WARREN
THE TORQUEMADA KILLER
$6.95/367-8
Detective Eva Hernandez gets her first "big case": a string of vicious murders taking place within New York's SM community. Eva assembles the evidence, revealing a picture of a world misunderstood and under attack—and gradually comes to understand her own place within it.

THE LOVING DOMINANT
$6.95/218-3
Everything you need to know about an infamous sexual variation—and an unspoken type of love. Warren guides readers through this world and reveals the too-often hidden basis of the D/S relationship: care, trust and love.

LAURA ANTONIOU WRITING AS "SARA ADAMSON"
THE TRAINER
$6.95/249-3
The Marketplace includes not only willing slaves, but the exquisite trainers who take submissives firmly in hand. And now these mentors divulge the desires that led them to become the ultimate figures of authority.

THE SLAVE
$6.95/173-X
One talented submissive longs to join the ranks of those who have proven themselves worthy of entry into the Marketplace. But the delicious price is high....

THE MARKETPLACE
$6.95/3096-2
The volume that introduced the Marketplace to the world—and established it as one of the most popular realms in contemporary SM fiction.

BUY ANY 4 BOOKS & CHOOSE 1 ADDITIONAL BOOK, OF EQUAL OR LESSER VALUE, AS YOUR FREE GIFT

MASQUERADE BOOKS

DAVID AARON CLARK

SISTER RADIANCE
$6.95/215-9
A meditation on love, sex, and death, rife with Clark's trademark vivisections of contemporary desires, sacred and profane. The vicissitudes of lust and romance are examined against a backdrop of urban decay in this testament to the allure—and inevitability—of the forbidden.

THE WET FOREVER
$6.95/117-9
The story of Janus and Madchen—a small-time hood and a beautiful sex worker on the run from one of the most dangerous men they have ever known—examines themes of loyalty, sacrifice, redemption and obsession amidst Manhattan's sex parlors and underground S/M clubs. A thrillingly contemporary love story, and a uniquely sensual thriller.

MICHAEL PERKINS

EVIL COMPANIONS
$6.95/3067-9
Set in New York City during the tumultuous waning years of the Sixties, *Evil Companions* has been hailed as "a frightening classic." A young couple explores the nether reaches of the erotic unconscious in a shocking confrontation with the extremes of passion.

THE SECRET RECORD: MODERN EROTIC LITERATURE
$6.95/3039-3
Michael Perkins surveys the field with authority and unique insight. Updated and revised to include the latest trends, tastes, and developments in this misunderstood and maligned genre.

AN ANTHOLOGY OF CLASSIC ANONYMOUS EROTIC WRITING
$6.95/140-3
Michael Perkins has collected the very best passages from the world's erotic writing. "Anonymous" is one of the most infamous bylines in publishing history—and these steamy excerpts show why! Includes excerpts from some of the most famous titles in the history of erotic literature.

LIESEL KULIG

LOVE IN WARTIME
$6.95/3044-X
Madeleine knew that the handsome SS officer was a dangerous man, but she was just a cabaret singer in Nazi-occupied Paris, trying to survive in a perilous time. When Josef fell in love with her, he discovered that a beautiful woman can sometimes be as dangerous as any warrior.

HELEN HENLEY

ENTER WITH TRUMPETS
$6.95/197-7
Helen Henley was told that women just don't write about sex—much less the taboos she was so interested in exploring. So Henley did it alone, flying in the face of "tradition" by writing this touching tale of arousal and devotion in one couple's kinky relationship.

ALICE JOANOU

BLACK TONGUE
$6.95/258-2
"Joanou has created a series of sumptuous, brooding, dark visions of sexual obsession, and is undoubtedly a name to look out for in the future."
—Redeemer

Exploring lust at its most florid and unsparing, *Black Tongue* is a trove of baroque fantasies—each redolent of forbidden passions. Joanou creates some of erotica's most mesmerizing and unforgettable characters. One of today's groundbreaking talents.

TOURNIQUET
$6.95/3060-1
A heady collection of stories and effusions from the pen of one our most dazzling young writers. Strange tales abound, from the story of the mysterious and cruel Cybele, to an encounter with the sadistic entertainment of a bizarre after-hours cafe. A complex and riveting series of meditations on desire.

CANNIBAL FLOWER
$4.95/72-6
The provocative debut volume from this acclaimed young writer.
"She is waiting in her darkened bedroom, as she has waited throughout history, to seduce the men who are foolish enough to be blinded by her irresistible charms.... She is the goddess of sexuality, and *Cannibal Flower* is her haunting siren song."
—Michael Perkins

PHILIP JOSÉ FARMER

A FEAST UNKNOWN
$6.95/276-0
"Sprawling, brawling, shocking, suspenseful, hilarious..."
—Theodore Sturgeon

Farmer's supreme anti-hero returns. "I was conceived and born in 1888." Slowly, Lord Grandrith—armed with the belief that he is the son of Jack the Ripper—tells the story of his remarkable and unbridled life. His story begins with his discovery of the secret of immortality—and progresses to encompass the furthest extremes of human behavior.

THE IMAGE OF THE BEAST
$6.95/166-7
Herald Childe has seen Hell, glimpsed its horror in an act of sexual mutilation. Childe must now find and destroy an inhuman predator through the streets of a polluted and decadent Los Angeles of the future. One clue after another leads Childe to an inescapable realization about the nature of sex and evil....

DANIEL VIAN

ILLUSIONS
$6.95/3074-1
International lust. Two tales of danger and desire in Berlin on the eve of WWII. From private homes to lurid cafés, passion is exposed in stark contrast to the brutal violence of the time, as desperate people explore their darkest sexual desires.

MASQUERADE BOOKS

SAMUEL R. DELANY
THE MAD MAN
$8.99/408-9
"Reads like a pornographic reflection of Peter Ackroyd's *Chatterton* or A. S. Byatt's *Possession*.... Delany develops an insightful dichotomy between [his protagonist]'s two worlds: the one of cerebral philosophy and dry academia, the other of heedless, 'impersonal' obsessive sexual extremism. When these worlds finally collide...the novel achieves a surprisingly satisfying resolution...." —*Publishers Weekly*

Graduate student John Marr researches the life of Timothy Hasler: a philosopher whose career was cut tragically short over a decade earlier. On another front, Marr finds himself increasingly drawn toward shocking, depraved sexual entanglements with the homeless men of his neighborhood, until it begins to seem that Hasler's death might hold some key to his own life as a gay man in the age of AIDS.

EQUINOX
$6.95/157-8
The Scorpion has sailed the seas in a quest for every possible pleasure. Her crew is a collection of the young, the twisted, the insatiable. A drifter comes into their midst and is taken on a fantastic journey to the darkest, most dangerous sexual extremes—until he is finally a victim to their boundless appetites. An early title that set the way for the author's later explorations of extreme, forbidden sexual behaviors. Long out of print, this disturbing tale is finally available under the author's original title.

ANDREI CODRESCU
THE REPENTANCE OF LORRAINE
$6.95/329-5
"One of our most prodigiously talented and magical writers." —*NYT Book Review*
By the acclaimed author of *The Hole in the Flag* and *The Blood Countess*. An aspiring writer, a professor's wife, a secretary, gold anklets, Maoists, Roman harlots—and more—swirl through this spicy tale of a harried quest for a mythic artifact. Written when the author was a young man, this lusty yarn was inspired by the heady days of the Sixties. Includes a new introduction by the author, detailing the events that inspired *Lorraine*'s creation. A touching, arousing product from a more innocent time.

TUPPY OWENS
SENSATIONS
$6.95/3081-4
Tuppy Owens tells the unexpurgated story of the making of *Sensations*—the first big-budget sex flick. Originally commissioned to appear in book form after the release of the film in 1975, *Sensations* is finally released under Masquerade's stylish Rhinoceros imprint. Tuppy Owens provides an unprecedented peek behind the scenes of a porn legend.

SOPHIE GALLEYMORE BIRD
MANEATER
$6.95/103-9
Through a bizarre act of creation, a man attains the "perfect" lover—by all appearances a beautiful, sensuous woman, but in reality something far darker. Once brought to life she will accept no mate, seeking instead the prey that will sate her hunger for vengeance.

LEOPOLD VON SACHER-MASOCH
VENUS IN FURS
$6.95/3089-X
This classic 19th century novel is the first uncompromising exploration of the dominant/submissive relationship in literature. The alliance of Severin and Wanda epitomizes Sacher-Masoch's dark obsession with a cruel, controlling goddess and the urges that drive the man held in her thrall. This special edition includes the letters exchanged between Sacher-Masoch and Emilie Mataja, an aspiring writer he sought to cast as the avatar of the forbidden desires expressed in his most famous work.

BADBOY

MIKE FORD, EDITOR
BUTCH BOYS
$6.50/523-9
A big volume of tales dedicated to the rough-and-tumble type who can make a man weak at the knees. From bikers to "gymbos," these no-nonsense studs know just what they want and how to go about getting it. Some of today's best erotic writers explore the many possible variations on the age-old fantasy of the dominant man.

WILLIAM J. MANN, EDITOR
GRAVE PASSIONS
$6.50/405-4
A collection of the most chilling tales of passion currently being penned by today's most provocative gay writers. Unnatural transformations, otherworldly encounters, and deathless desires make for a collection sure to keep readers up late at night—for a variety of reasons!

J. A. GUERRA, EDITOR
COME QUICKLY: FOR BOYS ON THE GO
$6.50/413-5
Here are over sixty of the hottest fantasies around—all designed to get you going in less time than it takes to dial 976. Julian Anthony Guerra, the editor behind the popular *Men at Work* and *Badboy Fantasies*, has put together this volume especially for you—a busy man on a modern schedule, who still appreciates a little old-fashioned action. Hassle-free quickies.

BUY ANY 4 BOOKS & CHOOSE 1 ADDITIONAL BOOK, OF EQUAL OR LESSER VALUE, AS YOUR FREE GIFT

MASQUERADE BOOKS

JOHN PRESTON

HUSTLING: A GENTLEMAN'S GUIDE TO THE FINE ART OF HOMOSEXUAL PROSTITUTION
$6.50/517-4
The very first guide to the gay world's most infamous profession. John Preston solicited the advice and opinions of "working boys" from across the country in his effort to produce the ultimate guide to the hustler's world. *Hustling* covers every practical aspect of the business, from clientele and payment options to "specialties," sidelines and drawbacks. No stone is left unturned in this guidebook to the ins and outs of this much-mythologized trade.

"...Unrivaled. For any man even vaguely contemplating going into business this tome has got to be the first port of call." —*Divinity*

"Fun and highly literary. What more could you expect from such an accomplished activist, author and editor?" —*Drummer*
Trade $12.95/137-3

MR. BENSON
$4.95/3041-5
Jamie is an aimless young man lucky enough to encounter Mr. Benson. He is soon led down the path of erotic enlightenment, learning to accept this man as his master. Jamie's incredible adventures never fail to excite—especially when the going gets rough!

TALES FROM THE DARK LORD
$5.95/323-6
A new collection of twelve stunning works from the man *Lambda Book Report* called "the Dark Lord of gay erotica." The relentless ritual of lust and surrender is explored in all its manifestations in this heart-stopping triumph of authority and vision from the Dark Lord!

TALES FROM THE DARK LORD II
$4.95/176-4
The second volume of John Preston's masterful short stories.

THE ARENA
$4.95/3083-0
There is a place on the edge of fantasy where every desire is indulged with abandon. Men go there to unleash beasts, to let demons roam free, to abolish all limits. At the center of each tale are the men who serve there, who offer themselves for the consummation of any passion, whose own bottomless urges compel their endless subservience.

THE HEIR•THE KING
$4.95/3048-2
The ground-breaking novel *The Heir*, written in the lyric voice of the ancient myths, tells the story of a world where slaves and masters create a new sexual society. *The King* tells the story of a soldier who discovers his monarch's most secret desires. A special double volume.

THE MISSION OF ALEX KANE

SWEET DREAMS
$4.95/3062-8
It's the triumphant return of gay action hero Alex Kane! In *Sweet Dreams*, Alex travels to Boston where he takes on a street gang that stalks gay teenagers. Mighty Alex Kane wreaks a fierce and terrible vengeance on those who prey on gay people everywhere!

GOLDEN YEARS
$4.95/3069-5
When evil threatens the plans of a group of older gay men, Kane's got the muscle to take it head on. Along the way, he wins the support—and very specialized attentions—of a cowboy plucked right out of the Old West.

DEADLY LIES
$4.95/3076-8
Politics is a dirty business and the dirt becomes deadly when a political smear campaign targets gay men. Who better to clean things up than Alex Kane! Alex comes to protect the lives of gay men imperiled by lies and deceit.

STOLEN MOMENTS
$4.95/3098-9
Houston's evolving gay community is victimized by a malicious newspaper editor who is more than willing to sacrifice gays on the altar of circulation. He never counted on Alex Kane, fearless defender of gay dreams and desires.

SECRET DANGER
$4.95/111-X
Homophobia: a pernicious social ill not confined by America's borders. Alex Kane and the faithful Danny are called to a small European country, where a group of gay tourists is being held hostage by ruthless terrorists. Luckily, the Mission of Alex Kane stands as firm foreign policy.

LETHAL SILENCE
$4.95/125-X
The Mission of Alex Kane thunders to a conclusion. Chicago becomes the scene of the right-wing's most noxious plan—facilitated by unholy political alliances. Alex and Danny head to the Windy City to take up battle with the mercenaries who would squash gay men underfoot.

MATT TOWNSEND

SOLIDLY BUILT
$6.50/416-X
The tale of the tumultuous relationship between Jeff, a young photographer, and Mark, the butch electrician hired to wire Jeff's new home. For Jeff, it's love at first sight; Mark, however, has more than a few hang-ups. Soon, both are forced to reevaluate their outlooks, and are assisted by a variety of hot men....

JAY SHAFFER

SHOOTERS
$5.95/284-1
No mere catalog of random acts, *Shooters* tells the stories of a variety of stunning men and the ways they connect in sexual and non-sexual ways. A virtuoso storyteller, Shaffer always gets his man.

MASQUERADE BOOKS

ANIMAL HANDLERS
$4.95/264-7
In Shaffer's world, each and every man finally succumbs to the animal urges deep inside. And if there's any creature that promises a wild time, it's a beast who's been caged for far too long. Shaffer has one of the keenest eyes for the nuances of male passion.

FULL SERVICE
$4.95/150-0
Wild men build up steam until they finally let loose. No-nonsense guys bear down hard on each other as they work their way toward release in this finely detailed assortment of masculine fantasies. One of gay erotica's most insightful chroniclers of male passion.

D. V. SADERO

IN THE ALLEY
$4.95/144-6
Hardworking men—from cops to carpenters—bring their own special skills and impressive tools to the most satisfying job of all: capturing and breaking the male sexual beast. Hot, incisive and way over the top

SCOTT O'HARA

DO-IT-YOURSELF PISTON POLISHING
$6.50/489-5
Longtime sex-pro Scott O'Hara draws upon his acute powers of seduction to lure you into a world of hard, horny men long overdue for a tune-up. Pretty soon, you'll pop your own hood for the servicing you know you need....

SUTTER POWELL

EXECUTIVE PRIVILEGES
$6.50/383-X
No matter how serious or sexy a predicament his characters find themselves in, Powell conveys the sheer exuberance of their encounters with a warm humor rarely seen in contemporary gay erotica.

GARY BOWEN

WESTERN TRAILS
$6.50/477-1
A wild roundup of tales devoted to life on the lone prairie. Gary Bowen—a writer well-versed in the Western genre—has collected the very best contemporary cowboy stories. Some of gay literature's brightest stars tell the sexy truth about the many ways a rugged stud found to satisfy himself—and his buddy—in the Very Wild West.

MAN HUNGRY
$5.95/374-0
By the author of *Diary of a Vampire*. A riveting collection of stories from one of gay erotica's new stars. Dipping into a variety of genres, Bowen crafts tales of lust unlike anything being published today.

KYLE STONE

HOT BAUDS 2
$6.50/479-8
Another collection of cyberfantasies—compiled by the inimitable Kyle Stone. After the success of the original *Hot Bauds*, Stone conducted another heated search through the world's randiest bulletin boards, resulting in one of the most scalding follow-ups ever published. Here's all the scandalous stuff you've heard so much about—sexy, shameless, and eminently user-friendly.

FIRE & ICE
$5.95/297-3
A collection of stories from the author of the infamous adventures of PB 500. Randy, powerful, and just plain bad, Stone's characters always promise one thing: enough hot action to burn away your desire for anyone else....

HOT BAUDS
$5.95/285-X
The author of *Fantasy Board* and *The Initiation of PB 500* combed cyberspace for the hottest fantasies of the world's horniest hackers. Stone has assembled the first collection of the raunchy erotica so many gay men cruise the Information Superhighway for.

FANTASY BOARD
$4.95/212-4
The author of the scalding sci-fi adventures of PB 500 explores the more foreseeable future—through the intertwined lives (and private parts) of a collection of randy computer hackers. On the Lambda Gate BBS, every hot and horny male is in search of a little virtual satisfaction!

THE CITADEL
$4.95/198-5
The sequel to *The Initiation of PB 500*. Having proven himself worthy of his stunning master, Micah—now known only as '500'—will face new challenges and hardships after his entry into the forbidding Citadel. Only his master knows what awaits—and whether Micah will again distinguish himself as the perfect instrument of pleasure....

THE INITIATION OF PB 500
$4.95/141-1
He is a stranger on their planet, unschooled in their language, and ignorant of their customs. But this man, Micah—now known only by his number—will soon be trained in every last detail of erotic personal service. And, once nurtured and transformed into the perfect physical specimen, he must begin proving himself worthy of the master who has chosen him....

RITUALS
$4.95/168-3
Via a computer bulletin board, a young man finds himself drawn into a series of sexual rites that transform him into the willing slave of a mysterious stranger. Gradually, all vestiges of his former life are thrown off, and he learns to live for his Master's touch....

BUY ANY 4 BOOKS & CHOOSE 1 ADDITIONAL BOOK, OF EQUAL OR LESSER VALUE, AS YOUR FREE GIFT

MASQUERADE BOOKS

ROBERT BAHR
SEX SHOW
$4.95/225-6
Luscious dancing boys. Brazen, explicit acts. Unending stimulation. Take a seat, and get very comfortable, because the curtain's going up on a show no discriminating appetite can afford to miss.

JASON FURY
THE ROPE ABOVE, THE BED BELOW
$4.95/269-8
The irresistible Jason Fury returns—this time, telling the tale of a vicious murderer preying upon New York's go-go boys. In order to solve this mystery and save lives, each study suspect must lay bare his soul—and more!

ERIC'S BODY
$4.95/151-9
Fury's sexiest tales are collected in book form for the first time. Follow the irresistible Jason through sexual adventures unlike any you have ever read....

1 800 906-HUNK

THE connection for hot handfuls of eager guys! No credit card needed—so call now for access to the hottest party line available. Pick up bad boys from across the country! (Must be over 18.) Pick one up now.... $3.98 per min.

LARS EIGHNER
WHISPERED IN THE DARK
$5.95/286-8
A volume demonstrating Eighner's unique combination of strengths: poetic descriptive power, an unfailing ear for dialogue, and a finely tuned feeling for the nuances of male passion.

AMERICAN PRELUDE
$4.95/170-5
Eighner is widely recognized as one of our best, most exciting gay writers. He is also one of gay erotica's true masters—and *American Prelude* shows why. Wonderfully written, blisteringly hot tales of all-American lust.

B.M.O.C.
$4.95/3077-6
In a college town known as "the Athens of the Southwest," studs of every stripe are up all night—studying, naturally. Relive university life the way it was supposed to be, with a cast of handsome honor students majoring in Human Homosexuality.

DAVID LAURENTS, EDITOR
SOUTHERN COMFORT
$6.50/466-6
Editor David Laurents now unleashes a collection of tales focusing on the American South—reflecting not only Southern literary tradition, but the many contributions the region has made to the iconography of the American Male.

WANDERLUST:
HOMOEROTIC TALES OF TRAVEL
$5.95/395-3
A volume dedicated to the special pleasures of faraway places. Gay men have always had a special interest in travel—and not only for the scenic vistas. Wanderlust celebrates the freedom of the open road, and the allure of men who stray from the beaten path....

THE BADBOY BOOK OF EROTIC POETRY
$5.95/382-1
Over fifty of today's best poets. Erotic poetry has long been the problem child of the literary world—highly creative and provocative, but somehow too frank to be "literature." *The Badboy Book of Erotic Poetry* restores eros to its rightful place of honor in contemporary gay writing.

AARON TRAVIS
BIG SHOTS
$5.95/448-8
Two fierce tales in one electrifying volume. In *Beirut*, Travis tells the story of ultimate military power and erotic subjugation; *Kip*, Travis' hypersexed and sinister take on film noir, appears in unexpurgated form for the first time—including the final, overwhelming chapter.

EXPOSED
$4.95/126-8
A volume of shorter Travis tales, each providing a unique glimpse of the horny gay male in his natural environment! Cops, college jocks, ancient Romans—even Sherlock Holmes and his loyal Watson—cruise these pages, fresh from the throbbing pen of one of our hottest authors.

BEAST OF BURDEN
$4.95/105-5
Five ferocious tales from this contemporary master. Innocents surrender to the brutal sexual mastery of their superiors, as taboos are shattered and replaced with the unwritten rules of masculine conquest. Intense, extreme —and totally Travis.

IN THE BLOOD
$5.95/283-3
Written when Travis had just begun to explore the true power of the erotic imagination, these stories laid the groundwork for later masterpieces. Among the many rewarding rarities included in this special volume: "In the Blood"—a heart-pounding descent into sexual vampirism.

THE FLESH FABLES
$4.95/243-4
One of Travis' best collections. *The Flesh Fables* includes "Blue Light," his most famous story, as well as other masterpieces that established him as the erotic writer to watch. And watch carefully, because Travis always buries a surprise somewhere beneath his scorching detail....

SLAVES OF THE EMPIRE
$4.95/3054-7
"A wonderful mythic tale. Set against the backdrop of the exotic and powerful Roman Empire, this wonderfully written novel explores the timeless questions of light and dark in male sexuality. The locale may be the ancient world, but these are the slaves and masters of our time...."
—John Preston

MASQUERADE BOOKS

BOB VICKERY
SKIN DEEP
$4.95/265-5
So many varied beauties no one will go away unsatisfied. No tantalizing morsel of manflesh is overlooked—or left unexplored! Beauty may be only skin deep, but a handful of beautiful skin is a tempting proposition.

JR
FRENCH QUARTER NIGHTS
$5.95/337-6
Sensual snapshots of the many places where men get down and dirty—from the steamy French Quarter to the steam room at the old Everard baths. These are nights you'll wish would go on forever....

TOM BACCHUS
RAHM
$5.95/315-5
The imagination of Tom Bacchus brings to life an extraordinary assortment of characters, from the Father of Us All to the cowpoke next door, the early gay literati to rude, queercore mosh rats. No one is better than Bacchus at staking out sexual territory with a swagger and a sly grin.
BONE
$4.95/177-2
Queer musings from the pen of one of today's hottest young talents. A fresh outlook on fleshly indulgence yields more than a few pleasant surprises. Horny Tom Bacchus maps out the tricking ground of a new generation.

KEY LINCOLN
SUBMISSION HOLDS
$4.95/266-3
A bright young talent unleashes his first collection of gay erotica. From tough to tender, the men between these covers stop at nothing to get what they want. These sweat-soaked tales show just how bad boys can really get.

CALDWELL/EIGHNER
QSFX2
$5.95/278-7
The wickedest, wildest, other-worldliest yarns from two master storytellers—Clay Caldwell and Lars Eighner. Both eroticists take a trip to the furthest reaches of the sexual imagination, sending back ten stories proving that as much as things change, one thing will always remain the same....

CLAY CALDWELL
JOCK STUDS
$6.50/472-0
A collection of Caldwell's scalding tales of pumped bodies and raging libidos. Swimmers, runners, football players... whatever your sport might be, there's a man waiting for you in these pages. Waiting to peel off that uniform and claim his reward for a game well-played....

ASK OL' BUDDY
$5.95/346-5
Set in the underground SM world, Caldwell takes you on a journey of discovery—where men initiate one another into the secrets of the rawest sexual realm of all. And when each stud's initiation is complete, he takes his places among the masters—eager to take part in the training of another hungry soul...
STUD SHORTS
$5.95/320-1
"If anything, Caldwell's charm is more powerful, his nostalgia more poignant, the horniness he captures more sweetly, achingly acute than ever."
—Aaron Travis
A new collection of this legend's latest sex-fiction. With his customary candor, Caldwell tells all about cops, cadets, truckers, farmboys (and many more) in these dirty jewels.
TAILPIPE TRUCKER
$5.95/296-5
Trucker porn! In prose as free and unvarnished as a cross-country highway, Caldwell tells the truth about Trag and Curly—two men hot for the feeling of sweaty manflesh. Together, they pick up—and turn out—a couple of thrill-seeking punks.
SERVICE, STUD
$5.95/336-8
Another look at the gay future. The setting is the Los Angeles of a distant future. Here the all-male populace is divided between the served and the servants—guaranteeing the erotic satisfaction of all involved.

QUEERS LIKE US
$4.95/262-0
"Caldwell at his most charming." —Aaron Travis
For years the name Clay Caldwell has been synonymous with the hottest, most finely crafted gay tales available. Queers Like Us is one of his best: the story of a randy mailman's trek through a landscape of willing, available studs.
ALL-STUD
$4.95/104-7
This classic, sex-soaked tale takes place under the watchful eye of Number Ten: an omniscient figure who has decreed unabashed promiscuity as the law of his all-male land. One stud, however, takes it upon himself to challenge the social order, daring to fall in love.

CLAY CALDWELL AND AARON TRAVIS
TAG TEAM STUDS
$6.50/465-8
Thrilling tales from these two legendary eroticists. The wrestling world will never seem the same, once you've made your way through this assortment of sweaty, virile studs. But you'd better be wary—should one catch you off guard, you just might spend the rest of the night pinned to the mat....

BUY ANY 4 BOOKS & CHOOSE 1 ADDITIONAL BOOK, OF EQUAL OR LESSER VALUE, AS YOUR FREE GIFT

MASQUERADE BOOKS

LARRY TOWNSEND

LEATHER AD: M
$5.95/380-5
The first of this two-part classic. John's curious about what goes on between the leatherclad men he's fantasized about. He takes out a personal ad, and starts a journey of self-discovery that will leave no part of his life unchanged.

LEATHER AD: S
$5.95/407-0
The tale continues—this time told from a Top's perspective. A simple ad generates many responses, and one man finds himself in the enviable position of putting these study applicants through their paces....

1 900 745-HUNG

Hardcore phone action for real men. A scorching assembly of studs is waiting for your call—and eager to give you the headtrip of your life! Totally live, guaranteed one-on-one encounters. (Must be over 18.) No credit card needed. $3.98 per minute.

BEWARE THE GOD WHO SMILES
$5.95/321-X
Two lusty young Americans are transported to ancient Egypt—where they are embroiled in regional warfare and taken as slaves by barbarians. The key to escape from brutal bondage lies in their own rampant libidos.

2069 TRILOGY
(This one-volume collection only $6.95) 244-2
For the first time, this early science-fiction trilogy appears in one volume! Set in a future world, the *2069 Trilogy* includes the tight plotting and shameless all-male sex pleasure that established him as one of erotica's first masters.

MIND MASTER
$4.95/209-4
Who better to explore the territory of erotic dominance than an author who helped define the genre—and knows that ultimate mastery always transcends the physical. Another unrelenting Townsend tale.

THE LONG LEATHER CORD
$4.95/201-9
Chuck's stepfather never lacks money or clandestine male visitors with whom he enacts intense sexual rituals. As Chuck comes to terms with his own desires, he begins to unravel the mystery behind his stepfather's secret life.

MAN SWORD
$4.95/188-8
The très gai tale of France's King Henri III, who was unimaginably spoiled by his mother—the infamous Catherine de Medici—and groomed from a young age to assume the throne of France. He encounters enough sexual schemers and politicos to alter one's picture of history forever!

THE FAUSTUS CONTRACT
$4.95/167-5
Two attractive young men desperately need $1000. Will do anything. Travel OK. Danger OK. Call anytime... Two cocky young hustlers get more than they bargained for in this story of lust and its discontents.

THE GAY ADVENTURES OF CAPTAIN GOOSE
$4.95/169-1
Hot young Jerome Gander is sentenced to serve aboard the *H.M.S. Faerigold*—a ship manned by the most hardened, unrepentant criminals. In no time, Gander becomes well-versed in the ways of horny men at sea, and the *Faerigold* becomes the most notorious vessel to ever set sail.

CHAINS
$4.95/158-6
Picking up street punks has always been risky, but in Larry Townsend's classic *Chains*, it sets off a string of events that must be read to be believed.

KISS OF LEATHER
$4.95/161-6
A look at the acts and attitudes of an earlier generation of gay leathermen, Kiss of Leather is full to bursting with the gritty, raw action that has distinguished Townsend's work for years. Sensual pain and pleasure mix in this tightly plotted tale.

RUN, LITTLE LEATHER BOY
$4.95/143-8
One young man's sexual awakening. A chronic underachiever, Wayne seems to be going nowhere fast. He finds himself bored with the everyday—and drawn to the masculine intensity of a dark and mysterious sexual underground, where he soon finds many goals worth pursuing....

RUN NO MORE
$4.95/152-7
The continuation of Larry Townsend's legendary *Run, Little Leather Boy*. This volume follows the further adventures of Townsend's leatherclad narrator as he travels every sexual byway available to the S/M male.

THE SCORPIUS EQUATION
$4.95/119-5
The story of a man caught between the demands of two galactic empires. Our randy hero must match wits—and more—with the incredible forces that rule his world. One o gay erotica's first sci-fi sex tales—and still one of the best.

THE SEXUAL ADVENTURES OF SHERLOCK HOLMES
$4.95/3097-0
A scandalously sexy take on this legendary sleuth. "A Study in Scarlet" is transformed to expose Mrs. Hudson as a man in drag, the Diogenes Club as an S/M arena, and clues only the redoubtable—and very horny—Sherlock Holmes could piece together. A baffling tale of sex and mystery.

DONALD VINING

CABIN FEVER AND OTHER STORIES
$5.95/338-4
Eighteen blistering stories in celebration of the most intimate of male bonding. Time after time, Donald Vining's men succumb to nature, and reaffirm both love and lust in modern gay life.

"Demonstrates the wisdom experience combined with insight and optimism can create."
—*Bay Area Reporter*

MASQUERADE BOOKS

DEREK ADAMS

PRISONER OF DESIRE
$6.50/439-9
Scalding fiction from one of Badboy's most popular authors. The creator of horny P.I. Miles Diamond returns with this volume bursting with red-blooded, sweat-soaked excursions through the modern gay libido.

THE MARK OF THE WOLF
$5.95/361-9
The past comes back to haunt one well-off stud, whose unslakeable thirsts lead him into the arms of many men—and the midst of a perilous mystery.

MY DOUBLE LIFE
$5.95/314-7
Every man leads a double life, dividing his hours between the mundanities of the day and the outrageous pursuits of the night. The creator of sexy P.I. Miles Diamond shines a little light on the wicked things men do when no one's looking.

HEAT WAVE
$4.95/159-4
"His body was draped in baggy clothes, but there was hardly any doubt that they covered anything less than perfection.... His slacks were cinched tight around a narrow waist, and the rise of flesh pushing against the thin fabric promised a firm, melon-shaped ass...."

MILES DIAMOND AND THE DEMON OF DEATH
$4.95/251-5
Derek Adams' gay gumshoe returns for further adventures. Miles always find himself in the stickiest situations—with any stud whose path he crosses! His adventures with "The Demon of Death" promise another carnal carnival.

THE ADVENTURES OF MILES DIAMOND
$4.95/118-7
Derek Adams' take on the classic American archetype of the hardboiled private eye. "The Case of the Missing Twin" promises to be a most rewarding case, packed as it is with randy studs. Miles sets about uncovering all as he tracks down the elusive and delectable Daniel Travis.

KELVIN BELIELE

IF THE SHOE FITS
$4.95/223-X
An essential and winning volume of tales exploring a world where randy boys can't help but do what comes naturally—as often as possible! Sweaty male bodies grapple in pleasure, proving the old adage: if the shoe fits, one might as well slip right in....

JAMES MEDLEY

THE REVOLUTIONARY & OTHER STORIES
$6.50/417-8
Billy, the son of the station chief of the American Embassy in Guatemala, is kidnapped and held for ransom. Frightened at first, Billy gradually develops an unimaginably close relationship with Juan, the revolutionary assigned to guard him.

HUCK AND BILLY
$4.95/245-0
Young love is always the sweetest, always the most sorrowful. Young lust, on the other hand, knows no bounds—and is often the hottest of one's life! Huck and Billy explore the desires that course through their young male bodies, determined to plumb the lusty depths of passion.

FLEDERMAUS

FLEDERFICTION: STORIES OF MEN AND TORTURE
$5.95/355-4
Fifteen blistering paeans to men and their suffering. Fledermaus unleashes his most thrilling tales of punishment in this special volume designed with Badboy readers in mind.

VICTOR TERRY

MASTERS
$6.50/418-6
A powerhouse volume of boot-wearing, whip-wielding, bone-crunching bruisers who've got what it takes to make a grown man grovel. Between these covers lurk the most demanding of men—the imperious few to whom so many humbly offer themselves....

SM/SD
$6.50/406-2
Set around a South Dakota town called Prairie, these tales offer compelling evidence that the real rough stuff can still be found where men roam free of the restraints of "polite" society—and take what they want despite all rules.

WHiPs
$4.95/254-X
Cruising for a hot man? You'd better be, because one way or another, these WHiPs—officers of the Wyoming Highway Patrol—are gonna pull you over for a little impromptu interrogation....

MAX EXANDER

DEEDS OF THE NIGHT: TALES OF EROS AND PASSION
$5.95/348-1
MAXimum porn! Exander's a writer who's seen it all—and is more than happy to describe every inch of it in pulsating detail. A whirlwind tour of the hypermasculine libido.

LEATHERSEX
$4.95/210-8
Hard-hitting tales from merciless Max Exander. This time he focuses on the leatherclad lust that draws together only the most willing and talented of tops and bottoms—for an all-out orgy of limitless surrender and control....

MANSEX
$4.95/160-8
"Mark was the classic leatherman: a huge, dark stud in chaps, with a big black moustache, hairy chest and enormous muscles. Exactly the kind of men Todd liked—strong, hunky, masculine, ready to take control...."

BUY ANY 4 BOOKS & CHOOSE 1 ADDITIONAL BOOK, OF EQUAL OR LESSER VALUE, AS YOUR FREE GIFT

MASQUERADE BOOKS

TOM CAFFREY
TALES FROM THE MEN'S ROOM
$5.95/364-3
From shameless cops on the beat to shy studs on stage, Caffrey explores male lust at its most elemental and arousing. And if there's a lesson to be learned, it's that the Men's Room is less a place than a state of mind—one that every man finds himself in, day after day....

HITTING HOME
$4.95/222-1
Titillating and compelling, the stories in *Hitting Home* make a strong case for there being only one thing on a man's mind.

TORSTEN BARRING
GUY TRAYNOR
$6.50/414-3
Some call Guy Traynor a theatrical genius; others say he was a madman. All anyone knows for certain is that his productions were the result of blood, sweat and tears. Never have artists suffered so much for their craft!

PRISONERS OF TORQUEMADA
$5.95/252-3
Another volume sure to push you over the edge. How cruel is the "therapy" practiced at Casa Torquemada? Barring is just the writer to evoke such steamy sexual malevolence.

SHADOWMAN
$4.95/178-0
From spoiled Southern aristocrats to randy youths sowing wild oats at the local picture show, Barring's imagination works overtime in these vignettes of homolust—past, present and future.

PETER THORNWELL
$4.95/149-7
Follow the exploits of Peter Thornwell as he goes from misspent youth to scandalous stardom, all thanks to an insatiable libido and love for the lash.

THE SWITCH
$4.95/3061-X
Sometimes a man needs a good whipping, and *The Switch* certainly makes a case! Packed with hot studs and unrelenting passions.

BERT McKENZIE
FRINGE BENEFITS
$5.95/354-6
From the pen of a widely published short story writer comes a volume of highly immodest tales. Not afraid of getting down and dirty, McKenzie produces some of today's most visceral sextales.

SONNY FORD
REUNION IN FLORENCE
$4.95/3070-9
Follow Adrian and Tristan on a sexual odyssey that takes in all ports known to ancient man. From lustful turks to insatiable Mamluks, these two have much more than their hands full!

ROGER HARMAN
FIRST PERSON
$4.95/179-9
A highly personal collection. Each story takes the form of a confessional—told by men who've got plenty to confess! From the "first time ever" to firsts of different kinds, *First Person* tells truths too hot to be purely fiction.

J. A. GUERRA, ED.
SLOW BURN
$4.95/3042-3
Welcome to the Body Shoppe! Torsos get lean and hard, pecs widen, and stomachs ripple in these sexy stories of the power and perils of physical perfection.

DAVE KINNICK
SORRY I ASKED
$4.95/3090-3
Unexpurgated interviews with gay porn's rank and file. Get personal with the men behind (and under) the "stars," and discover the hot truth about the porn business.

SEAN MARTIN
SCRAPBOOK
$4.95/224-8
From the creator of Doc and Raider comes this hot collection of life's horniest moments—all involving studs sure to set your pulse racing! A brilliantly sexy volume.

CARO SOLES & STAN TAL, EDITORS
BIZARRE DREAMS
$4.95/187-X
An anthology of stirring voices dedicated to exploring the dark side of human fantasy. *Bizarre Dreams* brings together the most talented practitioners of "dark fantasy," the most forbidden sexual realm of all.

CHRISTOPHER MORGAN
STEAM GAUGE
$6.50/473-9
This volume abounds in manly men doing what they do best—to, with, or for any hot stud who crosses their paths. Frequently published to acclaim in the gay press, Christopher Morgan puts a fresh, contemporary spin on the very oldest of urges.

THE SPORTSMEN
$5.95/385-6
A collection of super-hot stories dedicated to the all-American athlete. Here are enough tales of carnal grand slams, sexy interceptions and highly personal bests to satisfy the hungers of the most ardent sports fan. These writers know just the type of guys that make up every red-blooded male's starting line-up....

MUSCLE BOUND
$4.95/3028-8
In the New York City bodybuilding scene, country boy Tommy joins forces with sexy Will Rodriguez in a battle of wits and biceps at the hottest gym in town, where the weak are bound and crushed by iron-pumping gods.

MASQUERADE BOOKS

MICHAEL LOWENTHAL, ED.
THE BADBOY EROTIC LIBRARY VOLUME I
$4.95/190-X
Excerpts from *A Secret Life, Imre, Sins of the Cities of the Plain, Teleny* and others demonstrate the uncanny gift for portraying sex between men that led to many of these titles being banned upon publication.
THE BADBOY EROTIC LIBRARY VOLUME II
$4.95/211-6
This time, selections are taken from *Mike and Me* and *Muscle Bound, Men at Work, Badboy Fantasies,* and *Slowburn*.

ERIC BOYD
MIKE AND ME
$5.95/419-4
Mike joined the gym squad to bulk up on muscle. Little did he know he'd be turning on every sexy muscle jock in Minnesota! Hard bodies collide in a series of workouts designed to generate a whole lot more than rips and cuts.
MIKE AND THE MARINES
$6.50/497-6
Mike takes on America's most elite corps of studs—running into more than a few good men! Join in on the never-ending sexual escapades of this singularly lustful platoon!

ANONYMOUS
A SECRET LIFE
$4.95/3017-2
Meet Master Charles: only eighteen, and quite innocent, until his arrival at the Sir Percival's Royal Academy, where the daily lessons are supplemented with a crash course in pure, sweet sexual heat!
SINS OF THE CITIES OF THE PLAIN
$5.95/322-8
Indulge yourself in the scorching memoirs of young man-about-town Jack Saul. With his shocking dalliances with the lords and "ladies" of British high society, Jack's positively sinful escapades grow wilder with every chapter!
IMRE
$4.95/3019-9
What dark secrets, what fiery passions lay hidden behind strikingly beautiful Lieutenant Imre's emerald eyes? An extraordinary lost classic of fantasy, obsession, gay erotic desire, and romance in a small European town on the eve of WWI.
TELENY
$4.95/3020-2
Often attributed to Oscar Wilde. A yung man dedicates himself to a succession of forbidden pleasures, but instead finds love and tragedy when he becomes embroiled in a cult devoted to fulfilling only the very darkest of fantasies.

HARD CANDY

KEVIN KILLIAN
ARCTIC SUMMER
$6.95/514-X
Acclaimed author Kevin Killian's latest novel examines the many secrets lying beneath the placid exterior of America in the '50s. With the story of Liam Reilly—a young gay man of considerable means and numerous secrets—Killian exposes the contradictions of the American Dream.

STAN LEVENTHAL
BARBIE IN BONDAGE
$6.95/415-1
Widely regarded as one of the most clear-eyed interpreters of big city gay male life, Leventhal here provides a series of explorations of love and desire between men.
SKYDIVING ON CHRISTOPHER STREET
$6.95/287-6
"Positively addictive." —Dennis Cooper
Aside from a hateful job, a hateful apartment, a hateful world and an increasingly hateful lover, life seems, well, all right for the protagonist of Stan Leventhal's latest novel. Having already lost most of his friends to AIDS, how could things get any worse? An insightful tale of contemporary urban gay life.

PATRICK MOORE
IOWA
$6.95/423-2
"Moore is the Tennessee Williams of the nineties—profound intimacy freed in a compelling narrative."
—Karen Finley
"Fresh and shiny and relevant to our time. *Iowa* is full of terrific characters etched in acid-sharp prose, soaked through with just enough ambivalence to make it thoroughly romantic." —Felice Picano
A stunning novel about one gay man's journey into adulthood, and the roads that bring him home again.

PAUL T. ROGERS
SAUL'S BOOK
$7.95/462-3
Winner of the Editors' Book Award
"Exudes an almost narcotic power.... A masterpiece." —Village Voice Literary Supplement
"A first novel of considerable power... Sinbad the Sailor, thanks to the sympathetic imagination of Paul T. Rogers, speaks to us all." —New York Times Book Review
The story of a Times Square hustler called Sinbad the Sailor and Saul, a brilliant, self-destructive, alcoholic, thoroughly dominating character who may be the only love Sinbad will ever know. A stunning first novel—and an eerie epitaph for the author, who died tragically in the very milieu he portrayed in his fiction.

BUY ANY 4 BOOKS & CHOOSE 1 ADDITIONAL BOOK, OF EQUAL OR LESSER VALUE, AS YOUR FREE GIFT

MASQUERADE BOOKS

WALTER R. HOLLAND
THE MARCH
$6.95/429-1
A moving testament to the power of friendship during even the worst of times. Beginning on a hot summer night in 1980, *The March* revolves around a circle of young gay men, and the many others their lives touch. Over time, each character changes in unexpected ways; lives and loves come together and fall apart, as society itself is horribly altered by the onslaught of AIDS.

RED JORDAN AROBATEAU
LUCY AND MICKEY
$6.95/311-2
The story of Mickey—an uncompromising butch—and her long affair with Lucy, the femme she loves.
"A necessary reminder to all who blissfully—some may say ignorantly—ride the wave of lesbian chic into the mainstream." —Heather Findlay

DIRTY PICTURES
$5.95/345-7
"Red Jordan Arobateau is the Thomas Wolfe of lesbian literature... She's a natural—raw talent that is seething, passionate, hard, remarkable."
—Lillian Faderman, editor of *Chloe Plus Olivia*
Dirty Pictures is the story of a lonely butch tending bar—and the femme she finally calls her own.

DONALD VINING
A GAY DIARY
$8.95/451-8
Donald Vining's *Diary* portrays a long-vanished age and the lifestyle of a gay generation all too frequently forgotten.
"*A Gay Diary* is, unquestionably, the richest historical document of gay male life in the United States that I have ever encountered.... It illuminates a critical period in gay male American history."
—*Body Politic*

LARS EIGHNER
GAY COSMOS
$6.95/236-1
A title sure to appeal not only to Eighner's gay fans, but the many converts who first encountered his moving nonfiction work. Praised by the press, *Gay Cosmos* is an important contribution to the area of Gay and Lesbian Studies.

FELICE PICANO
THE LURE
$6.95/398-8
"The subject matter, plus the authenticity of Picano's research are, combined, explosive. Felice Picano is one hell of a writer." —Stephen King
After witnessing a brutal murder, Noel is recruited by the police, to assist as a lure for the killer. Undercover, he moves deep into the freneticism of Manhattan's gay highlife—where he gradually becomes aware of the darker forces at work in his life. In addition to the mystery behind his mission, he begins to recognize changes: in his relationships with the men around him, in himself...

AMBIDEXTROUS
$6.95/275-2
"Makes us remember what it feels like to be a child..." —*The Advocate*
Picano's first "memoir in the form of a novel" tells all: home life, school face-offs, the ingenuous sophistications of his first sexual steps. In three years' time, he's had his first gay fling—and is on his way to becoming the widely praised writer he is today.

MEN WHO LOVED ME
$6.95/274-4
"Zesty...spiked with adventure and romance...a distinguished and humorous portrait of a vanished age." —*Publishers Weekly*
In 1966, Picano abandoned New York, determined to find true love in Europe. Upon returning, he plunges into the city's thriving gay community of the 1970s.

WILLIAM TALSMAN
THE GAUDY IMAGE
$6.95/263-9
"To read *The Gaudy Image* now...it is to see firsthand the very issues of identity and positionality with which gay men were struggling in the decades before Stonewall. For what Talsman is dealing with...is the very question of how we conceive ourselves gay."
—from the introduction by Michael Bronski

ROSEBUD

THE ROSEBUD READER
$5.95/319-9
Rosebud has contributed greatly to the burgeoning genre of lesbian erotica—to the point that our authors are among the hottest and most closely watched names in lesbian and gay publishing. Here are the finest moments from Rosebud's contemporary classics.

LESLIE CAMERON
WHISPER OF FANS
$6.50/542-5
"Just looking into her eyes, she felt that she knew a lot about this woman. She could see strength, boldness, a fresh sense of aliveness that rocked her to the core. In turn she felt open, revealed under the woman's gaze—all her secrets already told. No need of shame or artifice...." A fresh tale of passion between women, from one of lesbian erotica's up-and-coming authors.

RACHEL PEREZ
ODD WOMEN
$6.50/526-3
These women are sexy, smart, tough—some even say odd. But who cares, when their combined ass-ets are so sweet! An assortment of Sapphic sirens proves once and for all that comely ladies come best in pairs. One of our best-selling girl/girl titles.

MASQUERADE BOOKS

RANDY TUROFF
LUST NEVER SLEEPS
$6.50/475-5
A rich volume of highly erotic, powerfully real fiction from the editor of *Lesbian Words*. Randy Turoff depicts a circle of modern women connected through the bonds of love, friendship, ambition, and lust with accuracy and compassion. Moving, tough, yet undeniably true, Turoff's stories create a stirring portrait of contemporary lesbian life.

RED JORDAN AROBATEAU
ROUGH TRADE
$6.50/470-4
Famous for her unflinching portrayal of lower-class dyke life and love, Arobateau outdoes herself with these tales of butch/femme affairs and unrelenting passions. Unapologetic and distinctly non-homogenized, *Rough Trade* is a must for all fans of challenging lesbian literature.

BOYS NIGHT OUT
$6.50/463-1
A *Red*-hot volume of short fiction from this lesbian literary sensation. As always, Arobateau takes a good hard look at the lives of everyday women, noting well the struggles and triumphs each woman experiences.

ALISON TYLER
VENUS ONLINE
$6.50/521-2
Lovely Alexa spends her days in a boring bank job, saving her energies for her nocturnal pursuits. At night, Alexa goes online, living out virtual adventures that become more real with each session. Soon Alexa—aka Venus—feels her erotic imagination growing beyond anything she could have imagined.

DARK ROOM: AN ONLINE ADVENTURE
$6.50/455-0
Dani, a successful photographer, can't bring herself to face the death of her lover, Kate. Determined to keep the memory of her lover alive, Dani goes online under Kate's screen alias—and begins to uncover the truth behind the crime that has torn her world apart.

BLUE SKY SIDEWAYS & OTHER STORIES
$6.50/394-5
A variety of women, and their many breathtaking experiences with lovers, friends—and even the occasional sexy stranger. From blossoming young beauties to fearless vixens, Tyler finds the sexy pleasures of everyday life.

DIAL "L" FOR LOVELESS
$5.95/386-4
Meet Katrina Loveless—a private eye talented enough to give Sam Spade a run for his money. In her first case, Katrina investigates a murder implicating a host of society's darlings. Loveless untangles the mess—while working herself into a variety of highly compromising knots with the many lovelies who cross her path!

THE VIRGIN
$5.95/379-1
Veronica answers a personal ad in the "Women Seeking Women" category—and discovers a whole sensual world she never knew existed! And she never dreamed she'd be prized as a virgin all over again, by someone who would deflower her with a passion no man could ever show....

K. T. BUTLER
TOOLS OF THE TRADE
$5.95/420-8
A sparkling mix of lesbian erotica and humor. An encounter with ice cream, cappuccino and chocolate cake; an affair with a complete stranger; a pair of faulty handcuffs; and love on a drafting table. Seventeen tales.

LOVECHILD
GAG
$5.95/369-4
From New York's poetry scene comes this explosive volume of work from one of the bravest, most cutting young writers you'll ever encounter. The poems in *Gag* take on American hypocrisy with uncommon energy, and announce Lovechild as a writer of unforgettable rage.

ELIZABETH OLIVER
PAGAN DREAMS
$5.95/295-7
Cassidy and Samantha plan a vacation at a secluded bed-and-breakfast, hoping for a little personal time alone. Their hostess, however, has different plans. The lovers are plunged into a world of dungeons and pagan rites, as Anastasia steals Samantha for her own.

SUSAN ANDERS
CITY OF WOMEN
$5.95/375-9
Stories dedicated to women and the passions that draw them together. Designed strictly for the sensual pleasure of women, these tales are set to ignite flames of passion from coast to coast.

PINK CHAMPAGNE
$5.95/282-5
Tasty, torrid tales of butch/femme couplings. Tough as nails or soft as silk, these women seek out their antitheses, intent on working out the details of their own personal theory of difference.

ANONYMOUS
LAVENDER ROSE
$4.95/208-6
A thrilling collection of some of the earliest lesbian writings. From the writings of Sappho, Queen of the island Lesbos, to the turn-of-the-century *Black Book of Lesbianism*; from *Tips to Maidens* to *Crimson Hairs*, a recent lesbian saga—here are the great but little-known lesbian writings and revelations.

BUY ANY 4 BOOKS & CHOOSE 1 ADDITIONAL BOOK, OF EQUAL OR LESSER VALUE, AS YOUR FREE GIFT

MASQUERADE BOOKS

LAURA ANTONIOU, EDITOR
LEATHERWOMEN
$4.95/3095-4
These fantasies, from the pens of new or emerging authors, break every rule imposed on women's fantasies. The hottest stories from some of today's most outrageous writers make this an unforgettable volume.

LEATHERWOMEN II
$4.95/229-9
Another groundbreaking volume of writing from women on the edge, sure to ignite libidinal flames in any reader. Leave taboos behind, because these Leatherwomen know no limits....

AARONA GRIFFIN
PASSAGE AND OTHER STORIES
$4.95/3057-1
An S/M romance. Lovely Nina is frightened by her lesbian passions, until she finds herself infatuated with a woman she spots at a local café. One night Nina follows her, and finds herself enmeshed in an endless maze leading to a world where women test the edges of sexuality and power.

VALENTINA CILESCU
MY LADY'S PLEASURE:
MISTRESS WITH A MAID, VOLUME I
$5.95/412-7
Claudia Dungarrow, a lovely, powerful, but mysterious professor, attempts to seduce virginal Elizabeth Stanbridge, setting off a chain of events that eventually ruins her career. Claudia vows revenge—and makes her foes pay deliciously....

DARK VENUS:
MISTRESS WITH A MAID, VOLUME 2
$6.50/481-X
Claudia Dungarrow's quest for ultimate erotic dominance continues in this scalding second volume! How many maidens will fall prey to her insatiable appetite?

BODY AND SOUL:
MISTRESS WITH A MAID, VOLUME 3
$6.50/515-8
The blistering conclusion! Dr. Claudia Dungarrow returns for yet another tour of depravity, subjugating every maiden in sight to her ruthless sexual whims. But, as stunning as Claudia is, she has yet to hold Elizabeth Stanbridge in complete submission. Will she ever?

THE ROSEBUD SUTRA
$4.95/242-6
"Women are hardly ever known in their true light, though they may love others, or become indifferent towards them, may give them delight, or abandon them, or may extract from them all the wealth that they possess." So says *The Rosebud Sutra*—a volume promising women's secrets.

MISTRESS MINE
$6.50/502-6
Sophia Cranleigh sits in prison, accused of authoring the "obscene" *Mistress Mine*. What she has done, however, is merely chronicle the events of her life. For Sophia has led no ordinary life, but has slaved and suffered—deliciously—under the hand of the notorious Mistress Malin.

LINDSAY WELSH
SECOND SIGHT
$6.50/507-7
The debut of Dana Steele—lesbian superhero! During an attack by a gang of homophobic youths, Dana is thrown onto subway tracks—touching the deadly third rail. Miraculously, she survives, and finds herself endowed with superhuman powers. Dana decides to devote her powers to the protection of her lesbian sisters, no matter how daunting the danger they face.

NASTY PERSUASIONS
$6.50/436-4
A hot peek into the behind-the-scenes operations of Rough Trade—one of the world's most famous lesbian clubs. Join Slash, Ramone, Cherry and many others as they bring one another to the height of torturous ecstasy—all in the name of keeping Rough Trade the premier name in sexy entertainment for women.

MILITARY SECRETS
$5.95/397-X
Colonel Candice Sproule heads a highly specialized boot camp. Assisted by three dominatrix sergeants, Col. Sproule takes on the talented submissives sent to her by secret military contacts. Then along comes Jesse—whose pleasure in being served matches the Colonel's own. This horny new recruit sets off fireworks in the barracks—and beyond....

ROMANTIC ENCOUNTERS
$5.95/359-7
Beautiful Julie, the most powerful editor of romance novels in the industry, spends her days igniting women's passions through books—and her nights fulfilling those needs with a variety of licentious lovers. Finally, through a sizzling series of coincidences, Julie's two worlds come together explosively!

THE BEST OF LINDSAY WELSH
$5.95/368-6
A collection of this popular writer's best work. Lindsay Welsh was one of Rosebud's early bestsellers, and remains one of our most popular writers. This sampler is set to introduce some of the hottest lesbian erotica to a wider audience.

NECESSARY EVIL
$5.95/277-9
What's a girl to do? When her Mistress proves too systematic, too by-the-book, one lovely submissive takes the ultimate chance—choosing and creating a Mistress who'll fulfill her heart's desire. Little did she know how difficult it would be—and, in the end, rewarding....

A VICTORIAN ROMANCE
$5.95/365-1
Lust-letters from the road. A young Englishwoman realizes her dream—a trip abroad under the guidance of her eccentric maiden aunt. Soon, the young but blossoming Elaine comes to discover her own sexual talents, as a hot-blooded Parisian named Madeleine takes her Sapphic education in hand. Desires are soon fully unleashed, as the two explore one another's young bodies without a care for convention....

MASQUERADE BOOKS

A CIRCLE OF FRIENDS
$4.95/250-7
The story of a remarkable group of women. The women pair off to explore all the possibilities of lesbian passion, until finally it seems that there is nothing—and no one—they have not dabbled in.

BAD HABITS
$5.95/446-1
What does one do with a poorly trained slave? Break her of her bad habits, of course! The story of the ultimate finishing school, *Bad Habits* was an immediate favorite with women nationwide, and remains an incredible best-seller.

"Talk about passing the wet test!... If you like hot, lesbian erotica, run—don't walk—and pick up a copy of *Bad Habits*." —Lambda Book Report

ANNABELLE BARKER
MOROCCO
$6.50/541-7
A luscious young woman stands to inherit a fortune—if she can only withstand the ministrations of her cruel guardian until her twentieth birthday. With two months left, Lila makes a bold bid for freedom, only to find that liberty has its own excruciating and delicious price....

A.L. REINE
DISTANT LOVE & OTHER STORIES
$4.95/3056-3
In the title story, Leah Michaels and her lover, Ranelle, have had four years of blissful, smoldering passion together. When Ranelle is out of town, Leah records an audio "Valentine:" a cassette filled with erotic reminiscences....

A RICHARD KASAK BOOK

SIMON LeVAY
ALBRICK'S GOLD
$20.95/518-2/Hardcover
From the man behind the controversial "gay brain" studies comes a chilling tale of medical experimentation run amok. LeVay—a lightning rod for controversy since the publication of *The Sexual Brain*—has fashioned a classic medical thriller from today's cutting-edge science.

SHAR REDNOUR, EDITOR
VIRGIN TERRITORY 2
$12.95/506-9
The follow-up volume to the groundbreaking *Virgin Territory* includes many essays inspired by the earlier volume's success. Focusing on the many "firsts" of a woman's erotic life, *Virgin Territory 2* provides one of the sole outlets for serious discussion of the myriad possibilities available to and chosen by many contemporary lesbians. Some of today's best writers 'fess up about the thrill of the first time.

VIRGIN TERRITORY
$12.95/457-7
An anthology of writing by women about their first-time erotic experiences with other women. From the ecstasies of awakening dykes to the sometimes awkward pleasures of sexual experimentation on the edge, each of these true stories reveals a different, radical perspective on one of the most traditional subjects around: virginity.

MICHAEL FORD, EDITOR
ONCE UPON A TIME: EROTIC FAIRY TALES FOR WOMEN
$12.95/449-6
How relevant to contemporary lesbians are the lessons of these age-old tales? Some of the biggest names in contemporary lesbian literature retell their favorite fairy tales, adding their own surprising—and sexy—twists. *Once Upon a Time* is sure to be one of contemporary lesbian literature's classic collections.

HAPPILY EVER AFTER: EROTIC FAIRY TALES FOR MEN
$12.95/450-X
A hefty volume of bedtime stories Mother Goose never thought to write down. Adapting some of childhood's most beloved tales for the adult gay reader, the contributors to *Happily Ever After* dig up the subtext of these hitherto "innocent" diversions—adding some surprises of their own along the way. Some of contemporary gay literature's biggest names are included in this special volume.

MICHAEL BRONSKI, EDITOR
TAKING LIBERTIES: GAY MEN'S ESSAYS ON POLITICS, CULTURE AND SEX
$12.95/456-9
"Offers undeniable proof of a heady, sophisticated, diverse new culture of gay intellectual debate. I cannot recommend it too highly."—Christopher Bram
A collection of some of the most divergent views on the state of contemporary gay male culture published in recent years. Michael Bronski here presents some of the community's foremost essayists weighing in on such slippery topics as outing, masculine identity, pornography, the pedophile movement, political strategy—and much more.

FLASHPOINT: GAY MALE SEXUAL WRITING
$12.95/424-0
A collection of the most provocative testaments to gay eros. Michael Bronski presents over twenty of the genre's best writers, exploring areas such as Enlightenment, True Life Adventures and more. Accompanied by Bronski's insightful analysis, each story illustrates the many approaches to sexuality used by today's gay writers. *Flashpoint* is sure to be one of the most talked about and influential volumes ever dedicated to the exploration of gay sexuality. Includes work by Christopher Bram, Samuel Delany, Aaron Travis, and many others.

BUY ANY 4 BOOKS & CHOOSE 1 ADDITIONAL BOOK, OF EQUAL OR LESSER VALUE, AS YOUR FREE GIFT

MASQUERADE BOOKS

HEATHER FINDLAY, EDITOR
A MOVEMENT OF EROS:
25 YEARS OF LESBIAN EROTICA
$12.95/421-6

One of the most scintillating overviews of lesbian erotic writing ever published. Heather Findlay has assembled a roster of stellar talents, each represented by their best work. Tracing the course of the genre from its pre-Stonewall roots to its current renaissance, Findlay examines each piece, placing it within the context of lesbian community and politics.

CHARLES HENRI FORD & PARKER TYLER
THE YOUNG AND EVIL
$12.95/431-3

"*The Young and Evil* creates [its] generation as *This Side of Paradise* by Fitzgerald created his generation." —Gertrude Stein

Originally published in 1933, *The Young and Evil* was an immediate sensation due to its unprecedented portrayal of young gay artists living in New York's notorious Greenwich Village. From drag balls to bohemian flats, these characters followed love and art wherever it led them—with a frankness that had the novel banned for many years.

BARRY HOFFMAN, EDITOR
THE BEST OF GAUNTLET
$12.95/202-7

Gauntlet has, with its semi-annual issues, always publishing the widest possible range of opinions, in the interest of challenging public opinion. The most provocative articles have been gathered by editor-in-chief Barry Hoffman, to make *The Best of Gauntlet* a riveting exploration of American society's limits.

MICHAEL ROWE
WRITING BELOW THE BELT:
CONVERSATIONS WITH EROTIC AUTHORS
$19.95/363-5

"An in-depth and enlightening tour of society's love/hate relationship with sex, morality, and censorship." —*James White Review*

Journalist Michael Rowe interviewed the best erotic writers and presents the collected wisdom in *Writing Below the Belt*. Rowe speaks frankly with cult favorites such as Pat Califia, crossover success stories like John Preston, and up-and-comers Michael Lowenthal and Will Leber. A chronicle of the insights of this genre's most renowned practitioners.

LARRY TOWNSEND
ASK LARRY
$12.95/289-2

One of the leather community's most respected scribes here presents the best of his advice to leathermen. Starting just before the onslaught of AIDS, Townsend wrote the "Leather Notebook" column for *Drummer* magazine. Now, readers can avail themselves of Townsend's collected wisdom, as well as the author's contemporary commentary—a careful consideration of the way life has changed in the AIDS era. No man worth his leathers can afford to miss this volume of sage advice.

MICHAEL LASSELL
THE HARD WAY
$12.95/231-0

"Lassell is a master of the necessary word. In an age of tepid and whining verse, his bawdy and bittersweet songs are like a plunge in cold champagne."
—Paul Monette

The first collection of renowned gay writer Michael Lassell's poetry, fiction and essays. As much a chronicle of post-Stonewall gay life as a compendium of a remarkable writer's work.

AMARANTHA KNIGHT, EDITOR
LOVE BITES
$12.95/234-5

A volume of tales dedicated to legend's sexiest demon—the Vampire. Not only the finest collection of erotic horror available—but a virtual who's who of promising new talent. A must-read for fans of both the horror and erotic genres.

RANDY TUROFF, EDITOR
LESBIAN WORDS: STATE OF THE ART
$10.95/340-6

"This is a terrific book that should be on every thinking lesbian's bookshelf." —Nisa Donnelly

One of the widest assortments of lesbian nonfiction writing in one revealing volume. Dorothy Allison, Jewelle Gomez, Judy Grahn, Eileen Myles, Robin Podolsky and many others are represented by some of their best work, looking at not only the current fashionability the media has brought to the lesbian "image," but considerations of the lesbian past via historical inquiry and personal recollections. A must for all interested in the state of the lesbian community.

ASSOTTO SAINT
SPELLS OF A VOODOO DOLL
$12.95/393-7

"Angelic and brazen." —Jewelle Gomez

A fierce, spellbinding collection of the poetry, lyrics, essays and performance texts of Assotto Saint—one of the most important voices in the renaissance of black gay writing. Saint, aka Yves François Lubin, was the editor of two seminal anthologies: 1991 Lambda Literary Book Award winner, *The Road Before Us: 100 Gay Black Poets* and *Here to Dare: 10 Gay Black Poets*. He was also the author of two books of poetry, *Stations* and *Wishing for Wings*.

WILLIAM CARNEY
THE REAL THING
$10.95/280-9

"Carney gives us a good look at the mores and lifestyle of the first generation of gay leathermen. A chilling mystery/romance novel as well."—Pat Califia

With a new introduction by Michael Bronski. First published in 1968, this uncompromising story of American leathermen received instant acclaim. Out of print even while its legend grew, *The Real Thing* returns from exile more than twenty-five years after its initial release, detailing the attitudes and practices of an earlier generation of leathermen.

ORDERING IS EASY

MC/VISA orders can be placed by calling our toll-free number
PHONE 800-375-2356/FAX 212-986-7355/E-MAIL masqbks@aol.com
or mail this coupon to:
MASQUERADE DIRECT
DEPT. BMMQ27 801 2ND AVE., NY, NY 10017

BUY ANY FOUR BOOKS AND CHOOSE ONE ADDITIONAL BOOK, OF EQUAL OR LESSER VALUE, AS YOUR FREE GIFT.

QTY.	TITLE	NO.	PRICE
			FREE
			FREE

We Never Sell, Give or Trade Any Customer's Name.

SUBTOTAL

POSTAGE and HANDLING

TOTAL

In the U.S., please add $1.50 for the first book and 75¢ for each additional book; in Canada, add $2.00 for the first book and $1.25 for each additional book. Foreign countries: add $4.00 for the first book and $2.00 for each additional book. No C.O.D. orders. Please make all checks payable to Masquerade Books. Payable in U.S. currency only. New York state residents add 8.25% sales tax. Please allow 4-6 weeks for delivery.

NAME

ADDRESS

CITY _____ STATE _____ ZIP _____

TEL( )

E-MAIL

PAYMENT: ☐ CHECK   ☐ MONEY ORDER   ☐ VISA   ☐ MC

CARD NO. _____ EXP. DATE _____